I0680279

THE
REHABILITATION
of *Angel Sinclair*

a pine bluff *novel*

NANCEE CAIN

Serrated Edge Publishing

The Rehabilitation of Angel Sinclair, Copyright © Nancee Cain, 2018
All Rights Reserved. Except as permitted under the U.S. Copyright Act of 1976,
no part of this publication may be reproduced, distributed, or transmitted
in any form or by any means, or stored in a database or retrieval system,
without prior written permission of the publisher.

Serrated Edge Publishing
PO Box 969
Jasper, AL 35502
www.nanceecain.com

First published April 2018

This is a work of fiction. Names, characters, businesses, places, events and
incidents are either the products of the author's imagination or used in a
fictitious manner. Any resemblance to actual persons, living or dead, or actual
events is purely coincidental

ISBN: 978-0-9976139-8-8

10 9 8 7 6 5 4 3 2 1

Editor: Jessica Royer Ocken
Line Editor: Coreen Montagna
Cover Design by Shannon Lumetta
Interior Book Design by Coreen Montagna

Printed in the United States of America

In memory of Dr. C who was my mentor, my boss and my friend for over twenty years. He taught me much more than the things I needed to work in the field of addiction. He gave hope to the hopeless and lived his faith through his actions. The world was a better place because of this man and won't be the same without him.

And in memory of Randy J, who fought the battle every day and won, only to be taken from us because of a heart attack. I think it's because his heart was too big for this world.

Chapter One

Why me, Lord?
Fuck, don't answer that.

Angel shifted his backpack and stared down the country road. Did the cashier say turn left or right at the bed and breakfast? *Dammit.* Was his Higher Power giving him a sign? He'd come to Pine Bluff, Alabama, to make amends, and now he stood literally at a crossroads, lost. Which pretty much summed up the story of his life.

Hands on his hips, he toed the ground, weighing his options. He could either push his male pride aside and ask for directions — yet again — or wander aimlessly.

Work a step; ask for help.

His growling, empty stomach made the decision easier. He was too damn hungry and too fucking cold to philosophize. Besides, if he ever arrived at Emma's, she'd feed him and direct him toward the bathroom. He'd just about give his right nut for a hot shower. Of course, he'd have to endure her lecture on showing up unannounced, but again, the meal and shower would be worth it. He would've called, but he was out of minutes and cash. He blew out a breath and watched it dissipate in the frosty air. *Focus, dumbass. Scattered thinking always leads to trouble.*

The unfinished sign in front of the farmhouse read *Sleep Inn on the Lake, Maggie Robertson, Proprietress.* Although the sign appeared new, the barely legible phone number and piss-poor lettering irritated him. He hoped this Ms. Robertson hadn't paid much for it.

Amateurs.

Admitting defeat, he trudged up the driveway. The old house appeared to be undergoing renovations. The smell of fresh paint permeated the air, though he immediately noticed the crooked, peeling shutters. *Who the crap paints a house without removing the shutters?* House painting wasn't his forte, but even he knew that.

The sound of Rick James singing "Super Freak" drifted through the front door. He peered through the narrow window beside the door and watched as a petite, dark-haired woman danced alone, immersed in the music. She caught hold of the newel post on the staircase, working it like a stripper pole. When she attempted to pop her moneymaker, he chuckled and shook his head. *Nice ass.* He'd give her a tip if he had a dollar to his name.

Still grinning, he pressed the doorbell and chuckled when she jumped and shrieked. After a moment, wide, emerald-colored eyes stared back at him through the glass. One hand covered her mouth and her cheeks bloomed the color of fall sumac. Throwing her shoulders back and raising her chin, she opened the door a crack, leaving the chain locked. Her brow furrowed as she clutched her robe closed, and a lock of hair fell over one eye.

"Are you Ms. Robertson?" he asked.

Her shoulders relaxed. Nervous laughter melted into a small smile, and she ran a hand through her tangled mess of hair. "Yes. That's me. My goodness, you're early."

Crimson and purple clouds dotted the sky, confirming her statement. *Oops.* Time meant nothing to him. It never had. He didn't even own a watch. Trying to stay warm, he'd been up for hours walking. *Emma will be pissed.* He was probably lucky this woman hadn't met him at the door with a shotgun.

"Yes, ma'am. I'm sorry."

The cool morning air seeped through his thin clothes. He shivered. This unseasonable October cold snap had caught him unaware, and he hadn't had the money for a coat at the Salvation Army. But this was the South — just stick around for twenty-four hours, and the weather would change again. He just hoped it would be soon. And warmer.

"I believe you're the only workman I've ever hired who's arrived earlier than promised. Come in, and I'll show you what needs to be done." She slid the flimsy chain across the lock and opened the door.

Hesitating, he stood on the porch, unsure what to do.

"Come in and shut the door. I don't want to heat the great outdoors." She disappeared around the corner.

He wiped his feet before entering her home. The temptation of getting warm, if only for a few minutes, overcame his initial inclination to tell her he wasn't her workman. He closed the door but didn't follow her.

"Would you like some coffee?" She poked her head out from what he assumed was the kitchen and smiled invitingly.

"Y-Yes, ma'am. Thank you."

Again he paused, not used to women smiling at him. An invisible thread pulled him toward the kindness in her voice. How long had it been since anyone had voluntarily spoken to him? Threats to leave the property or a reading of his Miranda rights didn't count.

It gave him a strange sensation when she looked him in the eyes without turning away in disgust, or embarrassment. Most folks didn't acknowledge the homeless. It made them uncomfortable. He swallowed the lump forming in his throat.

Even with her uncombed hair, she was beautiful. As a bonus, she had some nice curves under her green robe. And damn if she didn't smell like vanilla.

Shoving his paint-stained hands into his pockets, he shifted nervously as she took in his frayed jeans and the stained blue T-shirt layered over his torn thermal shirt. His clothes were clean, but they didn't appear so, and that was likely a little off-putting for this nice, soccer mom-type lady. Sink baths in public restrooms were a poor substitute for a hot shower. When she turned to pour the coffee, he sniffed his pits. At least he didn't stink.

Maggie turned around and handed the man a mug of coffee, feeling a little self-conscious that those startling blue eyes had witnessed her silly dance moves. He shook his head when she offered cream and sugar. Tall and lanky, he appeared to be in his twenties, maybe a little older than Phillip. But he looked nothing like her preppy son. He positively oozed urban sexiness and street cred with his long, Nordic-blond dreads. His beard was scruffy but didn't hide his finely chiseled jaw and cheekbones. He shivered and rubbed his arms. *Where is his coat?*

"So, um, Mister, uh…" Biting her lip, she racked her brain, trying to remember the name he'd given her on the phone yesterday.

He flashed a smile. "Angel." His smooth, Southern accent sent a warm thrill through her body like good Irish whiskey. He held out his hand and looked at the floor for a second before meeting her gaze.

She glared as she shook it. *Cheeky devil.* Better to set the employer/employee boundaries immediately. She drew herself up to her entire five-foot-four height and replied with a cool voice. "Maggie or Ms. Robertson will suffice. Calling me angel is not okay. Do you understand? Or is this conversation over before we've even begun?"

Shoving his hands back in his jeans pockets, his eyes crinkled, and one side of his mouth twitched upward. "Ma'am, I wasn't calling *you* angel. *My* name is Angel. Angel Sinclair."

Dubious, she lifted one eyebrow. *Right.* He certainly looked like a fallen angel. She paused at his self-deprecating smile. *He's not kidding?*

"Seriously?"

"Yup, 'fraid so. Made my life hell in school." He finished his coffee but held on to the mug.

He can't have been out of school for long. How old is *he?* "I bet it did. Um, look, I'll be right back. After I get dressed, I'll show you what needs to be done outside. Help yourself to more coffee."

"Okay, thanks." His gaze dropped from her face to her chest and lingered an awkward second before he averted his gaze. He moved toward the coffee pot, his duffel and backpack bouncing against his lean hips.

Did he just stare at my breasts? Maggie looked down and wanted to die. A toothpaste stain seemed to highlight her hard nipple. She scurried to her room, shutting and locking the door for good measure.

In a hurry, she grabbed clothes from the floor, threw them on, and yanked her hair into a messy ponytail. She paused to check her reflection in the mirror. Wiping away leftover mascara from under her eyes, she wondered for the hundredth time if she should give in and color her hair to hide the recently sprouted streak of gray.

Feeling more presentable, she returned to the kitchen and found him staring out the window.

"Penny for your thoughts."

He spun around to face her, nostrils flared, pupils dilated.

"Whoa. I didn't hear you come in. Sorry. Believe me, my thoughts aren't worth a penny." Face red, he mopped at the coffee that had sloshed on his shirt and looked everywhere but at her.

"Did you just steal my silver?" she asked, only half-joking. *Why does he look so guilty?*

"No, ma'am," he replied softly.

Looking defeated, he put his cup down and unzipped his duffel and backpack, pulling out dirty clothes, a handful of pictures, a toothbrush, and a sketchbook. He stood and pulled the lining from his empty jeans pockets. His face was red, and his lips pressed in a straight line as he looked out the window, a study in humiliation.

Guilt flushed her cheeks. "I-I'm sorry. You didn't need to do that. I was just kidding." *Sort of.* "Do you need help with your things?"

"No, ma'am." He squatted and quickly repacked his belongings.

Embarrassed and relieved, she poured herself a cup of coffee.

"You don't need to 'ma'am' me. I know it's a Southern thing, but it makes me feel ancient. As I told you on the phone, I'm turning this place into a bed and breakfast. The last guy I hired skipped town without completing the job. I need some interior painting done, and the shutters outside need to be scraped and painted. Did you say you could do minor repairs as well?"

His brow furrowed, and he nodded once, zipping his duffle bag. He stood and faced her, looking slightly confused. "When does everything need to be done by?"

"No later than the first week in December. Can your crew handle that?"

"Crew?" His brow rose for a few seconds, and he gave a nervous laugh. "Sorry, no crew."

Maggie frowned. "You don't have a crew? Can you complete this work in a little over a month by yourself?"

"I, um, yeah. I believe so."

She poured him a refill on his coffee. He took a sip and licked his lips, seeming to savor every drop.

"God, that tastes good. Thank you."

The room seemed brighter as she fell under the spell of his genuine, warm smile. Weather lines or a hard life creased the sides of his eyes, and she wondered again how old he was.

"You have experience painting?"

His blue eyes appeared to dance, and he smiled like he knew an inside joke. "Lots. Mostly, uh, urban renewal, but I think I can handle this. Show me everything you want done, and I'll try to give you a better idea of the timeframe."

Maggie pressed her lips together, disappointed. She should have known it wasn't going to be as easy as he'd alleged over the phone. He'd made profuse promises about completing everything ahead of schedule for a reasonable price. However, to the young man's credit, he *had* arrived early for their appointment.

"All right, follow me. You're welcome to bring your coffee with you. I'm not fully human until I've consumed at least a pot." Smiling, she waved her hand around the large, open, farm-style kitchen. It was her pride and joy. "As you can see, the kitchen has already been renovated."

He followed her into the dining and living area, where she pointed out what needed to be painted. The room was empty except for a couch, lamp, and big screen television.

He whistled appreciatively. "Nice TV."

Typical male. Most of her furniture was in storage until after the renovations were complete. They walked upstairs, and he remained silent as she explained what she wanted. When she showed him the paint chip samples, his grin widened.

"Excellent. Great colors. Crown molding and windowsills white?"

"Of course."

Standing with his work-worn hands on his hips, he surveyed the room and nodded. He knelt to look at the baseboards and caressed the woodwork. "Stellar."

Those hands on my body... Where did that thought come from? She swallowed and shifted, wondering if the heat needed to be adjusted. It felt like a sauna.

"All four bedrooms and baths need to be painted," she stammered. "I'd also like the faucets changed out in two of the bathrooms, and one bath needs some caulking done as well."

He nodded and offered a small smile.

He's beautiful. When was the last time she'd noticed a man? Her heart stuttered like an old rusty engine turning over. *Old* being the key word. This guy looked considerably younger than she was. A sad huff escaped her lips. She didn't need to add *cougar* to the list of labels others had imposed on her. The memory of Brian, her ex-husband, taunting her as the *Frigid Ice Queen* crept in, adding to her discomfort.

"Wanna show me what you want done outside and any tools, ladders, and stuff you already have?"

"Sure, I just need to slip on some shoes. You can refill your coffee." She followed him down the stairs, admiring his easy gait.

Angel refilled his coffee mug, ignoring his rumbling stomach. He should tell this nice woman he wasn't her handyman. But self-preservation kept him quiet as he assessed the situation. He didn't want to lie to her, but he needed a job, and he could do this. Plus, if he worked here, he'd be close to Emma, the only person he really gave a damn about.

And Ms. Robertson seemed genuine. He liked looking at her sleepy green eyes, tangled mess of black hair, and beautiful smile. Not to mention her great ass. Following her up the stairs, he'd had plenty of time to admire it. Nice and curvy.

He found it strange she hadn't asked him for any identification, or noticed he was hoofing it. Didn't anyone ever teach her about stranger danger? It spoke volumes about their differences; she lived in a place where trust still existed—something he hadn't had in years. And yet he sensed they were alike in some ways. The way she gave him her full attention said she wanted human contact and kindness. Maybe it was her reason for opening a bed and breakfast. He fought the lure of isolation every damn day. In my experience, being alone led to trouble.

Sipping his coffee, he walked to the window overlooking the lake. He liked the serene energy of this place. Once the renovations were done, a bed and breakfast should do well here. He'd love to explore the woods and swim. If he were Ms. Robertson, he'd put a gazebo in the backyard and add on a screened-in back porch with a hot tub.

This time, he heard her behind him and spun to face her. Being caught unaware earlier was unlike him. Usually he was vigilant, whatever his surroundings, as it was survival of the fittest on the street. His stomach growled, and he grimaced, totally embarrassed.

"Oh, my goodness. How rude of me. Are you hungry? Of course you are; you're a kid. My son's a bottomless pit. I'll cook some breakfast." She opened the refrigerator and pulled out eggs, butter, and what looked like a jar of homemade strawberry jam. His mouth watered.

"I'm not a *kid*. Please, ma'am, you don't need to cook breakfast for me." His stomach disagreed, letting out another humiliating rumble. Ms. Robertson shook her head as if amused.

He looked away, wondering about her motive. *Am I a charity case to her?* Feeding him could be her good deed for the day, a chance to ease her middle-class guilty conscience.

"I'm not a ma'am, and I want to," she assured him. "I haven't had anyone to cook for in a while. This will be fun. I need the practice, and I'm going to eat anyway, so you might as well join me. Besides, you can repay me by giving me honest feedback on my cooking."

She continued to chatter, gathering the items needed to prepare breakfast. He shrugged the tension out of his shoulders and relaxed. *No angle; she's just a nice person.*

"Okay. Thanks." He struggled to make small talk, not having done so in a while. "Um…where's your family?"

"Oh, it's just me here."

Her sunny, trusting smile worried him. *Dammit, I bet she takes in stray animals, too.* He frowned, concerned for her safety. She shouldn't let strangers in her home and tell them no one was around. He'd lay odds her last handyman had stiffed her.

"Phillip, my son, goes to college in Boston. It's a beautiful city — have you ever been there? Like me, he didn't like Atlanta. It was tough being the new kid his senior year, so he went to college where the majority of his friends did. He's a freshman at Tufts. Anyway, this was my grandfather's house. When I was a little girl, I would spend my summers down here on the lake. They were the happiest days of my life. Gramps passed away last year and left the house to me…" She bit her lip. "Sorry, I'm just chattering away. Where are you from?"

His childhood had been privileged but hardly happy. And he had to agree with her thoughts on Atlanta, where his family remained. He hadn't thought about them in weeks. *Tell her you're not her handyman, dumbass.* His empty stomach kept him silent as he watched her quiet, efficient motions. As soon as she knew the truth, she'd throw him out like yesterday's garbage. He'd be lucky if she didn't call the police.

"Um, yeah, I've been to Beantown. My best friend was from that area. I grew up in Atlanta, but I haven't been there in a while. I'm a gypsy; I roam all over. So, what made you decide to turn this place into a bed and breakfast? I like the name. Although the sign out front is for shit. A four-year-old could've done a better job."

She pursed her lips, clearly disappointed. "I know. I'm not happy with it, either. Can you fix that, too? This house is way too big for one person. This way I can make a little money and stay busy." Standing on tiptoe, she removed a bowl from the cabinet.

"I'd rather re-do the sign, make it better."

"Really? That would be great. How many eggs, and how do you want them?"

"Not runny, please. Just one is fine. Thank you, ma'am."

"One? Don't be silly." She shook her head, laughing softly while cracking four eggs into a bowl and whipping them to scramble. "Just Maggie is fine. Or if you insist, Ms. Robertson."

"Yes, ma'a—er 'just' Maggie."

When she laughed, the worry around her eyes softened. He wondered how old she was. Maybe late thirties since she said she had a son in college? Pouring the eggs into the pan, she leaned over to start the toaster. Angel moved to help, brushing against her by accident. Maggie's cheeks flushed as she inched away.

"Sorry, I was just going to help," he mumbled, stepping out of her personal space.

"Thank you. That's sweet. Do you mind setting the table?"

He bit back his laugh. He hadn't been called *sweet* since he was four years old. Maggie handed him the napkins and silverware. Her simple touch and faith in him stirred emotions he used to numb with drugs…*Not today.*

Pulling himself together, he placed the silverware and cloth napkins on the table. He fiddled with a fork. He couldn't remember the last time he'd eaten at a table, much less set one. A memory of his mother instructing him on the uses of the different utensils made him uncharacteristically nostalgic. He could still remember her tapping his hand when he used the wrong fork. Foreign born and an artist, she had beautiful, expressive hands that she used when speaking. And she always wore an emerald ring that would catch the light… He mentally shook himself for tripping down memory lane. *Not going there.*

"How long have you been painting?" she asked with a glance over her shoulder.

The toaster popped, and he chuckled as he buttered the toast. "All my life, it seems, in one fashion or another."

She touched his arm and he froze.

"No butter on my toast, please."

Her hand moved away, leaving him feeling strangely cold and bereft. *Am I that starved for human contact?*

"Is painting a family business?" she asked.

The thought of his father or brother removing their gold cufflinks, rolling up their starched white sleeves, and picking up paintbrushes to paint the family home—all eighteen-thousand square-feet of it—made him laugh outright.

"Uh, no. I, um, took this up on my own."

Maggie served the eggs, and he added the toast. His mouth watered. He longed to dive into his plate but managed to restrain himself as she topped off their mugs. Manners drilled into him as a boy kept him standing until she was seated.

"I'm sorry I don't have any sausage or bacon. I'm on a perpetual diet." Maggie handed him the homemade strawberry jam. "I'll have some when I have guests, of course."

His stomach growled, again. "I, uh, left this morning without eating." *Like most mornings and evenings lately.* "It all looks and smells great. Thanks."

"That explains why you were so early. I hope it tastes as good as you're expecting. Please, dig in, and enjoy." Maggie nibbled on half a piece of dry toast.

Tasting the first bite, he closed his eyes for a second, humming his appreciation. It took every ounce of good breeding his mother had instilled in him to refrain from shoveling the rest of the food into his mouth. Fluffy scrambled eggs, strong coffee, and strawberry jam to die for reminded him of breakfasts from his childhood, before things became unbearable.

"These eggs are wicked delicious. I'll knock a hundred bucks off your bill for this meal alone."

Her laughter filled the kitchen. "Wicked delicious? There's that Boston influence. And a hundred bucks? What are you doing for lunch, then?" She offered him the other half of her toast.

Angel frowned. She'd only eaten a half piece of toast and a small spoonful of egg. "Look, I just inhaled more than my share. You need to eat."

"My fat butt doesn't need this. Go ahead."

Snorting with derision, he looked at her. "You're not fat."

"You haven't seen me naked." She covered her mouth and blinked. Her cheeks were now the color of her delicious jam.

The image of her hard nipples in the silk robe came to mind, and he gave her a slow smile. *I wouldn't mind that.*

"You're not fat," he reaffirmed. "But if you don't want it, I'll eat it. Thanks."

He slathered jelly on the toast. Maybe she'd let him work out a plan to have meals included with this job. Looking up, he found her staring at him, and he quickly wiped his mouth.

Pain softened her face, and she looked away, but not before he'd seen his own loneliness reflected in her eyes. Or was it something else? Her hand shook as she pushed a loose strand of hair behind her ear and looked away. Abruptly, she stood to clear the table.

"How old are you?" She didn't look at him, focusing her attention on loading the dishwasher. Dropping a fork, she reached to get it and brushed his leg as he brought her his plate. "Shi—I mean, shoot. Sorry."

He stood with his back to the counter, sipping his coffee, watching her. "I'm legal." He didn't think it possible, but she turned four shades redder. "To work," he added, kind of enjoying her awkwardness. "Almost twenty-five. You?"

The stunned look on her face made him smile. "I'm clinging to thirty-nine for a few more months—maybe forever if I can get away with it." She laughed, drying her hands before straightening her shoulders, all business-like again. "Let's go outside, and I'll show you what needs to be done. Then you can give me your quote, so I can see what I can afford."

"Trust me, I'm cheap."

She opened her mouth, blinked, and shut it again before scurrying out the back door.

He grinned. *Well, well, well, does Ms. Robertson have a dirty mind?* He followed, enjoying the gentle sway of her hips as she shuffled through unraked leaves. Inside the garage, he found drop cloths, rollers, paintbrushes, and two ladders. He wondered if he could bunk here while he worked...

As they walked back toward the house, she explained her plans, and he half listened while taking in the peaceful surroundings. It was so damn quiet here. No sirens, no traffic, no temptation, at least for now.

One dark curl slipped from her ponytail and blew across the back of her long neck, captivating his attention. *Well, maybe one temptation...*

Geese flew by, and she grabbed his arm, pointing at the birds. The brush of her fingertips across his sleeve made his breath hitch. No one had touched him casually in a long time. On the streets of any major city, he was avoided as scum. She saw him differently, and he doubted it was because she'd shared his painful journey. Her willingness to see him as a person magnified his past isolation to the point of being physically painful.

He refused to meet her gaze, not wanting her to see his vulnerability. Walking away, he distanced himself to pull his shit together. *What the hell is wrong with me?* He didn't care what people thought of him. People always let him down, or he disappointed them.

To his surprise, she didn't ask questions, seeming to sense he needed time to collect himself. Or did she feel this strange connection, too? Maybe she was just as confused as he was. He wandered toward the back of the house.

She followed him and then took the lead as they made their way to the lake. Only the sounds of crunching leaves beneath their feet and the scampering of squirrels broke the silence. She tripped on a tree root, and instinctively, he caught her. As he steadied her on her feet, the scent of warm vanilla teased his nose.

She had the prettiest green eyes he'd ever seen. They stared at him for a few seconds before lowering, her dark lashes fanning across her pink cheeks. "Thank you. Grace certainly isn't my middle name."

She was definitely beautiful. But it was her trust and kindness that beckoned to him like a siren's song. For the first time in ages, he found himself at ease with another human being.

"I have two left feet most of the time, too," he murmured, letting go of her arm and staring out at the lake.

Prior to this moment, his life had been a series of bad choices and serious mistakes. The sound of the wind in the stately pines and the water lapping the shore called to his restless spirit, urging him to pause and simply be. Closing his eyes, he stood still and breathed in the fresh, crisp air. A momentary peace filled him.

Chapter
TWO

Maggie handed Angel a pad of paper, pencil, and calculator. She turned to wipe the already clean counters, praying his quote wouldn't be too high. On their tour she'd shown him everything that needed to be done, plus the extras she knew she probably couldn't afford. They'd discussed this over the phone, but now that he'd seen how much work would be required, it might end up being way over her budget. *Oh well. Dream big or go home.*

But going home was no longer an option, and she didn't think she could bear failing at anything else right now. She had funds from her divorce settlement, but money remained tight. Hell would freeze over before she asked her ex for further assistance.

Strumming the counter, she waited for the second pot of coffee to finish brewing. She smiled, remembering how Angel had devoured her "wicked delicious" eggs. He'd demolished the meal like he hadn't eaten in a week. Would a sandwich be enough for lunch? Today was grocery shopping day. Refilling his coffee, she peeked at the legal pad and frowned at the blank page. The calculator remained untouched.

Angel tapped the paper with the pencil, pulling on his scruffy beard. Just when she didn't think she could stand the suspense any longer, he scribbled on the pad and shoved it across the table toward her. Heart racing, she picked it up, holding it at arm's length before squinting and drawing it forward.

"Where did I leave my glasses?"

Grinning, he pointed with his coffee mug. "On top of your head."

She sighed. Her memory was getting as bad as her eyesight. "Thanks. I can't get used to needing them. My arms seem to be shrinking with age." She settled the reading glasses on the end of her nose, gasped, and glanced back at him.

"Uh, if it's too much, you can cut the salary some. I'm not married to the quote."

"Too much?" She reread his proposal.

> Let me bunk down in the garage, meals, phone use (local calls only) + $100 cash/week, to be held until the job is complete. If I need cash for personal needs prior to completing the job, I'll ask for it against my salary. Weekends + evenings off. If I get behind, I'll work daily until the job is done, no overtime pay. You pay for all materials needed to complete the job.
> -Angel Sinclair

Maggie peered over her glasses. "Who did you say your references were?"

The doorbell rang, interrupting her train of thought. Shoving the glasses back on top of her head, she left the kitchen, wondering who it could be. She hadn't reacquainted herself with many people in town, preferring to lick her wounds in peace and quiet. Opening the door, she found a large, bald man dressed in coveralls.

"You the lady needin' some paintin' done? I'm Andy Simpson. We spoke on the phone yesterday." He could barely talk around the tobacco lodged in his lower lip, and he thumbed over his shoulder toward an old, rusty truck.

A magnetic sign on the side read *Simpson's Home Improvements.* Two disheveled men stood next to it, smoking and laughing.

Maggie looked back at the portly man. "What time did you agree to be here?"

"I dunno. An hour ago, I guess? Bill was late meetin' me for a ride."

On closer inspection, Maggie thought one of them looked hung over. Andy spat tobacco juice off her porch. *Disgusting.*

"I'm sorry. The job has already been filled. Thank you for stopping by." She started closing the door, only to have Andy force it back open with one dirty fist.

"Now hold on, lady. I drove all the way out here 'cause you said you needed some work done. You can't go and blow me off like this. We had a verbal agreement."

Unease trickled down her spine. No way she'd ever let this man into her home.

"I believe Ms. Robertson asked you to leave."

She jumped at the lethal-sounding voice behind her, but then felt relieved.

Angel stepped in front of her. He needed to answer a lot of questions, but his presence at this moment made her feel much safer.

"Hey, Goldilocks, who the hell do you think you are? This is between me and her. You low-ballin' my job?" He jabbed his beefy finger into Angel's chest.

"You need to get the fuck out of here. Ms. Robertson has already asked you to leave. I won't be as polite." Angel stepped forward, forcing the other man out of the doorway. He closed the door behind him, leaving Maggie inside. Peering through the window, she watched Angel continue to press the rude man backward until he stood in the yard. With a scowl and an obscene gesture, the disgusting Andy finally rounded up his crew and left, scattering gravel in his wake.

A frown creased her forehead when she realized there was no other vehicle parked in the driveway. *How did Angel get here?*

Maggie opened the door and stood with her arms crossed, blocking Angel's return to the house. "Who are you?"

Stroking his beard, he looked up, appearing to contemplate the question. He grinned. "Your new handyman and bodyguard?"

She didn't budge, but it took everything in her not to smile.

"Or how about Goldilocks? The porridge was just right, but I still need to try out the bed." At her shocked gasp, the corners of his mouth twitched.

The thought of him in her bed stole her breath. She didn't dare look up, afraid he'd know where her mind had strayed.

"You lied to me," she pointed out.

"Not technically. You *assumed* I was your handyman. My offer still stands, although the salary is negotiable. I really do need a job."

"Why were you on my doorstep this morning?" she demanded, feeling anger surge through her. Had she been taken advantage of yet again?

Brian had always complained that she was too trusting. His point had been brought home in a personal way when he'd left her for someone she knew.

"I was lost." He placed one arm on the doorframe and leaned against it, smiling as if he had all the time in the world.

"Lost? Nobody gets lost here." She shoved aside the thought that this was precisely why she'd moved here — to get lost, far away from her former life.

"I stopped with the intention of asking for directions to a friend's house. But hey, it's okay. She doesn't know I'm coming, so she won't mind if I'm later than I planned to be."

I'd mind if I was his girlfriend.

"You really know how to paint? And do minor repairs? How did you get here?"

"Yes, I can paint. Yes, I can do minor repairs, and I walked."

"Where are you from?"

He shivered as a gust of wind blasted them, blowing leaves off the trees. "'Just' Maggie, can we talk about this inside, maybe over another cup of your badass coffee?"

"But I don't know you!"

"You didn't know me this morning either, but you still gave me coffee and made me breakfast. Which I appreciated."

"I, well, uh…I guess that's true," she sputtered. She tightened her arms around her chest.

"Yes, *ma'am*." He flashed a mischievous grin.

Impertinent and *irresistible.* Another breath of cold air swirled amber leaves around them. Angel shivered and blew on his hands for warmth. *He doesn't even have on a coat.* Her resolve melted, and she stepped aside.

After wiping his feet, he entered and closed the door behind him. He waited for her to lead the way to the kitchen, and once again, he stood until she was seated. She liked his good manners, and he didn't give her the creeps like that other guy had. Glancing over his written proposal one more time, she exhaled a deep breath. Her dreams of a bed and breakfast were about to be realized.

"What do you mean 'bunk down in the garage'?"

"I don't have a place to stay. I was wondering if it would be okay if I slept in the garage—there's that part that I guess was the tackle room when it was a barn? But I understand if the answer is no. I don't want to make you uncomfortable."

"In the garage? But there's no heat out there." The suggestion shocked her. She wouldn't leave an animal in the garage.

Angel shrugged. "I slept under a bridge last night."

She blinked, not knowing what to say.

"What about the friend you're here to visit?"

"I don't want to impose on her. The garage is fine. It's out of the elements."

"Don't be ridiculous. You can sleep in the room off the kitchen. I mean, you aren't a serial killer or anything, are you?" She gave a half-hearted laugh and immediately wondered if she'd lost her mind. But it wasn't like she'd be screening her customers; there was really no difference. "Any legal problems?"

"Not now."

"Meaning?" She raised one eyebrow and waited.

"Meaning I ran into some trouble when I was a kid. But I'm not in any trouble now. And I haven't murdered anyone yet."

"Yet?" she squeaked. "And you're still a kid."

He shrugged, but his blue eyes twinkled. "I get annoyed with questions and being called a kid."

She bit her lip, unsure.

"I'm joking."

"Drug or alcohol use?"

"You can drug test me. I'm clean." His blue eyes held hers, unwavering. "And I've never abused an animal in my life. Also, in case you're wondering, even if I sleep under a bridge, I brush my teeth and floss daily."

"May I see your driver's license?"

"I don't have one. That's why I was walking." He pulled his empty wallet out and showed her his Non-Driver Georgia State ID.

Putting her glasses back on, she looked at the ID. In the picture, he looked younger and a little out of it, his hair long and loose instead of in dreads. Of course, who was she to judge? She looked like a wanted felon on her driver's license. The DMV wasn't known for its flattering photos.

"You can't drive?" *What twenty-five year old doesn't drive?* "And you walked all the way here from…?"

"Memphis, and I hitched some. I can drive, but I don't." A hint of a smile played across his lips.

"Why not?"

"I don't own a car, so why bother with a license?"

"You want me to hold all of your salary until the job is complete?"

He nodded and looked at the floor. "Yeah, unless I'm going to need to find a cheap motel."

"I don't mind paying you weekly."

"No. Please, I'm not good with managing money. If I need some, I'll ask." He finally looked her in the eye.

Maggie sighed and looked at the paper again. At this ridiculously low rate, she could get all the renovations done, including some of her wish list. It wouldn't cost her anything but food and a hundred bucks a week. Brian would have a stroke if he knew she hired someone without references and allowed him to stay *in* her home. That very thought sealed the deal.

Smiling, Maggie shoved her glasses back on top of her head and held out her hand. "You're hired. But be warned, I sleep with a gun under my pillow, and I'm a good shot."

He raised his eyebrows and chuckled. "I'll remember that. Thank you. You won't regret it." Taking her hand in his, he gave it a firm shake. With the contact, a tingle zipped through every nerve ending in her body. Startled, she bolted from the chair so fast it tipped and would have fallen if Angel hadn't caught it.

"Wow, you're shocking," he teased, shaking his hand.

It wasn't just static electricity; it had felt like something more, and it rattled her. Nervous, she patted her hair, knocking her glasses to the floor. Like synchronized swimmers off their mark, they both stooped to retrieve them, bumping their heads in the process. Rubbing her sore temple, she laughed and promptly fell on her butt. Angel chuckled as he helped her to her feet. She found herself staring at his smile.

"Sorry," he murmured, letting go of her arm and stepping back. "I've been told more than once I have a hard head."

"I-I told you my middle name isn't Grace. I'll show you your room, and you can make a list of materials you'll need. Once you're settled, we'll drive in to town for supplies and groceries."

Angel picked up his duffel bag and backpack, following her to the bedroom just off the kitchen. Although small and sparsely furnished, the room was clean, with a private bathroom—and a window overlooking the lake.

Angel looked around, smiling. "This is sick. Thank you, ma'am—I mean 'just' Maggie."

Maggie laughed. "Sick?"

"It's great."

"Oh, right. Is lasagna okay for supper? Do you have any special requests for meals?"

"Sure, that's fine. I'm not picky. I'll eat anything. I appreciate it."

"I see." Maggie paused. "Liver and onions it is." The color drained from his face, and she burst out laughing. "I'm teasing."

"Oh fuck, that's cruel."

"I'm not a big fan of the F word," she cautioned.

"Sorry, ma'am."

She crossed her arms and glared.

"Maggie." He laughed and stretched. His two shirts rose, displaying cut abs and a nice, tempting happy trail below his navel. Averting her eyes, she hurried out the door. It was probably a good thing their rooms were on opposite ends of the house.

Yesterday, if someone had told Angel he'd go from being homeless, hungry, and broke to being employed with room and board, he would have laughed and accused the person of hiccuppin' the powder. The thought of sleeping in a bed tonight—not under a bridge or on a park bench—put a grin on his face. And Maggie's cooking sure beat begging for scraps at a fast food restaurant.

Always restless, and itinerant by choice, he had to admit at times he missed creature comforts—especially when the weather turned cold and nasty. Maybe he was getting too old for his lifestyle.

Starting to unpack, he wondered if Maggie would care if he ran a load through the washer. He was wearing the last of his clean clothes. Throwing the dirties on the floor, he placed his few toiletries in the bathroom. A hot shower would be the best part of this deal.

He threw his black book in the desk drawer, but left his gloves, respirator, markers, cannons, and caps in his backpack, storing it in the back of the closet. For once, luck had been on his side, and she hadn't asked him to dig under his clothes earlier. There was no need to leave this shit around for Maggie to see and ask questions about.

Later, when he rode with her to the store, he'd check and see if there were any galleries in town. He'd know by looking at the writing if they were gangbangers, dumbass kids defacing property, or actual street artists. Hopefully by this weekend he'd be able to put down a few tags to get established—and soon, he'd hit a throwup. Pine Bluff was a small town, hardly worth bothering with, but writing was a compulsion. It wouldn't be hard to establish himself as king of Pine Bluff's subculture of graffiti writers, if one even existed.

Tucking his dirty clothes under his arm, he went in search of the washing machine. Maggie looked up from her list and pointed toward the laundry room. Embarrassed, after a moment he had to ask for her help in figuring it out. It was new and much more complicated than the Laundromat. After thanking her, he headed to the detached garage to check out the state of the paintbrushes and rollers.

Maggie found him an hour later, shaking old cans of spray paint, which he hastily put down. He hoped to hell guilt wasn't written on his face.

"Ready?" She still wore the jeans and sweatshirt under her coat, but had added large gold hoop earrings and a touch of makeup, which enhanced her green eyes.

"Yes, ma'am, er, 'just' Maggie." He climbed in the old Ford truck, raising his brows with surprise when she gunned the engine. She tore down the driveway and headed toward town. He never would have taken her for a lead foot. His neck snapped, and he hastily buckled his seatbelt.

"You said you grew up in Atlanta? How long since you've been back?" she asked, keeping her eyes on the road.

Ah, here we go, time for Twenty Questions. "Awhile. I've breezed through but not lived there in years. I agree with your son. It sucks ass. Do you like it here in Hicksville? It's quite a change from Boston and Atlanta." Two could play this game.

Maggie snorted, which made him laugh. He liked how she didn't put on airs.

"I do. I haven't worn a pair of heels or pearls since I left the city. If I never attend another cocktail party where I'm required to make nice conversation with an insipid smile on my face, I'll die a happy woman."

Angel roared with laughter. "I'm right there with you."

Maggie glanced at him before returning her attention to the road. "Where did you go to school?"

"You're joking, right?"

This time, when she momentarily turned her attention to him, she wore a look that said she was not joking at all.

"I never went to college. I was kicked out of several high schools before managing to somehow get a diploma." He volleyed the questions back to her court. "How old is your son?"

"Nineteen. He's never been kicked out of any schools. Phillip's very much like his father, an overachiever."

"You don't have an accent. You always live in Boston? And you sure as shit don't sound like a Georgia peach."

Maggie laughed. "No, I grew up in the Midwest. My mother was from Pine Bluff. This was her childhood home. I met my husband in college." As an afterthought she added, "I was his one careless mistake."

"Careless mistake?"

Biting her lower lip, she nodded as if embarrassed she'd said it aloud. "I, uh, didn't finish college. Phillip was born six months after we married."

He shrugged. "So?"

"We *had* to get married." Her knuckles whitened.

"Again, so? I'm pretty damn sure you're not the only couple to say grace after dinner. You were in love. What's the big deal?" Angel surveyed the expanse of empty walls on the sides of derelict buildings while she drove down Main Street. This place was a series of blank canvases ready for his writing.

"In love? Yes, I suppose so. For a while…" She paused and sighed. "It's hard to remember."

The resulting silence signaled the conversation was over, leaving him with more questions. Fair enough. Everyone was entitled to secrets. Still, the loneliness lingering in her eyes drew him in. He'd not felt this connection to another human being in quite some time. His gut told him she was as lost as he was.

Pulling into the parking lot, she pasted a bright smile on her face. "We're here." She had the door open before he could get around to her side of the truck to open it for her. Heat flushed his cheeks when she handed him some money with specific instructions to buy a coat, along with the renovation supplies. He vowed he would somehow, someday pay her back for this kindness.

Angel walked toward the hardware store to purchase the things he needed to start the home renovations. Having money made him squeamish. It was a trigger of the worst kind, and he didn't want to look like a fool if he didn't have enough. He couldn't add or subtract for shit.

A bell on the door jangled as he entered. He smiled, taking it all in. It was like stepping back in time. The store seemed to be an organized mess and had everything from hardware to cookie cutters to plastic snakes.

Several people shot him wary looks. His appearance was likely something of a novelty in this small town. The owner didn't even attempt to hide the fact that he was on the phone with the police. He'd forgotten how hard it was to blend in when in rural America. In the city, he went unnoticed. People were either too busy or too uncomfortable to make eye contact with street people.

Not that he gave a rat's ass. Public opinion didn't matter to him. He'd always been a nonconformist. If you asked his old man, it was the source of all his problems.

But for some reason, he cared what Maggie thought about him. And her reactions had been nothing like this. She'd been so nice to him, accepting. This was not the norm.

He reined in his rambling thoughts and found what he needed, even digging through the camouflage and bright orange hunting hoodies until he found a black one.

On the way out the door, he racked a few cans of spray paint.

Some old habits were hard to shake.

Chapter
Three

Maggie looked up from reading the caloric and fat content on the bread package as Angel came toward her. She bit her lip to keep from laughing at the startled looks on the patrons of Hudson's One Stop Grocery.

Her return to Pine Bluff six weeks ago had been enough to spark the local rumor mill, but this would send it into overdrive. She hadn't volunteered any information other than that she was Maggie Robertson, granddaughter of Gerald and Pauline Thompson, whose family had been founders of Pine Bluff. Maggie had quickly learned that in this tiny town, lineage meant everything. Everyone wanted to know "who your mama and 'em were" so they could wrap you up in a nice, predetermined niche. Your pedigree defined your station in life, making rural Alabama not so very different from Beacon Hill or Buckhead.

She shoved her reading glasses to the top of her head. "Is there anything special you want to eat? I know my son has specific cereal likes and dislikes." She accepted the change and receipt Angel handed her and was happy to see him wearing a new black hoodie and beanie.

"No, ma—uh, 'just' Maggie. I'll eat anything." He quickly added, "Except liver and onions. Do you mind if I get a few personal items? You can deduct everything from my paycheck. Just a few things—nothing much, I promise." He looked around at the people staring and nodded. Two girls giggled and ducked behind a row of shelving.

"No, not at all. Get what you need."

"Thanks." Whistling, he meandered to another aisle.

Maggie chuckled as two more girls followed him, pretending to shop, but clearly on a reconnaissance mission. By the time she met Angel at the checkout line, she'd counted a total of six girls eyeing him, ranging in age from about fourteen to twenty-five. Ignoring the whispering ladies, Angel dropped an eclectic assortment of items in her shopping cart—a package of markers, shaving cream, razor blades, chewing gum, and condoms.

Holy crap, condoms?

There was only one cashier available, and it *would* have to be Pine Bluff's biggest busybody, Lydia Meadows. Maggie hid the condoms under the other items on the conveyor belt and smiled nervously as Lydia began to scan the purchases with her usual lack of enthusiasm. Her bland expression turned animated when she gave Angel a lingering look as she swiped the condoms.

"Ribbed for her pleasure" condoms, no less.

"Hello, Ms. Robertson. Is this your son?" Lydia asked. Her gaze raked over him like he was a piece of Kobe beef.

"No." Maggie hoped a clipped, one-word answer would prevent any further questions.

Not to be thwarted in her quest for information, Lydia simply quit scanning the groceries and waited. Only the sound of her popping gum broke the silence.

Maggie sighed. "My son, Phillip, is in college and won't be home until Thanksgiving. This is Angel Sinclair. I've hired him to help me get the bed and breakfast ready to open in a few weeks."

"Ohhhh, *I see.*" Her eyebrows disappeared into her hairline, her tone suggesting she'd heard something entirely different from what Maggie had said.

What made it worse, Lydia's implication mirrored Maggie's daydream since Angel's arrival on her doorstep this morning.

"Are you from around these parts, Angel?" Lydia asked in a breathy voice, batting her pale eyelashes.

Maggie dug through her purse for her debit card, trying not to laugh. Lydia was older than she was.

"Do I *look* like I'm from around these parts?" He flashed a megawatt smile.

"N-No." Lydia's jaw worked faster around the gum.

When it became apparent the cashier was too busy poking her nose in their business to do her job, Angel started bagging the groceries. Maggie smirked, impressed with his smooth deflection of the meddling clerk. Swiping her card, Maggie was unprepared for his next comment.

"Hey, Boss Lady, did you remember the can of whipped cream? Oh, and I forgot to tell you I got the rope we need at the hardware store."

Lydia almost choked on her chewing gum.

"W-What? N-No," Maggie croaked.

An image of being tied to her antique brass bed with Angel licking whipped cream off her body sent shivers up her spine and heat to her face.

"I'll get it." Before she could stop him, Angel darted to the back of the store. He returned with not one, but two cans, flipping them in the air before handing them to the now-scandalized Lydia.

"Can't have pie without whipped cream." He winked at the cashier.

Maggie refused to look anyone in the eye as she hurried out of the store. Buckling her seatbelt, she asked through clenched teeth, "What is your game? Why did you do that?"

He shrugged. "She's a nosy busybody. I figured I'd give her something worthwhile to post on Spacebook or Twatter."

"I'll never be able to show my face in there again," she complained. "I don't want scandal; it could ruin my business."

He snorted. "They'd talk regardless. Don't worry about it. Besides, scandal would probably bring in business."

"You embarrassed me. Don't *ever* do that again." Throwing the truck in drive, she spun out of the parking lot, ignoring his muttered gripes about whiplash.

At home, she slammed the truck door, still furious. Angel stopped her before she grabbed the groceries.

"I'm sorry. Really, I am. I wasn't thinking."

She took a few seconds to think before speaking—something this guy needed to learn how to do. But although young and impetuous, she didn't believe he was malicious.

Hands on hips, he looked at the ground.

Before she could speak, he took off the beanie and shrugged out of the coat, handing them to her. "I'll just get my stuff and leave. I'll, uh, get you the money I owe you, somehow."

Something in his stance reminded her of a rescue dog her father had once brought home. It had taken them weeks of patient love to get the dog to trust them.

"You'll do no such thing."

Glancing at her, his brows knit together and his shoulders braced, as if expecting bad news.

"You have work to do, starting with unloading these groceries. Just never embarrass me like that again."

He smiled and nodded. "Thank you, ma'am, er, Maggie."

Hours later, Maggie continued to rehash the One Stop Grocery brouhaha in her head. The scene at the checkout would have appalled Brian. Heaving an exasperated sigh, she mentally kicked herself. *Why do I care what that jerk would think?* She was no longer his concern, nor a reflection on the perfect persona he portrayed to his business associates and family.

But she was a mother, and Phillip would be home for Thanksgiving and Christmas. *Hopefully, he'll be home,* she amended. Although he'd been upset by his father's affair, he'd forgiven Brian, something she still struggled to do. Phillip and his father had always been close. Driven to succeed, Brian worked a lot, so the time he spent with Phillip had been for the fun things, like football games. Discipline had been left to her.

Phillip was much like his father, gregarious and good at making friends. Maggie never had been. As a child, she didn't want friends to come over, never knowing if her father would be drunk or sober. In Boston, she'd had a few close friends, but once they moved to Atlanta, contact dwindled due to busy lives. She'd never formed a close bond with the women of the country club set during her year in Atlanta. Old insecurities, followed by the knowledge that everyone knew Brian had cheated on her, left her withdrawn.

Here in Alabama, a fresh start in a small town was an answer to prayer. She could just be Maggie and leave the baggage behind. Though she still had to figure out how to go about that…

Pushing the memories aside, she set the table. When the timer on the oven buzzed, Maggie went to the back door to call Angel in for dinner. He'd been busy all afternoon taking down the shutters and hauling them to the detached garage, which used to be a barn. She stepped out on the back stoop and flipped on the light so he'd be able to see his way back to the house. Crossing her arms in front of her chest against the biting night air, she yelled, "Dinner's ready!"

The light in the garage flicked off, and he appeared, shrugging into his hoodie as he loped toward the house. Whistling, he waved and smiled when he saw her. For some inexplicable reason, it made her happy.

She stepped aside so he could enter, but he motioned her in first. Again, his manners impressed her. He shrugged out of his coat, hanging it on the peg by the back door, and kicked off his shoes, leaving them on the mat. Still whistling, he washed his hands as she served dinner.

"That smells good." He motioned for her to sit first.

"Thank you. You mother raised you with excellent manners."

Without commenting, he seated himself across from her. She passed him the plate of garlic bread. He took a bite of the lasagna and nodded his approval, eating with gusto. But in a few minutes, he frowned.

Nibbling on her dressing-free salad, she paused. *Did I over-season the sauce?* "What? Is something wrong? I can make something else for you to eat."

"No. Everything's perfect. Is that all you're having?" He stared at her bland salad.

"Yes. Too many carbs in bread and lasagna."

Angel shook his head and returned to eating. "You're just like my mother."

"Like your mother?" she croaked. *Thanks a lot.*

"Too worried about what you look like to enjoy food; it's stupid."

Maggie rolled her eyes. "You're male, not fat, and twenty-four. You don't have to worry about putting on weight or what society dictates is beautiful. Thin is in."

"I'm almost twenty-five, you're not fat, and you're only thirty-nine. Why the hell do you care what others think? I bet if you asked, you'd find most men think curves are sexier."

"Oh, really?" The knowledge that she hadn't been good enough for Brian was still too fresh to curb her sarcasm. "That hasn't been my experience. My ex-husband left me for a size-zero woman nine years younger than I am."

Angel shrugged. "Then he's a fool, 'cause you're a *yummy mummy*." He grinned and helped himself to another piece of garlic bread.

"What did you call me?" Sometimes she felt as if he spoke a foreign language.

"Yummy mummy. You're appealing. I'd lay down money your son's friends think you're a MILF."

"MILF?"

He grinned. "Mom I'd like to F-word."

"Uh, thank you...I think." She laughed and tried not to blush.

He shrugged. "It's the truth. You're pretty." He waved his slice of bread. "You're not high-maintenance looking."

She picked up her fork and poked her lettuce. He had a lot to learn. Most men did not want old, fat women. Brian hadn't been the only one to dump his wife for a younger, sexier, thinner option. From celebrities to sports figures to politicians, headlines screamed every day of men doing the same thing.

They ate the rest of the meal in silence. When he finished, Angel stood to take his plate to the sink. One bite of lasagna remained on his plate.

"That was great. Thank you." Resting his hip against the table next to her chair, he said, "Open up."

Maggie glanced at his crotch displayed before her. *Oh yeah, baby.* Blushing, she squelched her lascivious thought and looked up. He held the bite of lasagna on his fork. He smiled, and she opened her mouth. Slowly, he fed her the forkful. It was delicious, and she licked her lips to get every drop of sauce.

She swallowed and admitted, "It is good."

"See what you missed?" He pushed away and placed his dishes in the sink. "Life's too short to count calories. Thanks for dinner. I enjoyed it. I'm just sorry you didn't. I can do the dishes if you want, or help."

"No. No, thank you. I've got it." She needed to time to process what had just happened.

"Okay. Thanks again, for everything."

Whistling, he disappeared into his bedroom and shut the door. The clunk and hum of the old pipes signaled he'd turned on the shower. She busied herself cleaning up the kitchen to keep her dirty mind in check.

Logically, she knew his outlook was right. But it was hard to erase years of daily criticisms from her ex. Still, Angel had a point. She had moved here to start a new life. Maybe it *was* time she discovered who she was as Margaret Mary Maguire Robertson, not Brian Robertson's wife. After loading the dishwasher, she took a bite of the last piece of garlic bread, savoring the buttery goodness.

Shirtless, Angel walked out of his bedroom fresh from the shower as she finished up in the kitchen. His body was covered in tattoos. With difficulty, she managed to pull her gaze from the V cut of his hips to his freshly shaved face. Just enough facial hair remained around his lips and chin to counteract his youthful appearance. He rolled his damp dreads in the palms of his hands, seemingly unaware of her ogling. Her eyes widened, and her mouth dropped open. She'd never seen pierced nipples before and bit her tongue to keep her nervous laughter in check.

He walked to the dryer, and she clamped a hand over her mouth as she looked at his back.

Retrieving his clean clothes, he paused when her giggle escaped.

"Geezuz, Maggie. Usually women wait until I'm naked to start laughing." He cast a self-deprecating smile over his shoulder.

"Oh, I sincerely doubt that." *What the hell is wrong with me? What happened to the filter on my mouth?* She flushed with embarrassment and again covered her mouth.

His flushed face betrayed an unexpected vulnerability before he turned back to the dryer, removing more clothes. "Then what's so funny?"

"Y-Your…" She pointed with one hand, the other still covering her mouth. "Your back," she managed to gasp between snickers.

Holding his clean clothes in his arms, he turned and faced her. "With my ridiculous name, what else could I have gotten?" Covering his entire back, shoulders, and the back of his upper arms was an intricate tattoo of angel wings, exquisitely drawn and shaded in black and gray.

"How did you get your name? I mean, I know from your parents, but was it a family name?"

He paused before answering. "My mom told me I was a gift from heaven. Not sure she'd still agree, but she chose my name."

Maggie's giggles left her. "Did your tattoos hurt?" She couldn't begin to imagine the pain involved.

"Yeah, some of the tats hurt, but in a good way."

In a good way? Is he into pain?

Without looking at her, he hurried to his bedroom with his clean clothes. He returned, wearing his now-clean thermal shirt with his jeans. "Are you sure I can't help you do anything?"

"No thanks, I'm done. I'm just going to relax in front of the fire. You can watch television if you'd like." *Put that can of whipped cream to use.* She pinched herself for the ridiculous thought.

He shrugged and shook his head. "I'm not much of a TV person. I'm never in one place long enough. I'd like to use your phone, though, if you don't mind. I'm outta minutes. It's local."

"Sure. And we'll get you some minutes next time we go to town. You should've said something." Maggie pointed to the house phone in the kitchen and left the room to give him some privacy. Sitting on the couch with an old romance novel she'd found in the attic, she strained to hear his conversation.

"Hey, Emma, it's me." He chuckled. "What do you mean who, *amiga?* I know you weren't expecting me, but I'm here. Give me directions to find you. No, I'm on foot. Yeah, yeah, I'm good, but you know what I need."

I'll just bet she does, Maggie thought uncharitably. There was a long pause.

"Tomorrow night? Damn, girl, you're on it. I'm ready and needy. Sure, great…Oh, crap, hold on a minute." She heard him put the phone down, and he appeared in the doorway.

"Uh, Ms., er, 'just' Maggie? What's the address here?"

"946 Pineywood Road."

"Thanks."

He disappeared into the kitchen and repeated the address to this Emma person. "Can't wait to see you. I've missed you and have something for you." He hung up the phone.

Emma is probably a size zero with ginormous fake boobs. I can only imagine what he has for her...

Maggie chastised herself. *I'm pathetic.* Sex-starved and pathetic. *Make that pathetically sex-starved.* When he returned to the living area, she plastered a bright, phony smile on her face.

Picking up her grandmother's old romance novel, she began reading about the hero's sword of truth piercing the heroine's inner secrets. Angel sank to the floor at her feet, pensively gazing into the fire. He fingered a dog tag hanging around his neck.

"You served in the military?"

He didn't answer for a moment, staring at the fire. "No, I couldn't pass the test to get in. My best friend did, though."

"I see. I take it he no longer serves?" she asked softly.

Angel shook his head and took a deep, shuddering breath. "No, a sniper attack got him. Ken never hurt anybody. It was me, Ken, and Emma. We were the three *amigos.* We might have been from three different worlds, but we trekked all over the country together. I never laughed more than when I was with them. After he died, everything went to shit..." His voice trailed off, lost in his memories.

She reached over and placed a hand on his shoulder, not knowing what to say or how to console him. He closed his eyes and leaned his cheek onto her hand, accepting her nonverbal comfort.

"I'm sorry for your loss." There wasn't anything else to say. Grief was a lonely business.

"God, I still miss him." He rubbed his eyes with the heels of his hands. "Being here, about to see Emma again, has stirred some old memories." Angel stared at the fire and sighed. "Now I only have her." Shaking his head, he stood and nodded to her before excusing himself.

Maggie watched him leave, her heart heavy. No one his age should feel so alone in this world. Loneliness should be reserved for bitter divorcées.

Chapter Four

"You're really good at this. I don't have the patience to paint." Maggie watched as Angel rolled the wall.

He worked quickly and was almost done with the bedrooms upstairs. His organizational skills put hers to shame. This morning over breakfast he'd suggested he whitewash the garage after the house repairs were completed. With barely a thought, she'd agreed—and not just because the garage needed work. She'd found she liked having someone around to talk to. Angel was charming, a little flirtatious, and a lot of fun.

He chuckled. "I've, uh, painted a wall or two. You've never painted anything?"

"Oh heavens, no. Brian always hired contractors. God forbid I have paint flecks mar my manicure."

"That's just so far from how I see you. I mean, yeah, going to the PTA and cocktail parties, but you're very down to earth. Not like…"

"Like?"

He paused, almost as if he'd said too much. "You know, high-society women."

"I never fit in. I grew up lower-middle class and married above my station."

He snorted. "You were better off where you were. Did you ever work?"

"Sure."

"Doing?"

"I was a pole dancer."

Angel swung around, surprise stamped on his face.

"What? You don't believe me?" She almost bit her tongue in two as he appeared to struggle with what to say. She licked her finger and made a sizzling noise as she touched her butt in her paint-stained yoga pants.

He grinned. "You certainly have the moves; I just kinda saw you as um…"

"A librarian?"

Again, he looked flustered.

She layered it on. "I mean, you've seen how neat and organized I am."

"You're shittin' me, right?"

"I am."

He laughed and returned to painting. Every so often he'd chuckle to himself.

"What's so funny?"

"I was trying to figure out what your stripper name would be."

"Yummy Mummy, of course."

They both laughed for a full minute.

The next evening, Angel glanced around the freshly painted living area with satisfaction, but also with an itch to write. *God, I love the smell of paint.* Paint fumes might have more to do with his memory and math problems than any stupid learning disability. He hoped Emma would indulge him for just a few minutes tonight. At a minimum, he needed to do a tag, but he really wanted to do a throwup somewhere downtown.

He rolled his shoulders, working out the kinks as he went to grab a quick shower before Emma arrived. Walking through the kitchen,

Angel glanced at the digital clock on the stove. *Fuck.* Already running late, he'd have to rush to get cleaned up, which was a shame. He loved the hell out of long, hot showers.

Maggie looked up from kneading bread and gave him a small smile. She looked cute with the flour smeared in her hair and on her face. Damn, he wished he had the time and the balls to smear some more on her and make her laugh. He loved her laugh. It was full, exuberant, and unpretentious—just like her. That was her biggest appeal. She didn't put on airs and had a surprising sense of humor. He just didn't get why she was so insecure. She was, in his opinion, the full package—complete with a great ass. Her ex-husband must be the dumbest dick around.

A loner by choice, Angel's lifestyle wasn't conducive to long-term hook-ups. He'd never had a relationship that lasted more than a few days. He was a scratch-the-itch-and-ditch kind of guy. And he didn't think Maggie was that kind of woman. The way she gave him her full attention—like he was somebody—told him she was the real deal.

She mopped her forehead with the back of her arm as she worked the bread.

"Hey, Maggie. Need help with that?"

She continued to pound into the dough without making eye contact with him. "No, thanks. This is my stress relief. Don't you have a date?"

A date? Oh crap, Emma will be here in five minutes.

Maggie slammed a fist into the dough. *What the hell is wrong with me?* He's a twenty-four-year-old, good-looking guy. Of course he has a date with this Emma person. Mentally picturing her as a statuesque blonde bombshell, she slapped the dough a little harder than warranted.

As she kneaded, she allowed her mind to take a twisted turn, imagining Emma tripping down the steps before she left with Angel. Maybe she'd break one of her long, Barbie legs. Maggie didn't wish her anything too serious or harmful, just a fracture that would leave her totally immobilized. She'd even make her a cake and wish her a speedy recovery. Then, with luck, this Emma would gain thirty pounds. Maggie snickered and continued to knead rhythmically.

The doorbell rang.

She continued working her dough, waiting for Angel to answer it. It rang again. With a sigh, she realized he was still in the shower. Grabbing a dishtowel, she wiped her hands and stood before the door, preparing herself to face the pin-up girl. *This is no different than meeting one of Phillip's girlfriends. Angel is closer to Phillip's age than yours.* Glancing down at her sweatshirt and jeans, both covered in flour, she thought about how mortified her son would be if she met any of his college friends, much less a girlfriend, looking like this. Oh well, Angel wasn't Phillip—far from it—and she was *not* his mother.

Maggie plastered a smile on her face and swung the door open, surprised to find an unassuming girl standing before her.

"Hi. I'm Emma Patterson. Is Angel ready?"

Not blond, nor buxom, nor statuesque, Emma appeared to be in her mid-twenties, and just a few inches taller than Maggie. Her hazel eyes seemed much too world-weary for her age. She wasn't skinny, but not fat either—totally average. Immediately, Maggie felt awful for assessing another woman this way. *I should have my feminist card revoked.*

"Not yet. Please come in. I'm Maggie Robertson. I'd shake your hand, but I've been making bread, and I'm a mess."

Emma entered the house, bundled up in a charcoal hoodie and gloves. With a warm smile, she pushed the hood back, releasing shoulder-length brown hair with auburn highlights.

"Thanks. Homemade bread, huh? I'm impressed. I can't make toast without burning it. And I'm not a bit surprised Angel's not ready. He'll probably be late to his own funeral."

Maggie laughed. "He was on time when I met him, but it was for a job interview he didn't know he had."

Emma laughed. "Figures."

"I was even born late, a week past my mother's due date," Angel quipped as he entered the room. "I've been a day late and a dollar short ever since."

"Angel!" Emma squealed and launched herself into his arms. Picking her up, he swung her around, giving her a loud, smacking kiss on the lips. With his dreads tucked under the black beanie, wearing black jeans and the new black hoodie, he looked darker and more forbidding—dangerous, even. He dropped Emma back to her feet, draping his arm around her shoulders.

"Maggie, this is Emma Patterson. Emma, this is my boss, Maggie Robertson. I'm doing her house painting and some minor renovations."

Age before beauty. Maggie gave the cute couple a resigned smile. "Emma already introduced herself."

Emma stared at Angel with wide eyes, and her mouth dropped open. "Painting? You mean, you have a job? Here? Oh my God! That's wonderful. I've missed you so much!" She hugged him again.

Maggie attempted to crack a joke. "You two look like you're about to rob a bank or something, all decked out in black."

Angel shifted and his eyes darted to Emma's. "Or something," he said with a smile, picking up his backpack. "See ya later, Maggie. I won't be too late, but don't wait up on me."

Maggie bit back her snide retort as she shut the door. They looked sweet together—so young, so full of life. She could well imagine what they'd be doing tonight, while she had her date with her vibrator and a romance novel. She sighed and went back to pounding the bread dough.

"Thanks for giving me a ride. Before we get there, I wanna hit something tonight, just a quickie." Angel placed the backpack full of spray paint and paint markers on the floorboard. "By the way, you look fanfuckintastic. Married life agrees with you. How are David and Kensington?"

"I wish you'd think twice about what you want to do. It's illegal. David's still teaching full-time and studying his butt off for seminary. Kenzie's almost five going on twenty-five."

Angel let out a whoop of laughter. "You're gonna be a preacher's wife? Damn, girl. That's fuckin' hilarious. Don't you know Ken's laughing his ass off? And as far as my writing being illegal, ever since I dumped my crew and went solo, I just hit abandoned buildings. You know, to make 'em look better."

"That's it?" She glanced over at him.

He shrugged. *Busted.* "Okay and an occasional dumpster or stop sign. They're my thing."

Emma rolled her eyes but chose not to comment. "I want you to meet David and Kenzie. That's why I suggested I pick you up a little early." She chewed her lower lip.

Despite looking nervous, the difference in her appearance amazed Angel. Gone was the haunted waif he remembered. In her place was a confident young woman—a wife and mother—who looked him in the eye and not at the ground. Ken would be proud of his girl.

"You mean I'm not late?" Angel chuckled. "I'd love to meet your family. One of the reasons I'm here is to see this kid. I want to give her Ken's dog tag."

Emma sighed and stared straight ahead while she drove. "You know I loved Ken. But he's dead, and he never knew I was pregnant. David's her father, in every way that matters. David knows about Ken, but Kenzie doesn't. Not yet."

Her quiet delivery made Angel pause. He glanced at the firm set of her chin and stormy eyes. "I understand, but she should have something of Ken's. He would've loved her. If he'd known—"

Emma cut the wheel sharply and pulled over to the side of the road. Trembling, she turned to face him. "No! I won't have you blindside David. Do you understand me? He's everything to Kenzie and me. He deserves to know ahead of time. David and I are her parents, and we will decide when and how to tell Kenzie. If your mind is set on doing this, you can get out of my car right now. I'll have no part of your plan!"

"Whoa, Mama Bear." Angel held his hands up. "It's not my intent to hurt anybody. Chill." Taking off the dog tag, he handed it to her. "I won't say a word, I promise. Ken's mother gave this to me. I just thought it belonged to your daughter. I'm not here to cause any trouble. I can tell by looking at you, you're in a good place. Seriously, Emma, I'm happy for you. I'd love to meet your husband and daughter, if you'll let me."

Emma stared at the dog tag, and a tear slipped down her cheek. In all the years he'd known her, Angel had only seen her cry three times—the day Ken shipped out, the day they found out Ken had been mortally wounded, and the day he'd prevented her from doing something irrevocably stupid.

She clutched the remembrance of her first love to her chest and whispered, "Okay." Shoving the tag in her jeans pocket, she dashed away the tear and put the car in drive, her mouth set in a straight line.

They drove in silence until she turned down a gravel drive.

"You live even farther out than Maggie," Angel commented, taking in the small, white house with a screened-in porch. It looked cozy and inviting.

"This is my home." Emma smiled, and her eyes softened.

Angel had never seen her look so serene, and he felt a pang of jealousy — but for what, he was unsure. *A home?* Not likely. He liked being nomadic, without roots to tie him down. Maybe it was the sense of belonging? When they'd been on the road, she'd been scrappy and full of piss and vinegar. She'd just as soon cut someone as give them a second glance. Being a mother and a wife had made her softer, more approachable.

"It's nice, Emma. So, are you, like, a soccer mom now?"

"Crazy, isn't it? More like a dance mom." Her smile widened. "And I love it."

He stopped her from opening the door. "Hey, Emma?"

"Yes?"

"I'm sorry. I wasn't always the best friend to you. I should've done more to get you out of your situation. I should've managed to get to your wedding. I'm here to make amends and apologize."

She squeezed his hand. "We both did the best we could. And it wasn't really a planned wedding. We're good, *amigo*."

He nodded, too emotional to say anything else, and followed her through the screened-in porch into a comfortable living area. Seated on the floor was a little girl dressed as a pirate with a princess crown on top of tangled brown curls. She looked a lot like her mother, but when she cocked her head to the side and grinned, Angel saw his friend Ken. He returned her smile.

"Daddy won't go outside and walk the plank," Kenzie complained with an annoyed huff.

"I'm not jumping into an ice-cold lake at night, Kenz," replied her father, attempting to get out of the silk scarves wrapped around his wrists.

"But you're supposed to be Wendy, *Daddy*." She fisted her hands on her hips and glared at him.

"I kind of like your daddy all tied up. Maybe I should try it."
Emma giggled.

Angel laughed when the beleaguered father broke through his
tied wrists and sat up with a hair bow in his wavy brown hair. Dressed
in a non-Wendyish old college sweatshirt and jeans, he winked at
Emma and murmured, "Could be interesting..."

The petite Captain Hook stomped her foot. The fact that it was
encased in a bunny slipper made it even cuter. Angel chuckled. Two
hazel eyes narrowed, and she pointed straight at him.

"You could be Wendy. *You* have long hair sticking out from your
hat."

Using his best pirate voice, Angel swept off his beanie. "Ah, but
have you never seen a real pirate, lass? These be dreads, not merely
long hair. I've just returned from the seven seas to meet the infamous
Captain Hook. I'm here to verify the tales of horror I've heard 'round
the world! Is it true you can demolish worms and never throw up?
And it's rumored you're a master of disguises, posing as an angelic
princess, while truly being a devilish pirate. And then there are the
tales of your infamous tantrums, and believe me, *miss*, they spark
fear and cause grown men to tremble." He gave her a smart bow and
kissed the top of her hand. "'Tis indeed a pleasure to meet you, Cap'n."

Kenzie's eyes rounded. "Th-They're gummy worms, not real
worms, sir."

Angel shook David's hand as Kenzie's parents laughed.

"Captain Angel Sinclair of The Broken Compass, at your service."

"David Patterson—"

"No, Daddy! You're *Wendy*."

David rolled his eyes. "Mommy's here. Why can't she be Wendy?"

Emma laughed. "Because Mommy and Captain Angel are headed
back out to pillage and plunder."

Angel raised his eyebrows. Her description wasn't too far off
the mark.

"I just stopped by to give Captain Hook a kiss good night. Now
say good night to Daddy, er...Wendy and Captain Angel."

Effortlessly, she swung Kenzie onto her hip and gave her daughter
a kiss on the cheek. After protests and kisses, Emma swept Kenzie
to bed, leaving him with David.

He turned to Emma's husband with a genuine smile. "Emma looks better than I've ever seen her. Being a wife and mom suits her. I'm happy for both of you."

David rubbed the back of his neck and looked down at the floor for a moment. "Thank you. I confess your presence here makes me nervous." His other hand remained on his hip.

Angel shook his head, disconcerted. "Me? I mean, we're just friends. That's all we've ever been."

David looked him straight in the face. "I know; she told me. It's *my* issue. I don't know you, just what Emma's told me about you. She swears you're doing okay, but I'm protective of her and Kenzie. I worry about your past problems. I want to be clear; I won't put up with anything that might hurt my family." The resolve in his eyes told Angel he was serious.

He dropped his eyes to stare at the floor. "I totally get it. I'm clean and here to make amends. I hope to prove to you both that I've changed. I'm a better man and a true friend now." Swallowing nervously, he held out his hand and waited.

David paused for only a fraction of a second before shaking it. "Apology accepted. But I mean it, if you ever hurt Emma—" He looked down as Emma wrapped her arms around his waist and smiled up at him.

"Forgiveness, preacher," she murmured, patting his chest.

"You're right. Sorry for coming on so strong. I'm far from perfect," he replied with a smile. "It's early. Won't you sit down and visit awhile? I can go to the bedroom to finish grading papers since my life has been unwillingly spared by the infamous Captain Hook."

"I'm, uh, going to give Angel the tour."

"Of Pine Bluff? That'll take all of ten minutes."

"I want to catch up. We might grab some coffee and talk. Little ears hear too much…"

"Ah, good point. Okay. Have fun." David kissed Emma goodbye and shook Angel's hand.

Buckling into his seatbelt, Angel commented, "He's a good man, Emma. I like him. It's just hard picturing you as a teacher's wife, much less a preacher's wife." He chuckled.

"I know, right?" She grinned back at him while she drove. "So, I absolutely can't get caught doing this. You hear me?"

"I won't get caught. If I do, just leave me. I mean it. I believe your husband when he says he'll kick my ass." Angel waited until she nodded in agreement. He looked out the car window, his heart racing. "I'm gonna hit the side of the abandoned building next to the hardware store. There's plenty of indirect light, so I should be good. How much time do I have?" He pulled up his hood, snapped on his black latex gloves, and placed the respirator on top of his head.

Emma snorted. "As if time ever meant anything to you. An hour, tops. I'll circle around every fifteen minutes. When I flash my head-lights, time's up or something's going down." She pulled up beside the store. "Be careful, do you hear me? Ken would've loved this."

Angel nodded. "He'd be right here helping me. I miss the hell out of him. Don't worry. If trouble goes down, leave. But it won't—care-ful is my middle name."

"Oh brother. I can't believe you said that with a straight face."

Laughing, he grabbed the backpack, and jumped out of the car, giving her a quick salute as she drove off. A quick scan of his sur-roundings assured him he was alone. Placing the respirator on his face, he started working.

He'd decided to do just a quick throwie using his tag to get estab-lished. His heart hammered with excitement as he put down the first line. Hearing the hiss and smelling the paint pulled him into his zone. The adrenaline kick from writing was almost on par with a heroin rush. Finishing before Emma returned for her second drive by, Angel stepped back to admire his efforts. BE KIND. It wasn't his best or most compli-cated work, but he wanted to get a feel for the area before bombing it.

Looking around, he decided to add a small tag with a paint marker on the stop sign, too. *ASINR* written with a flourish and a halo over the *I*. He was entitled to a crown but never used it—too pretentious. He loved stop signs. *Stop a sinner, or stop a signer, or stop a Sinclair*—all of them worked as the meaning of his tag. *As if I can be stopped.*

With speed born from doing this more times than he could count, he cleaned his caps while he waited on Emma. Dumping the empty cans and gloves in a dumpster, he ran to the curb just as her car turned to make its way toward him.

Emma pulled up, and he jumped in, ducking as a car turned and passed them. The panicked look on her face made him laugh so hard tears streaked down his face.

"Stop laughing at me! Oh my God, that car nearly gave me a heart attack." She gave him a high five while she admired his work. "You're still king, Angel."

"Damn straight," he agreed with a wide grin. "God, that felt good."

"I wonder, do they have a 12-step program for graffiti writers?" She giggled as she began to drive. "If so, you'll never make it."

"We all have our vices. I've given up the one that'll kill me. Let me keep this one."

Looking out the window, he prepared himself for the rest of the evening. Emma's gloved hand squeezed his. He swallowed and bounced his leg, taking some deep breaths. Even after all this time, he still struggled every damn day.

"We're here. It's open tonight, so I can go with you if you'd like." She cut the engine and turned toward him, waiting, allowing him to make the decision.

Angel nodded. "Thanks, Emma, but even though it's supposed to be anonymous, this *is* a small town. I don't want to risk it."

"David knows, and he's fine with it. But it's your choice. I'll wait in another room in the church and read. I brought a book. Come on, you can do this. I'm awfully proud of you. Ken would be, too." She opened the door, and he joined her on the sidewalk, stuffing his hands in the pockets of his hoodie.

He looked down at her and grinned. "You seem to be familiar with this church."

"It's David's, um, yeah. I'm a member now…"

"I'm really happy for you."

And he was. Would he ever find that kind of peace and happiness? Looking down, he eyed the clean concrete, pausing until he felt Emma nudge his elbow with her shoulder.

She giggled. "Stop it. You can't write anything else tonight, I'm starting your 12-step program for graffiti right now."

He laughed and held open the door to the church for her. "Hi, my name is Angel, and it's been ten minutes since my last tag…"

Ten minutes later, he looked around the room at those who shared in his true struggle. Taking a deep breath, he introduced himself. "Hi, my name is Angel, and I'm a heroin addict." With a wry grin he added, "And yes, that's my real name." Several chuckled as he continued, "It's been…" *Oh damn, math.* "Uh, eighteen months and some change since I last slammed any dope…"

Angel tiptoed into the house, touched that she'd left the light on for him in the living area. To his surprise, he found Maggie curled up, asleep on the sofa. Her book lay open on her chest, her glasses crooked on her nose. The fire had died down to glowing embers. A half-empty bottle of wine and an empty wineglass remained on the end table. Her pink flannel pajamas decorated with green frogs and fuzzy orange socks made him smile.

Moving her book to the table, he placed her glasses on top of it. She stirred and twisted, looking like a human pretzel. He shook his head, unsure what to do. If he left her like this, she'd be sure to wake up with a terrible crick in her neck. If she woke with his hands on her, he could end up without a job and tossed out on his ass. He decided to risk the job and the roof over his head.

"Ms. Robertson?"

"Maggie," she murmured, without really waking up.

"You need to go to bed."

"Yes, I'd like that." She didn't open her eyes or move.

He nudged her to get up, but she didn't move.

Unsure what else to do, he scooped her into his arms, and she snuggled into his neck with a soft sigh. Her sweet, warm vanilla fragrance tugged at his heart. It reminded him of the homemade cookies Elise had made just for him when he was a boy. The scent was comforting, just like Maggie.

The bedside lamp in her bedroom cast a cozy light, and he looked around, shaking his head. When he first met Maggie, he never would've guessed her to be such a slob. Grinning, he kicked his way through dirty clothes and nearly knocked over a stack of bodice-ripping romances beside her bed. There were at least six pairs of shoes — no, make that five and two unmatched shoes — scattered across the room.

The bedside table drawer was open and revealed an interesting-looking vibrator with an extra gizmo thingie on it. He wondered how the damn thing worked but didn't want to risk getting caught looking at it. Using his leg, he pushed the drawer closed.

Pulling her covers back, he laid her on the bed and brushed her hair out of her face. She opened her eyes, and her full lips curved in a sleepy smile.

"You're home. What time is it?" Yawning, she sat up and looked around, clearly startled to find herself in her bedroom with him.

"I dunno. Ten or so, I guess."

"That's not very late for a date. Did you have fun?" she murmured, rubbing her eyes. Then she went stiff and scooted to the far side of the bed. "Oh! I, um, don't think you should be in here."

"Probably not, but you'll thank me in the morning when you don't wake up stiff from sleeping on the couch. And it wasn't a date."

"She's very pretty. I hope you used the condoms you bought." She stretched and blinked her eyes.

Angel gave a soft chuckle. "Emma *is* pretty. She's also very *married*. Not a date."

"Married?" She blinked again. "Oh. That's…I mean, I don't approve, but of course it isn't my business. But married or not, you need to protect yourself."

"Is this the wine talking? You're not listening to me." He picked up her dirty clothes and placed them in the laundry basket in her bathroom. She pulled her knees tight to her chest, wrapping her arms around them.

"This is awkward. You're in my room."

"Yep, I am. I didn't have sex with Emma. That's gross."

"You're touching my things."

He dropped the socks he'd been folding. "Sorry," he said. "I'm not stealing them. Your socks wouldn't fit me. And some of them have ridiculous animals on them."

"I didn't think you were stealing. It's embarrassing. This is my *bedroom*." She looked at him thoughtfully. "Gross?" She paused, looking confused. "Why is it gross? You stare at *my* butt," she blurted and then covered her eyes, blushing as red as the stop sign he'd tagged earlier.

"Huh? Well, um, yeah. You have a nice ass."

She peeked at him through her fingers. "I do? I'm sorry. Yes, you're right; it's the wine talking. I have no filter when I drink."

"May I?" Angel pointed at the bed and chuckled when her eyes nearly bugged out of her sleepy face. "I just want to get comfortable to talk, nothing else." He crossed his heart and held up his hands.

She snorted and dove under the covers. "Okay, but you have to stay on top of the comforter."

"Will do."

Angel kicked his shoes off as he unzipped his hoodie. Shrugging out of it, he folded it neatly, placing it and his beanie on her dresser. He stretched out beside her, hands behind his head.

"Now, back to the topic of your sexy butt. Yes, *ma'am*, it is one fine ass." He gazed intently at her, and grinned when she wrinkled her nose.

She nudged him as she scolded, "Don't ma'am me, just Maggie. Why are we even having this conversation?"

"Why don't you think you're attractive, 'just' Maggie?"

Her eyes fell, and she picked at a loose thread at the hem of her pajama sleeve.

"What did your ex do to you? Why is your self-confidence so far in the ground?"

She shrugged. "I, uh…I told you. He cheated on me. I wasn't enough for him — not pretty enough or young enough."

"You weren't enough for him? What a crock of bullshit. He's the one who committed adultery. I can just about guarandamntee you he couldn't handle the guilt. He belittled you so you'd think it was your fault. Be glad you're rid of the dumbass."

"What did you do tonight? You and Emma?" Her voice sounded strained as she veered the conversation away from herself.

"Not much. Mostly just talked. I met her family. She has a cute kid." He didn't see a need to go into his writing, and it wasn't a lie — he and Emma *had* talked.

Maggie lay down and turned to face him. "You met her family? You're really just friends?"

"Just friends."

She grinned and looked away, color blooming in her cheeks.

Was that interest or curiosity he'd witnessed in her face? *Does she also feel this — whatever this is — between us?* He rolled over, propping his cheek on his hand, and faced her, taking in her honest green eyes and that long, exquisite neck. Sex with Emma was the furthest thing from his mind. Maggie, however, was moving into the forefront.

"I think you need to leave," she whispered.

"We're just talking. Want to go back to the living room?"

She hesitated. "I-I guess not. Why dreads? Do your tats have special meanings?"

"They're easy to care for when you're homeless. And yes, but I'm not up to explaining their history right now."

Luckily, for him, she was still sleepy and didn't pursue the topic.

She yawned. "You've spoken about your family. Why are you homeless?"

He shrugged. "My father threw me out of the house due to some mistakes I made when I was a teen, but now it's by choice. I'm a restless person. I don't have roots."

This questioning was not going where he wanted it to.

"Thrown out? Who throws a child out?" She sat up, seeming more fully awake. "When did this happen? How old were you?"

Her outrage touched him, but he didn't want to talk about his family. He hadn't gotten that far in his recovery, and his hatred still burned.

Scrubbing a hand over his face, he stood. He felt like a coward, but sometimes it was best to just walk away. "It was a long time ago. I think I'll call it a night." Grabbing his things, he left her room without looking back.

Chapter
Five

Stunned by his abrupt departure, Maggie wondered what she'd said to make him bolt from her room. Had her un-employer-like interest in him been apparent? Probably. Brian had hated partnering with her for bridge because she had no poker face. She sighed.

Pulling the pillow over her head, she groaned. What was wrong with her? She was a responsible adult—a responsible, *boring* adult. Make that a responsible, boring, *frustrated* adult.

A nagging thought crossed her mind, and she sat up with horror. Looking around, her room was a mess, as usual…Thankfully, her vibrator was tucked away in a drawer and not sitting out. Relieved, she sank back onto the bed. *That would have been beyond humiliating.* She turned out the light, hugging a pillow close to her chest, but sleep eluded her.

Angel was unlike any man she'd ever known before. In high school she'd dated nerdy, scholastic boys. When she went to college, Brian Robertson had been the boy every girl wanted—tall, athletic, intelligent, and oozing charm. Years later, she'd realized all that charisma was an illusion.

Older and in his last year of law school, he'd swept her off her feet in a haze of sexual awareness and attention. One careless night had left her a sad, terrified statistic—it only takes once with unprotected sex. Brian and his family pushed for her to have an abortion, but she'd refused. When she came home in tears, her father took matters into his own hands.

An Irish Catholic immigrant, with fists the size of small hams and a quick temper, Mick Maguire had proved quite persuasive during his visit to the Robertsons' home. Maggie never knew what her father had said—or threatened—but the next thing she knew, she was not only pregnant at age twenty, she was also married. Brian's family did "damage control" by telling everyone it had been a whirlwind romance and elopement. To this day, his parents believed she had entrapped their only son for his money.

After the honeymoon, Brian caved to the pressures of school and focused his energy on his career. Once he passed the bar, he landed a job with a prestigious law firm in Boston, and she'd packed and moved with a newborn. At the office, he was affable and controlled. At home, he'd taken his frustrations out on her, verbally assaulting her about her failings as a woman and wife. That scenario had replayed numerous times during their marriage.

Despite his failings as a husband, Brian was a good father, but intent on molding his son to emulate every male Robertson in the family. Maggie was convinced the family motto was *No tears, no compassion, no sense of humor.* How she wished she'd had the courage to defy her father, defy the Robertsons, and raise Phillip on her own.

Maybe if she had, she wouldn't hate herself so much.

Maybe she would've been happy.

Three nights later, Angel drew in his black book with his markers. He did his best thinking when working, and he didn't want to wake Maggie by painting upstairs. The urge to claw his skin and a need to shut down his mind consumed him. *To use, or not to use*—his daily struggle. The 12-step meetings had helped; they always did. But he felt confused and overwhelmed. Maggie's questions about his family the other night had stirred the dragon within, not to mention his convoluted interest in his boss. Why couldn't he quit thinking about her?

It was surprising to him how easily and quickly a level of comfort had developed between them. It was as if he'd known her for years. And he also really liked having a routine that didn't involve chaos. The itch to keep moving had receded. He no longer slept during the day when it was warm, or stayed up all night writing. Nope, his late nights were now spent thinking about the woman asleep down the hall.

Was he delusional to wish for something more with her? He couldn't blame drugs; he was clean. Maybe that was the problem. When channel swimming, he'd had no sex drive. The heroin suppressed that along with the feelings. *Maybe I'm just horny as fuck.*

Dammit, he knew in his gut it wasn't just loneliness. Being alone was nothing new. The fact was, with her, he didn't feel *as alone.* It was as if his soul cried out for hers, filled with a longing to connect with someone more intimately, not just sexually. He sighed and threw down the marker, rubbing his eyes.

Not today, heroin. Today I choose to be clean. I'm not slammin' dope.

Having over eighteen months clean helped, but the dark thoughts still emerged when he faced new or stressful situations. And being around the beautiful, kind Maggie Robertson was both new and stressful. Maybe he was just starved for attention. And drugs were no longer the answer. First thing tomorrow, he'd buy some minutes so he could talk to his sponsor, Randy.

He picked up another marker, switching colors. Quickly he added a bold stroke here, a dash of color there, working out the piece. The first throwup he'd ever done was on the back of his father's office building in downtown Atlanta when he was fourteen. He'd been tagging since age ten. Caught red-handed, he'd been hauled down to the police station. Dad had been less than pleased, and his mother handled it by putting him in art lessons. No one ever asked why he did it, or why he continued to bomb his neighborhood with tags.

Instead, his parents turned a blind eye to him, to his struggles, and to his pain. He began drinking his father's liquor and quickly moved on to the prescription meds found in his parents' closet. He was picked up more than once for disorderly conduct, but his parents bought his way out of trouble with the law. They never delved deeper into why he was acting out, choosing to ignore his aberrant behavior. Only good behavior was acknowledged in the Sinclair household, and his brother had the monopoly on that. He'd drifted through his impressionable teen years, sinking further and further into the abyss of emotional abandonment, drug use, and depression.

He was the proverbial black sheep, a disgrace to his family, and the polar opposite of Damien, his perfect older brother. The only time he felt like himself was when he snuck out to write. God, he'd been such a snotty toy writer, thinking he knew everything, until he hooked up with a crew and went through the ropes, honing his craft until he was king. The summer after his seventeenth birthday, he ran away. He went north and found himself in Boston, New York, and then Philadelphia, where he continued to improve his skill and creativity. In his new world, he established a name for himself as a gifted writer who took risks that paid off.

When he came home a year later, boasting of his accomplishments, his parents had been appalled. Graffiti was not considered art. It was defacement of public property and illegal. His father ignored him completely, and his mother begged him to stop for his father's sake—and then went on about her charity work, never mentioning it again. They moved him to a new school, a year behind. Drug use masked his self-hate, and he disappeared within his own tortured mind. He remained invisible to his parents and classmates—until graduation day, when he mainlined prescription opiates and overdosed in the school bathroom, still wearing his cap and gown.

Suddenly, everyone knew who he was, and it wasn't the sort of accolade a Sinclair was supposed to garner. Finally giving him the attention he'd sought, his father issued an ultimatum—rehab or get out. So he left and never went back. Why go home where he wasn't wanted or loved? And at the time, he'd felt rehab was for quitters.

That was unfair. He supposed his mother loved him, but he'd disappointed her so often he couldn't bear to see the hurt in her eyes. *Someday…* He knew he needed to work through that step and make amends to his family. Just not today.

Angel threw down the marker. He'd found a new family on the streets—Emma and David "Ken" Kensington. The three of them were inseparable until Ken got caught doing a wildstyle on the overpass. His parents had coerced him into joining the army to avoid serving time, and to prevent him from marrying an unsuitable girl like Emma Devine. Angel had tried to enlist with him, but he couldn't pass the entrance exam—yet another failure to add to his growing list.

Instead of a few months in jail with probation, Ken had received a purple heart and a death sentence, while Angel joined the ranks of the walking dead in the depth of his addiction.

Tossing the markers and sketchbook back in the desk, Angel turned off the lamp by his bed and went to the window. Moonlight rippled across the inky blackness of the lake, mirroring his mood. He had to think of something positive to get out of this funk.

Maggie's smile surfaced first. He wanted to get to know her. The real her, not that soccer-mom divorcée façade she hid behind. The light in her eyes was like a beacon to his miserable, dark soul. But he was afraid.

He feared her rejection once she learned of his dark, shameful past. If she knew about his addiction and trouble with the law, she'd probably throw him out. He'd come to Pine Bluff to make amends with Emma and face his fears. He needed to be sure those things got done.

Maybe this fear of intimacy was another one he could overcome. Leaning against the window, he stopped his thoughts from going down the miserable path that always led him to trouble. Was he becoming obsessive? Was Maggie now his drug of choice? His need to connect with her rivaled being dope sick. *This is insane. I barely know her.*

Angel frowned and squinted when a movement outside caught his eye. Bundled in a coat, Maggie walked slowly toward the lake. She moved like a specter to the boat dock, where she sank down to sit and dangle her feet over the side.

Looking out over the water, her loneliness reached out and touched him, almost palpably. He could sense it, and everything in him wanted to comfort her, lighten her load. Maybe they could help each other heal from the past. Or would they just end up a co-dependent mess?

Angel turned away from the window to take a shower. Maggie deserved nothing but the best. Hell, most of the time she didn't even see him as a man. In her eyes he was a boy, an employee, sometimes an embarrassment. He didn't want to ruin their tenuous friendship, but dammit, he wanted more. And restraint just wasn't in his nature.

Chapter Six

Maggie woke up to the mouthwatering aroma of fresh coffee, a loud clattering of pans, and a sworn oath that would have earned Phillip a mouthful of soap when he was a kid. Although she'd slip and cuss when stressed, in general, she hated crude language; it brought back memories of her father's drunken rages. Shrugging into her robe, she made her way to the kitchen. She found Angel picking up the pots and pans now strewn across the floor. Organization was not her forte, and her cupboards were a mess.

He looked up and stared at her with such open longing she almost forgot to breathe. It was gone in an instant and left her feeling even more confused and unsettled. She poured herself a cup of coffee and closed her eyes. *Did I just imagine that?*

"I'm sorry." His husky voice sounded full of promises that shouldn't be kept.

Sorry for waking her? Sorry he left her the other night? She jumped when she realized he now stood behind her, his chest a mere fraction of an inch from her back, his warm breath on her neck. Stepping to the side, he refilled his coffee cup, and her breathing leveled out again.

"I didn't mean to wake you. Geezus, Maggie, these cupboards are a disgrace. How do you find anything?"

Her eyes narrowed, and her head snapped up at the criticism. "I know exactly where everything is, and you had no business rummaging around in there," she spat. Immediately, she regretted her knee-jerk reaction. *He's not Brian.*

He slammed his coffee cup down on the counter. "I just wanted to make you breakfast. Again, I'm sorry. I'm sorry I woke you up. I'm sorry I made a bigger mess—which I might add was pretty damn hard to do—and I'm sorry I criticized your fuckin' crazy cupboards."

For a second she wondered if he was talking about the mess on the floor or their fuzzy personal boundaries. Backing her into the cabinets, Angel placed a hand on the counter on either side of her, trapping her so she couldn't flee. With a nervous swallow, she slowly raised her eyes to gaze into his. Caught in this almost-intimate position, she prayed he didn't notice how hard her nipples were.

"You're so damn pretty…"

She laughed nervously. "Yeah, I bet. No need to be sarcastic."

"I'm not. I'm being honest. Don't you feel this thing between us? If I'm imagining it, tell me so."

"A-Angel. I'm old—"

"Yeah, yeah, you're fuckin' ancient. Almost old enough to be my mother. I know, Maggie. Put the goddamned walker away. I don't give a rat's ass that you're closer to forty than thirty. Kiss me. Let's just do it and get it out of our system." Leaning in closer, he whispered, "Please?"

Her eyes widened. "Kiss you?" she squeaked, sounding like she'd sucked on a helium balloon. She lowered her eyes from his powerful gaze to his blue-plaid flannel shirt.

"Kiss me."

"I-I, no, Angel. We can't."

"Why not? I know you want to. Your pupils are dilated, your breathing is shallow, and you keep wetting that delicious bottom lip with your tongue." His smooth voice drizzled over her like icing on a hot cinnamon roll. The pulse at the base of his neck pounded, and when she raised her eyes to his, the vulnerability reflected there made her look away.

"B-Because…" *Dammit,* she couldn't think with him so close. She drew in a deep breath. "I haven't brushed my teeth."

It was the only thing she could come up with. *I'm so lame.*

He threw his head back, roaring with laughter, and kissed her on her forehead. "Damn you're cute, 'just' Maggie."

Cute? She hadn't been cute since grade school Was he teasing or taunting her? Memories of Brian's insults haunted her. Shoving Angel out of her way, she began picking up the pots and pans from the floor.

"Quit laughing at me." Her voice didn't crack, but her hands shook as she stacked the cookware.

"Go brush your teeth and come back and kiss me, Maggie May."

"What did you call me?" She stood with the pans in her hand, stunned. No one had called her that since her father died.

"What?" Angel took a sip of his coffee.

"Maggie May. My father used to call me that. My full name is Margaret Mary." She smiled, feeling nostalgic. When sober, her father had been a great dad.

"It fits you. I think it's an old song or something."

"It is. Da used to sing it with his Irish lilt and dance with me. It's a good memory."

"Please don't be sad. Look, go get dressed, brush your teeth, and I'll cook breakfast, okay? I overstepped, and I'm sorry." Angel smiled at her and took the pots and pans, placing them on the counter. Grabbing the coffee pot, he topped off her cup. "Go." He motioned her to leave the kitchen.

An old song or something. Yes, an old song about a young man and an older woman. Maggie nodded and fled the room, wondering if fate was truly that ironic.

Angel shoved all the pots and pans back in the cabinet and found the frying pan for the eggs he'd planned to make for breakfast. Remorse coursed through his veins. Who did he think he was? Some hot, A-list movie star? No self-respecting woman would want a homeless junkie. Hell, he couldn't even do simple math.

Drumming his fingers on the countertop, he decided to back off. It was never his intention to make her uncomfortable. If Maggie wanted to pretend she was his mama, fine. But she was nothing like his mother. His mother was cold and distant. And she sure as hell didn't have a fine ass.

Angel cracked three eggs into the frying pan and groaned. Pieces of eggshell had gone in with one of the eggs. He couldn't even fry a damn egg without fucking it up. Taking a fork, he began digging the eggshell out of the pan.

"Ack! Stop, you'll ruin my frying pan." Dressed in jeans and a white blouse, her hair pulled up in a messy knot, Maggie hurried over.

Angel backed away when she grabbed the fork out of his hand.

"Sorry," he mumbled.

A nudge to his shoulder made him look at her. "You don't use a metal fork, silly. You'll scratch the coating on the pan." She smiled, and he relaxed his clenched fist. With a rubber spatula, she expertly removed the shells. "Leave the cooking to me; you can take out the trash."

She isn't mad. Angel let out an exaggerated sigh and gave her a smart salute. "Yes, ma'am."

"Next time you 'ma'am' me, I'm going to smack you with this spatula."

Angel raised his eyebrows and gave her a wicked grin. "Yes, *ma'am.*" He laughed at the startled look on her face as he pulled the garbage bag from the can. Giving her a naughty wink, he left the kitchen, whistling.

He returned as Maggie plated the perfectly cooked eggs with ham and toast. Her arm brushed his shoulder when she placed his food on the table, and she pulled away like she'd been burned. Her cheeks reddened, and she almost spilled the orange juice.

"Calm down, Mags. I promise not to ravish you until after breakfast." *Shit! Filter, dumbass. What happened to backing off?*

"That's not funny. We n-need to talk." After refilling their coffee, she sat and rearranged the silverware by her plate three times.

"I'm not going to force you to kiss me, so quit panicking." He spoke matter-of-factly, hoping to ease her fears.

"This isn't right. You're an attractive, sweet young man. But the fact remains, the age difference is significant, and I'm your employer. People would talk." Maggie picked up her fork, turning it over and over. Looking at the table, she added softly, "And I don't do casual sex."

Angel shrugged. "I don't buy the excuses. Maggie, please *look* at me." She hesitated before raising her eyes. "And I don't want a hit and run. I know you're not that kind of woman. You mean too much to me already, and I don't want to risk our friendship. If that means no sex—*okay*."

He went back to eating. Maggie watched him for a moment and nodded. He bit his lip to keep from laughing at the look of disappointment that flitted across her face.

There's still hope.

One week later, Maggie walked into the kitchen carrying groceries and found her pantry completely emptied, with Angel on his back under the sink.

"What are you doing?"

His T-shirt was hiked up just enough to reveal his happy trail. A path she was quite sure lead to heaven. *Good thing he can't see me staring...*

"Cleaning out the trap. It's pretty damn gross."

"But why is everything out of the pantry?" The cupboard doors stood ajar, and she realized he'd also neatly stacked all the pots and pans. She actually had more room than she realized.

He crawled out from under the sink.

"I found some scrap lumber in the garage. I had an idea to build some step shelves, so you can actually see what's in there. I'll need you to help me figure the measurements, though. Then we can make a master list for when you go get supplies."

"It's a great idea, but I'm not sure..."

"Why? This is a business, Maggie. Organization can only help."

When she started to protest, he held up his hands. "Look, I know you got pissed about this very issue last week. I'm not criticizing. I'm trying to help. I want this place to succeed. You deserve it."

She put the sacks of groceries down on the floor. What he was suggesting would be helpful. "You're right, it's just that..."

He waited.

"I feel like I'm taking advantage of you. You're doing more work than we agreed upon."

He grinned. "I am, aren't I? Guess that means you owe me a pie."

She laughed. "Maybe I could increase your salary a little? And you could stay on a bit, um, you know, until things are up and running? You can be my handsyman."

Oh, dear God.

She covered her mouth and closed her eyes, mortified. "Handyman. I meant handyman…"

Angel guffawed so hard he had to sit down. Wiping the tears of laughter from his eyes, he said, "Deal. But no increase in salary. You can't afford it — yet. But your handsyman wouldn't mind that pie, and if you'd get me some minutes for my phone, I'd appreciate it. I keep forgetting."

"Of course. And thank you." Despite her embarrassment, her heart felt lighter. *He's staying…*

Chapter
Seven

Two weeks later, Maggie followed Angel through the completed rooms of her bed and breakfast, impressed with his work. Everything was ahead of schedule because on several days he'd continued to paint late into the night, telling her he needed to keep busy. He hadn't been kidding when he said he was a restless spirit. He and Emma went out once or twice a week, especially on the days when he seemed antsy. Maggie felt a small pang of jealousy and a lot of concern when she thought of Angel with Emma. She'd met Emma's family when they came to the house trick-or-treating. David seemed like a nice man, and she hoped Angel and Emma didn't have something going on behind his back.

Maggie hated to acknowledge her jealousy, but in truth, she longed to be the one Angel confided in, to be there for him. He talked with her about a variety of subjects, but rarely about himself. She didn't know much more about him today than she had when he'd arrived on her doorstep.

After the embarrassing slip when they discussed extending his duties, they'd fallen into an easy rapport that wasn't too formal or distant, yet didn't cross the line, except for the occasional flirting. She quickly realized she had no skills in that department; she always ended up feeling embarrassed. Thankfully, he hadn't asked her to kiss him again. On occasion, Maggie would find him staring at her like a hungry wolf, but he would quickly look away and deflect the awkward moment with humor or leave the room.

His restraint should have made her happy. After all, it was what she wanted.

Liar.

Truthfully, she found herself increasingly frustrated, which in turn kept her focused on decorating the inn. Angel's knack for organization created a more streamlined approach to running the bed and breakfast. Just this morning, she'd booked her first reservation in the notebook Angel had designed and gifted to her, complete with sketches of scenes around the inn. And working also helped squelch the occasional dreams of her handyman in bed with a can of whipped cream and rope.

"I'll begin hanging the shutters today, and the yard needs to be raked…Maggie?"

She ran into his back, lost in thought. "W-What?" The impact caught her off guard, and heat rose in her cheeks.

"Are you okay? You look flushed. Are you coming down with something?"

Angelitis. "No, I'm fine. It's just awfully warm in here." *Has anyone ever died from sexual frustration?*

He raised an eyebrow. "Yeah? I guess it is. But I don't think the temperature has a thing to do with it." His eyes slowly raked down her figure.

She rubbed her sweaty palms on her jeans. Good grief, the way he was staring, you'd think she was wearing lingerie instead of work clothes.

"You've done a wonderful job on the house. Thank you." Unable to meet his stare, she straightened the white eyelet duvet on the antique four-poster bed that had belonged to her grandparents.

"I aim to please."

Aim that thing and please me. "I booked our first guests in December…"

"That's great, Maggie."

Feeling his presence behind her, she whirled to find herself cornered, with her back to the bed.

Thump, thump, thump. She wondered if he could hear her heart hammering. A deep, stuttering breath assured her that her lungs still worked. His eyes darkened a second before he picked her up, placing her on the bed. As she sank into the mattress, he crawled on top of her, caging her body with his arms. A smile formed on his perfect lips, and she found herself longing to feel his beard on her neck.

"Maggie, Maggie, Maggie…" His low voice rumbled with longing.

She closed her eyes, not wanting him to see her fear, her desire. Her breathing escaped in shallow puffs, and her skin burned as if on fire. *No, no, no…*

He leaned in and nibbled on her ear. She sighed as her body temperature shot up by at least another five degrees. *Yes, yes, yes…*

"You're so fuckin' beautiful," he whispered, his warm breath sending a shockwave all the way to the pit of her stomach. The sensations swirled lower and lower until even her toes curled.

Tentatively, with the back of her fingers, she stroked his beard. The intensity of the moment scared her, and she dropped her hand.

"I want to kiss you," he rasped. "But if you say no, I won't, and I'll understand."

She lowered her lashes, not wanting him to see her desperation.

"You can't hide, Margaret Mary."

Maggie shifted away a bit and gave a nervous laugh. "I'm not." She paused. "I am. Angel, we can't—"

"Why not?"

He's right. Why not? I'm single… "It's not that I don't want to," she admitted.

"Yeah?" He gazed at her, questioning.

"Yes, okay…" she whispered.

He took his time and trailed kisses along her jaw until he captured her lips, coaxing her mouth open so his tongue could delve inside. "You're perfect."

She scoffed, and he placed a finger over her mouth.

"You are." His other hand crept under her old, ratty sweatshirt. He gentled her with soft, easy strokes on her stomach and kissed her neck.

"I need you, and I'm not just talking physically."

Their kiss deepened, and his tongue explored in tandem with his hand. She shifted so his knee was between her legs. When his hand squeezed her breast, she whimpered, wanting more. She wrapped her free hand around his neck, returning the kiss.

"Oh, God, Maggie…" He inched her sweatshirt up. "I want to see you."

She kept her eyes closed as embarrassment encroached on her happiness. *What am I doing? I'm almost old enough to be his mother!*

Maggie turned her head away from him, feeling lost and exposed. "No."

"No? Why not? Don't…" He turned her face toward his, cradling her cheek in his palm. "Don't turn away from me."

Maggie stared at his strong jaw line before slowly raising her eyes. The depth of emotion she found in his face reassured her. But she couldn't stop shaking.

"Okay. I'm stopping." He rolled to his side and pulled her into his arms, stroking her back, kissing her forehead, her hot cheeks.

Hiding her face in his neck, she broke down and wept. She wasn't even sure why she was crying. Was it because this attraction felt so right, or because it was so very wrong?

"Shh…Hush, baby. It's okay," he crooned in her ear. His strong hands soothed her on some level, but her mind worked overtime, listing the reasons she shouldn't allow this.

"N-No, it's not. It isn't okay. I don't see how this can work."

Her body rejected her words, and she found herself snuggling in closer, as if she could hide from the powerful emotions washing over her. She desperately wanted to give in and draw strength from his words and arms.

"There's nothing we can't overcome together. We'll take it slow. I promise. We won't do anything you don't want to; I swear it." He kissed her forehead, and the phone rang from downstairs. "Don't answer it," he murmured, brushing her hair out of her face.

"I have to. It might be my son." *My son. Dear God.*

She got up and ran downstairs to answer the phone. Sunshine poured in through the kitchen window, revealing a beautiful, crisp autumn day. With a quick glance at the caller ID, she answered. "Hello, Phillip." She prayed her voice sounded cheerful and not strained.

"Hi, Mom."

Angel walked into the kitchen and stretched, his shirt inching up to reveal a hint of abs. *Definitely never let him see me without clothes in any kind of light. Why can't he be blind?*

Wait—did this mean she was thinking about pursuing a relationship with him? She snapped out of it when Phillip asked if she was still on the line. What had he been saying?

"Mom, are you there? So is that okay?"

"What? I'm sorry. What did you say?"

Phillip gave an exasperated sigh, sounding a lot like his father. "I asked if it would be okay if I went skiing with Dad and Tiffany over Thanksgiving."

The new Mrs. Brian Robertson was tall, blonde, tiny, and had the personality of a cur bitch. Tiffany had been married when she'd started her affair with Brian. And she'd been one of Maggie's so-called friends at one time, which made it harder. This was one of Maggie's biggest regrets. She'd laughed at Tiffany's catty gossip at the country club, until she became the target. As far as she was concerned, the two cheaters deserved each other. Maggie made a gagging motion with her finger down her throat and then regretted acting so immature.

"Not at all, if that's what you want to do. I'll miss you, but I'll look forward to seeing you at Christmas. It might be best all around for you to wait to visit. The renovations will be completed by December." She looked up to see Angel beaming at her and doing a victory fist pump.

"Thanks, Mom. See you next month."

"I love you, Phillip. Be safe." She hung up the phone and knit her brows together as Angel let out a whoop of joy.

"What is that all about?"

Angel picked her up and twirled her around. "What a great Thanksgiving. I'll have you all to myself and won't have to share the pumpkin pie!"

"Typical man. You just want me for my cooking. So you'll be here for Thanksgiving?" She pulled one of his dreads.

"I mean, if you'll have me. Where else would I go? The Pattersons are going to see his family down south. And I want you for more than your cooking." His voice sounded serious.

"I'll have you... for Thanksgiving, I mean." She smiled nervously. Unsure what else to say, she kept quiet.

"I want so much more, Maggie. I'm not kidding. I wish you'd give us a chance." He hoisted her onto the kitchen counter, standing between her legs.

He held her face and slowly brought his mouth to hers. "Please?" he whispered before taking her lips, tenderly exploring, asking for more without any further words. It was the kiss to end all kisses. His hold tightened, and she wrapped her legs around his back. As the kiss grew more passionate, she found herself wanting more, too. He pulled back and gazed into her eyes, his hands now tangled in her hair as he waited.

"Yes," she answered, breathlessly.

He grinned. "Thank you." He gave her one more kiss before setting her back on her feet. "And for the record, pumpkin pie is my favorite, especially with whipped cream on top." He winked at her before heading toward his room.

Maggie laughed, feeling carefree and — dare she think it — *happy?* A spark of hope took flame. *Could this possibly work?*

Angel shut the door to his bedroom and leaned against it with his eyes closed. He smiled. *Thanksgiving alone with Maggie. Yes!* For once he'd have a lot to be thankful for. With a grimace, he shifted his jeans, easing the pressure on his erection. Kissing Maggie had been sublime and nearly his undoing after weeks of friendly flirting. He wanted more. She was all he could think about.

Was this dangerous? He pondered who to call. His sponsor? Or Emma. He pulled out his phone and sent a text.

I need to talk.

Emma: You OK?

I dunno. Tonight okay?

Emma: Sure. But no writing.

Spoilsport.

Emma: I'm serious.

K, cya @ usual time

"Maggie gives me weird looks when I pick you up." Emma sipped her coffee.

They'd parked outside a convenience store on the edge of town. Emma didn't want to go to the diner where she used to work, and he understood.

"Really? Why? Do you think she's jealous?" Angel asked, frowning. "How old is this coffee?"

"Maybe. I mean, what do you tell her when you go off at night a couple times a week? Have you told her you're in recovery?"

"No." *Maybe it was a mistake to call Emma.* And ditching his meeting probably was too. His palms itched to write.

Emma sighed. "Angel…"

"I know. I know. I just want her to get to know me for *me* before I give her all the sordid details. Things are complicated. She's no longer just my boss. And before you go jumping to conclusions, I'm not going to say more because we're still defining our relationship. But I'm terrified that once she knows, she'll throw me out. I mean, who trusts a junkie?"

"Oh…wow. But regardless, you're in *recovery.*"

"Yeah, and we both know the stats on me relapsing." He finished the horrible coffee and crumpled the cup. Looking over at the dumpster next to the convenience store, he grimaced. Some toy had gone over his piece and hit it with a really lousy tag, using a crown, which was fuckin' ridiculous. He wondered who wanted a turf war. He didn't get into that shit…If the guy or girl was willing, he'd give 'em some pointers instead…

"Stop looking at the dumpster and talk to me. I didn't leave my nice, warm home for the hell of it."

"Tsk, tsk, such language from a preacher's wife," he teased.

"Quit skirting the issue. Tell me what you're feeling."

"Like I'm freefalling. I mean, what the fuck is this? Maggie's gorgeous, but it's not her looks, it's her…" He shrugged. "It's everything about her. She pays attention when I speak, she's kind, she's funny, she snorts when she laughs, she's messy as hell, disorganized as fuck, and just so goddamned perfect. She's my new heroin. I can't get enough of her. I'm worried that I might be hopelessly co-dependent."

Emma's smile widened into a grin. "Angel, have you never felt this way about a girl before?"

"She's not a girl; she's a woman. And I've had a few girlfriends, but nothing like this. Those were disasters, bound together and split up by drugs. Plus, I've never been in one place long enough — and as you know, I suck at communication."

Emma laughed outright. "Dumbass, you're falling in *love*. It's *normal*." She patted his hand. "There, there, you'll learn to adjust. It really isn't so bad. I promise."

Angel closed his eyes and let out a deep breath. She'd just verbalized what he knew in his gut.

"And Angel?"

"Yeah?"

"You deserve it, *mi amigo*."

He wasn't so sure about that. But she was right. He was falling balls deep in love with Maggie Robertson.

Chapter
Eight

Dragging himself into the kitchen, Angel sank into a chair. Dog-ass tired, he put his head down on the table, unable to move. The shutters were hung, most of the yard was raked, and he'd even helped the mover get the rest of Maggie's furniture out of storage.

If she'd asked us to move that damn piano one more time, I swear to God, I would've buried her in it.

The mover yelled goodbye and the door slammed as the scent of warm vanilla entered the room. Capable hands massaged his aching shoulders, and he smiled, relaxing.

Damn if I wouldn't move that stupid piano by myself if she asked.

"Thank you for all your hard work today. Everything's perfect."

Her thumbs hit a tense spot, and he moaned at the mixture of pleasure and pain. "God, that feels good."

"It might be better if you were lying down."

"Ms. Robertson, you're trying to seduce me," he quipped as he sat up. He laughed when she smacked him on the back.

"That's not funny."

"Come on, yes, it is. I loved *The Graduate*, but you're ten times hotter than Mrs. Robinson, and I know without a doubt that I'm way cuter than Benjamin. I wish you weren't so damn sensitive about your age." He pulled her into his lap and wrapped his arms around her waist. Leaning his head into her shoulder, he closed his eyes. "You always smell good enough to eat, *yummy mummy*."

"It's late, and we haven't eaten," she replied crisply, maneuvering her way off his lap. Her hand shook as she tucked a loose strand of hair behind her ear. "Sandwiches okay?"

"Fine," he snapped.

His sexual frustration was almost to the point of being unbearable. He immediately regretted his ill temper when her eyes grew wide. "I'm sorry. Sandwiches would be great. I'm just tired."

And horny as hell and fucking tired of blue balls.

He walked out, intent on watching some television to take his mind off sex with Maggie, but instead gravitated toward the piano.

How many hours had he sat with his mother at her grand piano as she tried to teach him to read music? Years later, he found out his dyscalculia was part of the problem. Instead he played by ear. Angel lifted the cover of the piano and hit middle C a few times. As a child, he'd loved watching his mother play. Her normally cold face would be full of expression as her manicured nails flew across the keyboard. Her diamond rings glittered. *Does she still play?*

Angel sat and softly played what he remembered of Beethoven's "Moonlight Sonata." It was his mother's favorite piece, but she would only play it when his father wasn't around. More than once, he'd seen her crying while she played. When he asked her why, she'd always shake her head, wipe her tears, and tell him to run along.

Maggie sat next to him on the piano bench as he continued to play.

When he finished, they sat in silence together. Wrapping his arm around her waist, he kissed the top of her head.

"That was beautiful. I didn't know you played." She rubbed circles on his back, as if knowing he needed the comfort of human contact.

"Not much. And not in a long time. My mother used to cry when she played that piece. She's a gifted pianist." He gave a self-deprecating smile and added, "She cried when I played it too, but it was because I couldn't read music for shit, despite her attempts to teach me."

Maggie smiled. "You play by ear? It sounded perfect to me."

"It was far from perfect."

"I think you're too hard on yourself."

Angel laughed. "Hello? Pot calling the kettle black? I've forgotten most of it. The truth is, I have no math skills, and I'm unable to read music. My old man called it laziness; my teachers called it a learning disability."

"I've never liked it being labeled a disability. It's a different way of learning."

"I like that. Thank you."

"At one time, I wanted to be a teacher."

He nudged her. "Give me some room."

Maggie hopped off the bench, and he made a great show of rolling his shoulders. He grinned. "Ready?"

She nodded, and he began playing a rockabilly piece. It used to make his mother cringe, especially when Damien would join in, fiddling. When he finished, Maggie clapped, and he took a bow.

"You ready for supper, Jerry Lee?"

"Whoa, I can't be Jerry Lee Lewis. I like my women old enough to at least drive a car."

Maggie burst out laughing. "Got that covered here. By the way, why don't you study and get your license back? You could use the truck while you're here."

Angel looked away for a second. "I don't know how much longer I'll be here."

"W-What?"

"My work here is just about done. You have your first guests booked. I don't think you really need a full-time maintenance man." He shrugged. *And the rate we're moving, I'm afraid you don't want me the way I want you.*

Pain flickered in her eyes.

Come on, Maggie. Say you want me to stay. Say you want me. He held his breath, his heart beating ninety to nothing.

"What about that deck and screened-in back porch you talked about? And whitewashing the garage?" She grabbed his arm, and her nails dug in almost to the point of pain.

He relaxed and gave her a slow smile. "Are you saying you want me to stay?"

"I, uh, well, I, er, have more work for you to do." She blinked and let go of his arm, twisting her hands together and looking everywhere but at him.

Angel tucked a loose strand of hair behind her ear. He hated that crazy knot on top of her head, preferring her hair down and loose. *God, how I want to wrap my fists in that hair and bury myself inside her.* He chuckled when she inhaled sharply. Had she read his thoughts?

"There's still work to be done," she reiterated.

"That's all? Just work?"

She shook her head. "N-No. I want you…"

The last sentence came out so softly he had to strain to hear it. But it was the one he'd been longing for.

"I guess maybe I better start studying, huh?" Wrapping an arm around her shoulders, he walked her into the kitchen. He kept his exterior cool and nonchalant, but inside, he was doing backflips and cartwheels.

Maggie stepped out of the shower and slathered her dry skin with lotion, admiring her red toenails. Yesterday she'd splurged on a pedicure.

Who did she think she was kidding? She was preparing herself for some serious sex. Why else would she have suffered through a bikini wax, too? Angel's kiss alone had made her short of breath. *Sex with him will probably give me a damn heart attack.*

Good grief, she could just imagine Phillip's embarrassment if he read a coroner's report documenting her death from cardiac arrest during sex. She paused and frowned at her reflection in the mirror. The streak of gray in her hair reminded her she was closer to forty than thirty. Thank God it was only on top of her head. If she ever found gray hair down *there,* she'd have to seriously consider a total Brazilian, not just a bikini wax.

She slipped into her striped pink flannel pajamas and sighed. Pajamas were not man magnets. Next time she went to town, she'd splurge on a sexy nightgown and underwear. Maybe even a thong? She dropped her pants and looked at her butt in the mirror.

Oh, hell no.

She quickly pulled her pajamas back up, promised for at least the millionth time to hit the gym, and brushed her teeth. At least she had nice teeth, and they were all there. She padded to the kitchen to set the coffee pot up for in the morning.

"No!"

The shout from Angel's room made the hair on the back of her neck stand on end.

Dear God, what's happened?

She found him tossing and turning in the throes of a nightmare.

"Angel, wake up. Everything's okay. Wake up," she crooned.

His body was drenched in sweat. Gently she stroked his chest.

"No, no, stop!" he whimpered.

"Wake up, Angel. It's just a nightmare." This time, she turned on his bedside lamp.

He woke with a start and jumped out of bed, fists raised. His eyes darted around like a trapped animal's as he struggled to breathe.

"It's me. Maggie." She backed away, unnerved, hands held where he could see them.

It took a full minute before he seemed to recognize her. He clutched his chest and collapsed on the side of the bed, hanging his head.

"Take some deep breaths and calm down. You're okay."

He closed his eyes and covered his face with his hands. "Fuck. I'm sorry, Maggie."

She sat next to him. "Shhh, don't apologize. It was a bad dream."

When he seemed to be breathing normally, he repositioned himself and wrapped both arms around her waist, leaning his head on her shoulder. She stroked his back and hummed until he visibly relaxed.

"You're okay," she murmured, over and over.

"D-Did I say anything?" He pulled away and rubbed his face.

"Not really. Just *no*. Do you want to tell me about your nightmare? It might help."

Angel pulled her down on the bed so they faced each other and threw an arm across her waist. "No."

He opened his eyes and gave her a small smile. "I would've tried to have a nightmare earlier if I'd known it would get you in my bed." His voice was teasing, yet husky and layered with need.

She tensed as his warm, rough hand worked its way under her pajama top and rubbed in sensuous circles on her back. But she didn't stop him. His beautiful eyes were hooded with desire as they locked with hers.

"I need you." He propped his head on his hand and moved his other hand out from under her pajama top. Slowly, he unbuttoned the first two buttons. She caught her breath but didn't move. Leaning over, he traced a kiss after each button he'd painstakingly unfastened.

"Mmmm…flannel pajamas. Major turn-on," he whispered. He placed soft kisses down her neck to her collarbone. His tongue dipped into the concave area, and she moaned in response.

Maggie let out a shallow breath, every nerve in her body on high alert. "Quit teasing me. I know what I'm wearing isn't sexy. P-Please, can we turn out the light?"

"Why? You're beautiful. Anything you wear is sexy. You, Margaret Mary Robertson, are the sexiest woman I've ever known."

His arm snaked across her and turned off the lamp.

"Better? Maggie, when will you believe me when I say you're beautiful?"

"I'm not twenty-five," she replied. "I need to lose ten pounds—"

"Hush."

He placed a hand over her mouth. "Don't talk about the woman I'm crazy about like that. It pisses me off, because she's perfect as is."

Pushing her top aside, he captured one breast in his mouth, tugging, licking, and kissing the nipple until it pebbled.

"I'm not going to listen to any negativity. You're right; you're not twenty-five. But you're also not ninety-nine."

She gazed at his face, lit by the dim light from the kitchen stove, and didn't see any derision. He caressed her breasts, circling the other nipple until it peaked.

"So sensitive. So pretty, just like you." He pulled it with his teeth and sucked.

Hot heat zipped through her body.

He really thinks I'm pretty? He could have anyone, but he wants me—Maggie Robertson—in my pink flannel pajamas. Still tense, she gave him a small smile.

Slipping her pajama pants off, Angel kissed her stomach. As he traced the stretch marks with his finger, he whispered, "You're a woman, Maggie. Not a girl—a woman whose body is to be caressed, respected, and loved. You have curves a man can sink into and enjoy. My God, you have no idea how you drive me fuckin' crazy. One smile from you can light up a room and make me forget what the hell I'm doing. Your eyes see me as a better man than I am and make me want to live up to your ideal. Your laughter is like music; your compassion, a balm to my soul. You're an intelligent, beautiful woman, and I want to make love to you."

Angel pulled her hand to the erection in his pajama pants. He smiled into her ear and whispered. "Does this feel like a man repulsed by your body?"

Maggie shook her head no, and with shaking hands, helped him shed his pants before rolling on top of him. With wild abandon she kissed, licked, and tasted his jaw, neck, and mouth. Skimming his body with greedy hands, she couldn't get enough of him. After years in the desert, he was her oasis. She knew she'd been thirsty, but she'd never realized she was so damn dehydrated.

Angel smiled, her cheek cupped in his hand. "You're perfect, 'just' Maggie."

"You look like a fallen angel." She nipped his lower lip with her teeth as her hands continued to roam the dips and crevices of his sculpted muscles. "With a perfect body."

He stilled for a moment. "Not perfect by any means. I have my scars and flaws. Everyone does." He reached into the bedside table drawer, and Maggie heard the foil packet rip.

Oh my God, I'm going to do this. She was going to have sex for the first time with someone other than her ex-husband...

Angel flipped her onto her back and kissed her forehead. Maggie ran her fingers over his pierced nipples, and he moaned into her lips when he kissed her.

"Do they hurt?"

"Hell no...God, it feels good," he murmured, nipping her earlobe. "You sure about this?"

"Yes." Her voice shook with emotion.

Capturing her nipple in his mouth, he sucked on it as his hand tweaked the other. "Totally...one hundred percent...sure?"

"Yes," Maggie hissed. She panted as he tracked warm kisses lower and lower.

His tongue flicked and licked her clitoris, causing her to moan as her hands clenched the bed sheets.

"I dunno, Maggie, maybe you're not ready. Maybe I should stop…" He chuckled and teased her unmercifully with his skilled tongue.

"Don't. You…" She gasped and bucked as his tongue continued to torture her with pleasure. "Dare. Stop…" Her body convulsed with the intensity of her orgasm. Kissing her stomach, he grinned and pried her hand from the dread she had clutched.

Angel pulled her legs up around his waist and entered her swiftly, possessively, with an animalistic groan. The moonlight dipped into the window, and she watched him close his eyes, clench his jaw. She dug her fingernails into his arms and raised her hips to meet each thrust, closing her eyes, not believing the tension was building again for another orgasm.

"Look at me," he rasped. Her eyes flew open, and he quickened the pace until her inner muscles began to quake and spasm. She screamed with her second release, which made her feel as if she was falling, falling, falling into an abyss of satisfaction. His soon followed, and he ground out her name, his gaze never leaving hers. Spent, he collapsed on top of her, slick with sweat.

"Maggie," he gasped again.

"Angel," she purred as she ran her nails down his back.

He didn't move for a few moments as they savored the moment. Then with a sigh of contentment, he rolled off and went to dispose of the condom. When he returned, he jumped back in bed on top of her.

"Damn, Maggie. That was fuckin' awesome!"

He brushed a damp curl off her forehead and kissed her, holding both of her hands.

"I can't think. My mind is mush," she whispered. "Two. Incredible. Orgasms."

He chuckled. "Your brain *is* mush. You didn't even fuss about my language. I'm sorry, baby. I'll do better next time. Just give me a minute to recuperate."

She snorted with disbelief.

"Okay, okay, call my bluff, heartless woman. Ten minutes, tops." Angel blew a raspberry on her stomach before rolling onto his back next to her. He pulled her close, and she rested her head on his shoulder as his fingers lazily caressed her skin.

"I want a cigarette."

Raising her head, she looked at him with confusion. "You smoke?"

"Nope. The sex was just that mind blowing."

They both laughed, and she curled into him again, her hand rubbing up and down his body.

"That was the best sex of my life," she whispered.

He kissed her forehead. "It was more than sex. So much more..." He smiled sheepishly. "But thank you. I have to admit—I was nervous as hell and worried."

She rolled on top of him and rested her chin on her folded hands, gazing into his eyes, surprised by his serious look. "Worried?"

"Well, I figured you have a lot more experience than me." He ran his fingers up and down her spine.

Maggie raised her eyebrows and tried hard to keep from laughing by biting her lip. But she couldn't help it. At first, it started as a chuckle, but soon erupted into a sidesplitting all-out whoop of laughter.

"Experienced? Me?" She wiped her eyes and continued to chuckle.

He grinned and pinched her nose. "You keep telling me how old you are..."

"Angel, you're only the second man I've ever been with in my entire, pathetic life. My ex-husband was my first and only, until you. I'm about as inexperienced..." Her voice trailed off and her cheeks heated with discomfort. "This was my first time in years. I'm practically a born-again virgin. Brian and I didn't even sleep in the same room the last five years of our marriage."

"Damn, you snore that loud?" he teased.

Giggling, she smacked him on the chest.

Angel brushed the hair out of her face and captured her lips. "I love that sound."

She knit her brows. "What sound?"

"Your laughter. I hope I can always make you laugh."

"Angel, have you ever been married, or in love?"

He chuckled. "Never married. Although I once proposed to an older woman named Elise."

"What happened?" She traced the tat that said Three Amigos above his heart. There were no names anywhere on his body, which made her happy.

"Nothing. She told me she was too old for me." He laughed and tapped her nose. "Sound familiar?"

He reached up and tickled her until she squealed and squirmed.

Her eyes grew wide when she realized what her squirming had caused. "Again?"

"Yes, ma'am. One of the advantages of a younger *man*," he replied with a wicked grin. "Be right back." He hopped off the bed and left the room, leaving her curious. She laughed when he entered the room shaking a can of whipped cream.

Maggie quietly pulled on her pajamas, wondering if she'd be able to walk today. Muscles she never even knew existed now ached deliciously.

"Where are you going?" Angel wasn't quite awake, lying on his stomach with the sheet low, his eyes still closed. To her surprise, he'd already redressed in his pajama pants and thermal top.

She leaned over, pushed the dreads out of his face, and kissed his scruffy cheek. "To put the dirty sheets in the laundry and start the turkey. Go back to sleep." She slipped on her slippers and grabbed the messy sheets they'd thrown in the corner after their dessert-in-bed sex.

"Mm'kay, you wore me out. You're an insatiable sex fiend," he added with a lazy smile, still not opening his eyes. "You taste even better than pumpkin pie."

Maggie shook her head, smiling. *He thinks I'm insatiable?* His stamina was remarkable, and he'd more than kept up with her. He was right. There were definite benefits to having a younger lover. Snidely, she hoped Brian had to use something for erectile dysfunction with the new Mrs. Robertson.

Angel went back asleep, and Maggie took a moment to stare and admire him. He looked so content—and still. He was never still when awake.

Humming to herself, she started the laundry. Her mind replayed the wicked look on Angel's face as he shook the whipped cream can. And the way he'd lapped it off her body. He was everything and more than she'd fantasized about since meeting him. Starting the coffee, she removed two mugs from the cupboard and sighed as reality overtook fantasy. Fears wormed their way into her thoughts.

Restless spirit. Gypsy. Her heart plummeted. She busied herself with getting the turkey ready to cook. *He agreed to stay and help with the bed and breakfast, but for how long? Will he tire of me? Find someone closer to his age? Stop! It's Thanksgiving. Be thankful for what you have.*

This beautiful man had done what she thought was impossible. He'd pieced her broken heart back together with patience and tenderness. She could no longer imagine her home without Angel's presence. Even just a quick trip to town left her feeling lonely without him. Maggie finished prepping the turkey and covered it with foil.

Bending over to open the oven, she shoved the turkey inside. When two strong hands grabbed her hips, she squealed. "Angel!"

"What do you expect me to do with that cute ass up in the air?" He smacked her butt, kissed the back of her neck, and pulled her upright against his chest. "You smell like vanilla, sage, and sex. Quite the aphrodisiac," he growled, nibbling on her ear.

"I, Angel…" She moaned when his hands crept under her pajama top and cupped her breasts, tweaking her hard nipples between his fingers. "Stop," she said with a giggle. "I need to make the pie."

His hands stopped moving, and she felt the smile on his lips when he asked, "Pumpkin?"

She nodded, unable to speak with the rush of need infusing her body.

"Hmmm, does pumpkin pie trump sex? That's a tough question."

"Pumpkin pie goes well with whipped cream," she choked out, turning in his arms to give him a quick kiss. She wrapped her arms around his neck.

"Ah, you do too." He leered, licking her neck with an exaggerated slurp. "However, I think pie, whipped cream, and Maggie all together will make me very thankful, so I'll let you get back to the pie making." Giving her a kiss, he poured himself a cup of coffee and went outside to the back stoop.

Maggie shook her head and peered out the window. The thermometer outside read 56°F, and there he was, barefoot. What was he thinking? She watched him shiver and meander down toward the boat dock, sipping his coffee. When he reached the dock, he put his coffee mug down, slipped out of his clothes, and dove into the frigid water.

Has he lost his mind?

Maggie threw on her sweater, grabbed his hoodie and ran to the dock, shivering in her flannel pajamas.

Treading water with his teeth chattering, he grinned when he saw her on the dock. "Wanna join me?"

"Are you insane? What are you doing? Get out of that water right now."

"Not yet." He slung his wet dreads out of his face and continued to tread.

"You're going to catch your death from cold."

He laughed. "Come in and join me. I'll warm you right up."

"There is no way I'm getting in that ice cold water." Dropping his hoodie next to his clothes and coffee, she turned to walk back to the house. She heard him behind her, climbing the ladder to the dock. The next thing she knew, she hit the lake with a shrill shriek of outrage. When she surfaced, her teeth chattered so hard she was afraid she'd crack them. Angel smirked at her, lazily treading water and ignoring her icy glare.

"Keep moving, baby. You'll warm up, and it feels great. When you swim in water like this, you know you're alive. Embrace the feeling."

Maggie sputtered, "Alive? We're going to die of hypothermia! I hate you!"

He laughed and splashed her. With another shriek, she splashed him back and dunked him under the cold water. She laughed when he surfaced, slinging water from his dreads and howling with laughter. She hated to admit it, but Angel was right.

She felt invigorated, young, and deliriously happy.

Chapter
Nine

"Seriously? Isn't Christmas like a month away?" Angel complained later that afternoon, after dinner, as he stretched and rubbed his stomach. "Let's get naked instead. I'll give you an early Christmas present." He waggled his eyebrows.

Maggie smiled. While tempting, she had things that needed to be done.

"I always start decorating for Christmas after Thanksgiving dinner. Plus, the place needs to have a holiday feel. Our guests will expect it."

"But I haven't had my pie yet." His tone wasn't quite a whine, but a definite pout lingered on his lower lip.

"At least put the wreaths up, okay?"

"Sure, that's no biggie. Front door, back door, no *problemo*. Then we can get naked. And eat pie."

Maggie laughed as his smile widened. "You have a one-track mind. I hate to disappoint you, but I have wreaths for all the windows, upstairs and downstairs."

"Fuck, er, I mean, shoot," he huffed. "Okay, I'll go get the ladder. Let's get this over with. I want my dessert. You and whipped cream with a little pie on the side." Standing, he stretched again. "I'll go change clothes."

Maggie considered ditching the decorating and going straight for dessert, but she really needed to get things done. The phone rang as she headed out of the kitchen.

"Hello?"

"Hi, Mom."

"Happy Turkey Day! Are you having a good time?"

"Yeah, it's okay." In a low voice he added, "Tiffany can't cook her way out of a damn can of ravioli."

"I hardly think her cooking is why your father married her. And don't talk that way, son. It sounds crass."

"I miss your bread. Will you make homemade bread for Christmas?"

"Let's get this over with," Angel said, walking back in the room.

She put a finger to her lips. But he already had his arms wrapped around her waist, nuzzling the side of her neck. Surprised, she gasped.

"Stop!" She tried to wiggle away.

Angel laughed, but he moved to the back door, whistling as he shrugged into his coat.

"Stop?" Phillip sounded puzzled.

"Nothing, Phillip. I wasn't talking to you."

Unfortunately, there was nothing wrong with her son's hearing.

"Is that a guy with you?" Phillip sounded incredulous.

Maggie clenched her teeth. She didn't want to discuss Angel with Phillip over the phone. She needed time to think about what to say.

"It's just my handyman. I love you. Be safe on the ski slopes, and call me when you get back to school, okay?"

"Uh, okay...Well, bye, Mom." He still sounded suspicious when he hung up.

She turned around, feeling guilty.

"Just the handyman, eh?"

"You're so much more, but I want to talk to Phillip in person about us—not spring it on him while he's with his father." She walked over to put her arms around him. "You make me feel alive and pretty, Angel. You've given me so much to be thankful for."

"I haven't given you anything, Maggie. You *are* pretty. But that's just a bonus. Your compassion and humor are what attracted me to you."

She raised an eyebrow.

He threw up his hands. "Okay, and your great ass."

She laughed. "Flattery won't get you out of hanging the wreaths."

"I'll gladly hang your wreaths. Anything, as long as I get a good-night kiss and pumpkin pie." He gave her a quick kiss on her brow and grabbed her butt.

"You're copping a feel now?"

"Yes, ma'am, I am. Lately, it's one of the perks of my job as your handsyman."

"Don't ma'am me!" But she couldn't quit grinning.

"Okay, 'just' Maggie. Get the wreaths out. Let's get this done. I'm ready for dessert."

Two hours later, Angel climbed the ladder to hang the last wreath. *Why the fuck does she need to hang the stupid things on the back of the house?* Every time he complained about it, she giggled. This led him to complain a lot, because he loved hearing her laugh. It was now dark, and they were working by the outside floodlights.

Angel's sleeve slipped, revealing old, scarred track marks barely concealed by his tats. His stomach clenched. He'd been careful keeping them covered. The thought of explaining his past to her still scared the shit out of him, but now that things were changing, he had to tell her. Just not yet…Not during the holidays…How many more excuses could he come up with? *Denial, not just a river in Egypt.* He wished he could get to a meeting tonight. Emma was out of town, and if he continued with this line of thinking, he was headed down a slippery slope. He supposed he could call someone from NA for a ride, but Maggie wouldn't understand him leaving tonight of all nights. *Shit, I'm overthinking.*

"Brrr, I think the temperature is dropping." Maggie shivered, working the wreath so the branches weren't so flat.

"Hey, sexy fluffer, got the last wreath ready?"

"Sexy fluffer?" She stared up at him.

"You know what a fluffer is, right?"

"No, should I?"

He laughed. "I'll, uh, tell you later, and you can demonstrate."

Her dark hair blew in the breeze, and she grabbed hold of the ladder as it shook with his movement. Bundled up in her gray coat, her cheeks bright pink from the cold air, his Maggie was indeed beautiful. And thoughts of her fluffing and decking his balls made him feel quite festive and jolly…

He stretched and reached a little too far to grab the wreath from her. The ladder swayed, and Maggie's terrified scream alerted him he was in trouble.

Big trouble.

Spatial reasoning was another of his many deficits. In a panic, he attempted to grab the gutter but missed. He'd always wondered what it would feel like to fly when not on drugs or cliff diving. He now knew.

And it was *terrifying.*

His shoulder hit the ground, his body cushioned by Maggie. Pain overtook all thoughts. He wasn't sure who screamed louder, him or her. *Dear God, is she hurt?* With a groan, he struggled to roll off of her. His right arm hung useless, his wrist throbbed, and he felt ready to pass out. Gasping, he maneuvered onto his back. Tears streamed down Maggie's face as she knelt beside him.

"Angel! Are you all right?" She ran her hands over his body as she assessed his injuries. "Hold still. Oh my God."

"Are you okay?" he managed to gasp. "Motherfuckinsonofabitch, I hurt."

"I'm fine, except you've aged me fifty years. What hurts?"

"My shoulder and wrist."

"Stay here. I'll be right back." Maggie darted into the house.

"Okay," he mumbled. Where did she think he'd go, Timbuktu? *Where the hell is Timbuktu, anyway?* A tear escaped down his cheek, and he hastily wiped it away, embarrassed to be crying. Gritting his teeth, he tried focusing on his breathing.

Maggie returned and eased his useless right arm into a sling she'd fashioned from a sheet.

"I think your shoulder's dislocated, but you'll be fine."

His breathing eased, and his anxiety lessened with her calm reassurance.

He managed a weak smile instead of whimpering like he wanted to.

She helped him to his feet, and he leaned on her, feeling a little woozy as she guided him to the front step. Air hissed between his lips as he sat.

"I'm going to go get the truck. Wait here. The hospital isn't that far away. Let me grab my purse."

"What? N-No. I don't want to go to the hospital!" His heart raced. He scrubbed his face with his unhurt hand. Ignoring him, Maggie ran and got her purse and started the truck. Leaving it running, she sprinted back to help him.

"Can't you put my shoulder back?" He refused to get up from the front step.

"Don't be ridiculous. Get in the truck, or I'll call an ambulance. We have to make sure it isn't serious." Holding him by his good elbow, she placed a steadying hand on his back as she helped him stand and walk.

A cold sweat broke out on his brow, and his teeth chattered uncontrollably as he settled in the seat. He struggled not to cry, afraid. This could be the beginning of the end…

She wrapped a blanket around him and drove like a bat out of hell to the ER.

"M-Maggie, please, I don't want to go." He was at the point of begging. "Please?"

"Don't be silly. They'll give you something for pain before they manipulate your shoulder back in place. Phillip had a similar injury playing football one time. You'll be fine. But you need x-rays."

His entire body shook all over. *Pain meds, needles…*

The dragon of his addiction roared, threatening to devour everything he'd fought so hard to achieve.

Twenty minutes later, Angel still felt sick. And not just because of his shoulder and wrist, or the fear of being here. After tonight, Maggie could very well kick him out, just like his parents had. Not that he could blame them. For too many years, addiction had ruled his life. It took losing everything for him to get his shit together and get clean.

Christmas carols played overhead, and a lopsided tree decorated the nurse's desk. *What the fuck? It's only Thanksgiving.*

And prior to falling, he'd had so much to be thankful for.

He hated Christmas and had for years. Few families lived up to the commercialized happiness portrayed in sappy movies and commercials meant to influence people to buy shit. His certainly didn't.

Holidays when he was a small boy had seemed magical, with the extravagant presents and parties. As he'd matured, he'd realized it was a fragile veneer of civility covering deep-rooted dysfunction. His parents didn't love each other. They tolerated each other, living separate lives. It was a mystery how he and Damien had ever come to be. He could never see his parents being in the same room long enough to procreate.

The one thing Angel wanted and needed from his parents, he never got: attention. To be heard. *To matter.* Instead, he and his brother were left to the care of the housekeeper and estate manager. Christmas was the only day the family was together. And it invariably ended with a fight between him and his father, or between his parents. He sighed. Turning, he vomited in the trash can.

He had so wanted this Christmas to be different.

Maggie wet a washcloth and attempted to bathe Angel's face. He swatted her away and closed his eyes. He'd been uncooperative and irritable since he was triaged, x-rayed, and placed in a cubicle in the ER. He'd asked her to leave, but she hadn't. She hoped that was the right thing to do.

A nurse came in to draw blood for the second time. The first time he'd refused.

His eyes narrowed. "If you come near me with that needle one more time, I'll fuckin' sue."

The nurse left in a huff, snapping the curtain closed. Maggie walked over and kissed Angel's forehead. "Don't you think suing over one tiny stick is overkill?"

"No needles. No meds," he snarled. Sweat lined his upper lip, and his leg bounced nonstop.

"I know you're hurting, but you need to cooperate. They're here to help you—"

The curtain shoved back, and the doctor entered.

He frowned, giving Angel a cursory glance before studying the chart. "I'm Dr. Raymond. I understand you've been uncooperative. There's no need to worry, son. You're not the first to be needle shy. Bigger men than you have passed out." He looked at the chart and x-ray and did a cursory exam. "The wrist has a minor sprain. But you have an anterior dislocation of your shoulder, though I don't see any fractures. You're lucky, considering the fall you took. A closed reduction will provide you relief. I know it won't be comfortable, but we'll give you something to relieve the pain and anxiety—"

"No!" Angel barked. "No meds. Just do it."

"You're having some swelling and spasms. There's no need to be stoic about this; it's going to hurt."

"I c-can't," Angel muttered through clenched teeth. "I'm a junkie. I used to bang heroin…So no meds, no needles! I have over eighteen months clean." His cheeks flushed. Hanging his head, he stared at the floor.

Shocked, Maggie sank into the chair. The news was a blow to the gut. A memory of helping her drunk father washed over her. He'd accidentally knocked her down a flight of stairs and broken her arm. She shivered and forced herself to deal with the present situation.

"I see." The doctor's attitude went from aloof to downright indignant, and he turned to Maggie. "Is that why your son didn't want blood drawn? He was afraid of the drug test? What was he using prior to the fall?"

"I haven't used a damn thing!" Angel shouted, anger blazing in his eyes. "But I'm as addicted to the fuckin' needle as I am the goddamned drugs. I don't want them near me."

"He's an adult in his right mind. You should address *him*, not me. I'm *not* his mother. I don't believe he's been using any kind of drug, and he's obviously in pain. After you do the procedure, I could give him the pain medications if they're needed and lock them up—" Maggie offered, still reeling from Angel's confession.

"Goddammit, no meds! And I'll piss in the damn cup for a drug test, but I don't want any fuckin' needles near me."

"I'm not giving an addict pain meds," the doctor replied brusquely. "Now, if you'll step outside, I'll get this shoulder back in place."

"No. I'm not leaving him." She crossed her arms. "And you might want to look around for the compassion you've obviously misplaced. This man is in pain and a human being. He told you he was an addict *not* to get pain meds, but to protect himself from *relapsing*. If you don't want an angry letter sent to the hospital board, check your damn attitude, Dr. Raymond."

Angel flashed a wan smile. "It's okay. Calm down, Maggie. Let's just get this over with."

"It's *not* okay," she reiterated, glaring at the doctor.

Dr. Raymond nodded, looking somewhat contrite. Maggie watched him maneuver Angel's shoulder with the help of a nurse. Angel withstood it in silence, but tears tracked down his pale face. Weak-kneed, Maggie collapsed into the chair. The doctor called for the nurse to bring an ice pack.

"You did well, son. You should feel better now. And the prescription I'm giving you is non-addictive. Don't be afraid to take it and use ice. The nurse will give you your discharge instructions. Wear the sling and take it easy for a while. If you have any problems, come back." He patted Angel on his good shoulder and left the room.

"I'm so sorry." Maggie moved to him and kissed his silent tears away, whispering soothing words of comfort.

"You were awesome, Maggie," he croaked.

"Me? You're the one who just went through hell without any pain medication. I'm proud of you, and you should be proud of yourself."

"The way you lit into that doctor for me? No one's stood up for me like that in a long damn time. Thank you." He closed his eyes and another tear escaped. With his good hand, he wiped it and turned away.

She reached out and held his hand, giving it a squeeze as they waited on the nurse to complete his discharge. She'd meant what she said to the doctor, but Angel's bombshell had left her feeling decidedly shaky.

Angel pushed the bite of pie back and forth across his plate. Out of the corner of his eye, he watched Maggie clean up the kitchen. She hadn't mentioned anything about him being an addict since they'd arrived back home. As a matter of fact, she'd been inordinately quiet. The elephant in the room needed to be addressed. He just hoped he wouldn't have to sleep under a bridge tonight. *Damn, it didn't take long for me to get soft and comfortable.*

He took a deep breath and said, "It's where I go at least once or twice a week. Emma takes me. To my NA meeting." Ice-cold fear gripped his heart.

Maggie stopped unloading the dishwasher. "I realize that now. I can take you while she and David are out of town. Didn't you say they would be gone a few days for the holiday?"

"Yeah. Thanks. I need to go to one soon. Holidays are hard enough. Now I've got pain fuckin' with my head, pushing me to use." He looked up at her and bit his lip, trying to keep the emotions in check. "It's an every-day struggle, but I swear, I'm fighting it. I won't let it beat me. If I don't stay clean, my ass is grass. I'll end up dead—or worse, in prison."

She stood at the sink, her back to him, staring out into the night.

The pain he'd witnessed on her face when he admitted he was a junkie had been ten times worse than the physical pain in his shoulder. "You can drug test me if you want."

She turned and faced him. The anger he saw surprised him. "Why would I need to do that?"

"Because now you don't trust me; I don't blame you." Angel stared at the table.

"I trust *you*, Angel. *You don't trust me.*"

Confused, he looked up, taking in her stormy green eyes. He returned to pushing the pie around his plate. "I don't understand."

"You didn't trust me enough to tell me the truth before you were injured. When did you plan to mention that? I feel like a fool. At one time, I seriously wondered if you and Emma Patterson were having an affair." She held up her hand when he started to protest.

"No excuses. Answer me. Why didn't you trust me enough to tell me the truth — that you're an addict in recovery?"

Staring at his hands folded on the table, he admitted, "I didn't think you'd give me a chance."

"Me not give you a chance? I guess it turned out the other way around, didn't it?" She shoved a plate in the cupboard and slammed it closed. "Why? When have I been less than open with you? I mean…" She struggled to find the words. "I trusted you by inviting you into my home — into my life…"

With a heavy sigh, she turned and wiped the counter for a moment before continuing. "I'm well aware of your struggles…of your pain. I was the child of an alcoholic. You could have trusted me. Let me rephrase that. *You should have trusted me.* But because you didn't, I don't know what to believe any more."

She threw down the rag and quietly left the room without looking at him, leaving him alone with his pie.

Angel shoved the plate away.

Chapter
Ten

Maggie sank to the side of her bed, covered her face with her hands, and let the tears flow.

She'd never been the type to cry dainty, quiet, romance-heroine tears, and she buried her face in her pillow to stifle her blubbering. In that split second when Angel fell, fear had engulfed her. And it wasn't just worry that he'd be injured—it was more. There was no denying how important he'd become to her. And now she knew he had a serious disease—one she knew only too well could steal him from her.

The thought saddened her.

Everything between them had happened in a flash. She needed to slow down and think about her life in a calm, rational manner. The age difference was no longer the only factor separating them. From an emotional standpoint, could she afford to get involved with someone in recovery? What if he relapsed? Her father had struggled with alcoholism until his painful death from cirrhosis. She and her mother had borne the brunt of his relapses and recovery time after time, and it had been a rollercoaster life—one she escaped by going away to college. For her own self-preservation, she should probably protect her heart and end the relationship, but a part of her rebelled, not wanting to be sensible and responsible. For once, couldn't she just go with her emotions? *He's clean.*

A knock at the door interrupted her thoughts.

"May I come in?" Angel slouched against the doorjamb, not making eye contact with her. He ran his thumb up and down the doorframe.

He'd changed into pajama pants, and she felt guilty for not helping him; it had to have hurt.

She dashed the tears from her eyes, knowing she looked a mess. "I'm sorry. I just needed to take a breather. I'm feeling a bit overwhelmed."

"I understand. Please, if nothing else I say matters, I want you to know I realize I was wrong. And I'm sorry. Really, really sorry. It was a sin of omission, but nonetheless dishonest."

"I believe you. I'm just…hurt."

"I know." He sighed. "It's not a past to be proud of. And it's ruined so many of my relationships…I was scared to tell you. I'm falling for you, Maggie, hard. But I'll understand if you want me to leave."

"I don't want you to leave, but I need a little time."

"Fair enough."

"Please be honest with me from now on."

He paused for a fraction of a second. "I'll do my best."

She gave him a small smile. "Are you okay? You need to rest and put ice on that shoulder and wrist."

Angel hesitated a second before crossing the room and sitting next to her. Placing his good arm around her shoulder, he kissed her forehead.

"Don't look at me." She hid her face in his neck.

"Why not?"

"I'm not a pretty crier."

His chest rumbled with laughter. "I think your red, splotchy face is sexy."

"Don't be ridiculous."

"Maggie?"

"Yes?"

"Who takes care of you?"

"Me?" She pulled away. "I don't understand what you mean."

"I bet you took care of your dad. I know you catered to Brian and Phillip. Who has ever taken care of you?"

"I'm f-fine. I can take care of myself."

"I know you can. But what if *I* want to take care of *you?* Would you trust me enough to let me?" He lifted his brows, waiting.

She gave him a small smile. "I'll do my best."

"That's all either of us can do."

"Do you want to sleep in here tonight? The bed is bigger."

He tipped her chin up so she was forced to look at him, and his smirk broadened into a grin. "Are you trying to seduce me, Ms. Robertson?"

"No! I just…" Flustered, she hopped off the bed.

He grinned. "I don't mind if you are. I don't think I'm really up to doing much, but you could show me how that gizmo thingie on your vibrator works."

"What?" Maggie's cheeks blushed hot. She screeched, "How? When?"

Angel burst out laughing and patted the bed. "The night I put you to bed, I saw it in your open drawer. I closed it so you wouldn't be embarrassed. But I've been curious ever since."

"Oh my God, stop! This is beyond embarrassing and more awkward than the time I walked out on the football field for homecoming with my dress tucked in my pantyhose," she muttered.

Angel grimaced as he laid back on the bed.

"I'm totally teasing. I'm done for the night."

She helped him under the covers and went to the kitchen, returning with an ice pack.

"Thank you."

"You're welcome."

"So tell me, Maggie May. Where did you learn to be all calm in an emergency and make a sling?"

"I guess it's a mom thing." She sighed as she helped him get comfortable. "They even thought I was your mother at the ER."

"They also thought I was drug seeking. I wouldn't worry about what they thought. They didn't exactly get gold stars in the bedside manner department. And trust me; you're nothing like my mom. My mom would've freaked out."

"I learned to make a sling in Boy Scouts. I was a den mother, and we had to learn basic first aid. I'm sure your mother would have done the same for you."

"I doubt it. I was never a Boy Scout. I was busy with, uh, other activities."

"Drugs?"

"Not at first." He rubbed his eyes with the heel of his good hand. "I promise to tell you about it, but right now, can we just go to sleep?" Yawning, he flashed a lazy smile.

"Of course. I'll sleep in your bed." Maggie moved to get up, but he caught her hand.

"I'm not staying in here unless the offer includes my private-duty nurse." He grinned and gave her an exaggerated leer. "Do you by chance have one of those cute little hats, white hose, and six-inch white high heels?"

"You're incorrigible."

"Yes, ma'am."

"You 'ma'am' me one more time and I'll go get the rectal thermometer."

"Kinky. Will you wear your homecoming crown?" He ducked for cover under her pillow, laughing.

Angel sat straight up, his heart pounding. He grimaced uncomfortably at the sudden motion. Thankfully, his nightmare hadn't awakened Maggie. Taking a deep breath, he slowly exhaled to steady his nerves. She'd left the light on in the bathroom so he wouldn't trip if he needed to get up in the middle of the night, which was still a distinct possibility with all her shoes scattered around the room. He tossed the ice pack to the bedside table and propped himself up against the pillows. He smiled, watching the woman who had laid claim to his heart.

She slept on her side, her dark hair spread out and her chin tucked onto one hand. Her lips were slightly parted, and she purred softly—she'd kill him if he said she snored. He couldn't get enough of her full lips, wanting to kiss them, tease them, bite them, and watch them smile at him, like he was something special.

After a few moments, his heart rate returned to normal, his breathing evened out. He was safe. And in bed with the woman he was pretty damn sure he was in love with, which was still hard to grasp. A feeling of peace settled over him. She'd been magnificent dealing with that asshole doctor at the ER. His family wouldn't have reacted like that. The doctor's comments would have been ignored. Unpleasant situations were not dealt with in the Sinclair household. They were quietly swept away.

Did his family even miss him at the Thanksgiving table this year? *I should've called them.* Maybe it was time to work step nine and make amends to his family. He had over eighteen months clean. His sponsor had repeatedly urged him to continue to work the steps and move forward. He really needed to touch base with Randy, especially now that he sort of had roots. Or maybe even get a local sponsor.

Restless and uncomfortable, he eased out of bed, torn on what to do. Maybe he'd sketch. He wandered into his room and pulled out his black book, but he felt uninspired. Giving up, he tossed it back in the desk and glanced at the clock.

It was after midnight, but for some strange reason, he longed to speak to his mom. It was his birthday, after all. He needed to hear her voice and pulled out his phone. Luckily, the number was stored, if they hadn't changed it. Pitiful, he couldn't even remember his own home phone number. He'd never been able to remember it, even though his parents and teachers had tried to drill it into his thick skull when he was younger.

Angel made the call.

After a few rings, his mother sleepily answered, "Hello?"

"Hi, Mom. Sorry it's so late…" The lump in his throat made it difficult to speak. He never dreamed that hearing his mother's voice after two years of silence would cause this much emotion.

"Angel?"

Is that worry in her voice? "Yes." He struggled with what to say next.

His mother sighed and whispered, "What kind of trouble are you in, son?"

"I-I'm not, Mom. I just wanted to hear your voice." *It's my birthday, dammit.*

"At three in the morning? Look, your father's waking up. I can't talk to you right now. Come see me soon and take care. I love you."

He held the phone for a full minute after she hung up, staring at the wall, lost in the memories of other times he'd been brushed aside by his mother because of his father. She hadn't even said *happy birthday*. He didn't know if he wanted to throw the phone or cry.

God forgive me, I hate that sonofabitch.

"Are you okay?" Maggie stood at the doorway.

"Yeah, I guess." He rubbed his eyes with the heel of his hand. *Oh well, like Dad says, the road to hell is paved with good intentions.* It shouldn't hurt like this. He should be used to being rebuffed by his family.

She moved to stand in front of him, and he pulled her onto his lap, holding her tight with his good arm. "I phoned my mom. Sorry if I woke you."

"The bed got cold. I was worried about you." She placed a tender kiss on his cheek.

"Yeah?" He buried himself in the softness of her breasts and pressed a kiss to the exposed skin above the button of her silly pajamas.

"Yeah." She echoed, rubbing his back.

"Thanks." That meant more than words could ever express. When had anyone besides Emma and Ken ever given a fuck about him?

"Did you tell your mom you got hurt?"

"I didn't get a chance. She wasn't exactly thrilled to hear from me."

"I'm sorry."

"It's okay."

As he spoke, it dawned on him that it really was. He had someone who cared about him. *I'm home. Home is with Maggie.* He hid his face in her lavender flannel pajama top and murmured brokenly, "I love you."

She stopped breathing for a moment and went still, so still he wondered if she was ever going to breathe again. *You spoke too soon, dumbass.*

"You're tired, in pain, and emotional. Come eat a bite of something and take your medicine." Maggie headed to the kitchen.

He followed and watched her pour a glass of milk. She motioned him to sit and sliced a piece of pie, even adding the whipped cream. She handed him the anti-inflammatory painkiller. "Eat and take your medicine."

Staring at the pie, he wondered if she hadn't heard him, or if she didn't believe him. Or worse, she didn't return the feelings. Judging by the way she avoided meeting his gaze, it was the last option.

Fuckin' great. She's probably trying to figure out how to let me down easy.

Why would she want some loser addict who couldn't even hold down a real job? He couldn't provide for her, not the way she'd been accustomed to in her previous marriage. Hell, he couldn't even balance a checkbook, or tell time unless it was a digital clock.

But I sure as hell wouldn't emotionally abuse her like her ex.

Angel took a bite of the pie. Friends with benefits…was that all they were destined to be? Or was he capable of changing, becoming the man she needed and wanted?

He had so many things to tell her, promises he wanted to make.

But he was desperately afraid he wouldn't be able to keep them.

"Are you coming back to bed?" Maggie yawned.

"Not yet. You go on."

"Okay." She kissed his forehead and headed back down the hall.

After finishing his pie, he got up and went to his room. Taking out his black book and markers, he sketched, trying to quiet his mind and keep the dragon at bay. A half hour later, his skin was crawling. Pacing, he picked up his phone.

"Hey, Randy. Sorry it's so late. I'm struggling, man…"

Eleven

Later that afternoon, Angel stood in the checkout line of Hudson's One Stop Grocery waiting on Maggie. She'd forgotten the milk and run back to get it, even though he'd offered to do that for her. He wore the sling to keep Maggie from fussing, but it was more of a bother than useful. Lydia, the nosy cashier, gaped at him with interest.

He stared back and shrugged. "That woman is hell with rope." He tossed an ace bandage on the belt.

Lydia's eyes grew wide. Turning red, she looked away, and he snickered.

Where is Maggie? His whole arm ached, and he was ready to go home. Perusing the gum selection, he grinned. Someone had left an interesting assortment of non-purchased items on the floor at the checkout. There was no one else in line, so he waited, staring at the cashier just to make her nervous.

Maggie arrived, and on a whim, he picked up the funniest of the left-behind items and added it to the belt moving toward Lydia. He would have been hard pressed to say whose expression was more stunned, Maggie's or Lydia's, when the personal lubricant was scanned.

"Angel! What the hell? Again?" Maggie screeched when they got to the parking lot.

"She's a nosy old bat, and I derive great pleasure in keep her guessing. Quit obsessing about what others think. Live in the moment; show me off. I don't mind being your boy toy."

He laughed so hard at the half-hearted tirade Maggie gave him all the way home, he had to sit in the truck a minute before he managed to get out and walk.

The next day, Angel poked the fire in the fireplace. He had an ace bandage wrapped around his wrist, but the sling lay folded on the couch, not on his arm.

"I'm tired of being stuck in this house," he announced. "I need to work on the sign out front." Flames leapt. Peeling his flannel shirt off, he folded it and placed it on top of the sling.

"I don't think that's a very good idea," Maggie countered. "Even though it isn't your painting arm that was affected, it will be too much. Just take it easy, at least through the weekend." She weaved the lights in and out of the Christmas tree branches. A roar from the television signaled another touchdown for Alabama, and she fell on her butt cheering.

Angel laughed and shook his head.

"What? I'm the woman most men dream about. I love football. And Alabama versus Auburn is the biggest rivalry in the SEC. You can't live in Alabama and not choose a side."

"Football is dumb. You didn't go to either school; why do you care?" He threw another log on the fire. "Fuck. That hurt," he swore under his breath.

"What happened? I heard that, Angel Sinclair." She stopped what she was doing. "What *is* your middle name?"

"I accidentally brushed the andiron. I will go to my grave before I reveal my middle name." He moved his finger toward his mouth.

"*Ew*, stop. What are you doing? Your mouth is dirty. Do you want an infection?"

"Relax, I'm just blowing on it. We've already established the fact that my mouth is dirty. However, I must point out, there are times I think you rather like my dirty mouth. As a matter of fact, I'm not the only one with a dirty mouth…" His lips curved into a wicked grin. "I do believe I remember hearing *someone*—I'm not mentioning any names—screaming *'Fuck me harder, Angel, harder,'* a few hours ago. I believe this was accompanied by some colorful language about my mad skills and crazy big package."

He adjusted his jeans around his *crazy big package* and snickered. She was certain her face now matched the red stockings hung on the mantle.

"I can't believe you talked me into it. I hope we didn't hurt your shoulder…"

"Nah, you did most of the work, cowgirl."

Maggie plugged the Christmas lights into the socket and looked up with anticipation as she half-heartedly protested, "I'm sure I don't know what you're talking about. You have such a vivid imagination. Well, *damnation.*" One side of the tree remained dark.

"Oh no, my virgin ears!"

She chucked the empty light box at him, which made him laugh. When he stood, Maggie caught her breath. Every defined muscle on his bare upper torso was perfectly highlighted by the firelight.

He came over and squatted next to the tree, testing the bulbs that didn't work. Maggie felt an incredible urge to tackle him right there and lick him from head to toe. *What's wrong with me?* She'd gone from "frigid" to insatiable in a New York minute.

Angel glanced up and smiled, unaware of her lascivious thoughts. It was part of his appeal. He seemed totally oblivious of just how handsome he was. The man didn't have a conceited bone in his body—unlike her ex-husband, who thought the sun rose and set on his very existence. Maggie reached out to touch him but pulled back. He'd told her he loved her, but she wondered if it had been his physical pain and the emotional letdown of the phone call to his family talking. *Why would this beautiful man, so full of life, love me? And just what are my feelings for him?*

She needed to think about all this—after she got the house ready for guests. "I wish you'd wear your sling. The discharge paperwork said two weeks, not two days."

"I'm fine, baby. I'll put it back on in a bit." He crawled around to test more bulbs, unaware of how that term of endearment made her heart race.

Perhaps there *was* hope for two lonely people, from two different backgrounds, with a significant age difference, to come together and be happy. But uncertainty still lingered, mainly because she knew so little about his past. Before the accident, whenever she asked, he'd shrugged and changed the subject.

Mentally she ticked off the known facts. He was an addict in recovery. His family didn't have anything to do with him. He possessed no sense of time or numbers, but judging by his doodlings on her grocery list and the beautiful reservation book he'd made her, he was artistic. Easygoing, he had a wicked sense of humor tinged with self-deprecation. And he was a free spirit who wandered through this physical world, embracing life seemingly without a care—except his recovery.

What must that be like? Since her one, irreparable lapse in judgment back in college, she'd been vigilant and responsible—or at least tried to look that way. She knew she put too much emphasis on what others thought and worried about being judged...

The tree lights flickered and lit.

Angel jumped up. "Let there be light!"

He grabbed her by the back of the neck and kissed her soundly, one fist wrapping in her hair, his other hand creeping under her shirt. She molded into his body. The kiss deepened, his tongue exploring her mouth.

In the background, the crowd roared on the television as someone scored another touchdown. She looked at him, her senses heightened. Their breathing was heavy, his eyes hooded with desire. He smelled like a crisp autumn day, and he tasted like sin. He smiled, and all her doubts about him faded.

"Come here. I want to unwrap that crazy big package," Maggie purred. She reached down and unbuttoned his jeans as her tongue flicked his nipple ring. Angel moaned in response, and his grip on her hair tightened.

The doorbell rang.

"Hell's bells," she swore softly and pulled away.

Angel smacked her butt and roared with laughter. "Such language."

Straightening her clothes, she threw the door open with a wide smile. Her hand went straight to her throat, where her heart now seemed to be permanently lodged. She gasped, horrified.

"Hiya, Mom. Surprise!"

Her handsome son stood on her front porch dressed in a white button-down starched shirt, tweed sports coat, and dark pants. Leaning down, he gave her a quick kiss on the cheek. From the living area, she heard Angel whistling behind her, shuffling boxes.

"Phillip! What are you doing here?" she hissed, stepping onto the porch and pulling the door almost closed behind her.

"I swear I could smell your bread all the way out in Colorado and thought I'd swing by and grab a slice on the way back to school." He brushed past her into the house, carrying his suitcase. His bright smile—the result of thousands of dollars of the best orthodontics money could buy—faded when he spotted Angel.

Angel sat on his heels, stacking some of the empty boxes. Looking over his shoulder, he nodded a greeting to Phillip.

He stood and turned to face them, and Maggie wanted to die a thousand deaths. *Lord, just strike me dead now.* The button on Angel's jeans remained undone. Phillip's double-take and sharp inhale would have been comical if he wasn't her son. She frantically motioned for Angel to button his fly.

Frowning, Phillip's dark eyes—the replica of his father's—cut toward her. "Is this the *handyman?*"

Angel juggled the boxes and held out his good hand. "I'm Angel. You must be Phillip."

He dropped his hand after Phillip stood there, unmoving, staring at him.

"You have got to be fuckin' kidding me. Mom? What the hell?"

"That really is his name," Maggie offered, knowing full well that wasn't what Phillip was referring to. "And I don't like you using language like that." She ignored Angel's snorted snicker.

Thankfully, he put down the boxes, buttoned his jeans, and shrugged into his shirt and sling.

"I don't care if his name is Rumpelstiltskin. Who is this guy, and why was he half naked in your living room?" Phillip dropped his suitcase.

Angel didn't say a word.

Phillip shook his head, still stunned. "How old are you?"

"Twenty-five."

"What?" he roared and turned to face her. "This is gross. *He's only six years older than me?*"

"Enough!" Maggie stepped forward and in between the two.

Phillip raised his eyes in disbelief. The pain on his face tempered her voice.

"You will not speak to me in my home like this, nor will you speak to Angel in that manner. He's important to me."

"Important to you. What the fu—What does that mean? Please tell me you're *not* sleeping with him."

Not exactly sleeping. "That's none of your business, son."

"Oh Jesus…" Phillip paced back and forth, his hands in his pockets jingling his change. Brian did the same thing when frustrated, and it drove Maggie nuts.

"Tell me something, does your father sleeping with Tiffany bother you this much?"

"That's different, Mom. They're married. And she isn't twenty-five. She's *thirty*."

Dying of a stroke was a real possibility as anger coursed through her. Clenching her teeth, she hissed, "He was *married* to *me* when he started his affair with her. And she was *married* to someone else. There's a big difference here. I'm not married. Your father and Tiffany cheated on their spouses. Your father broke his wedding vows. And those vows were important, at least to me."

"That's a crock, and you know it! I can count, Mom. You *had* to get married. Did you even want me? You two were never happy together. You were both so damn miserable you made me miserable, too. You *hated* each other…" Phillip's voice broke. He turned his back to her.

Maggie placed a hand on his arm and turned him to face her. Her heart felt like it was being run through a meat grinder. She and Brian had tried to keep their arguments private, but of course he knew. And he was right. Though they were outwardly civil to one another, Phillip must've seen there was no love between them. He was bound to have heard the violent diatribes Brian flung at her behind closed doors, and after the affair was revealed, her equally venomous replies.

"Of course we wanted you. We love you. Both of us love you. You're everything to us." She tried to embrace him, but he shrugged away.

Bowing her head, she sucked in a painful breath as she tried to deal with her guilt and her child's pain. Angel slipped from the room, giving them privacy.

"Phillip, I love you. Please, let me show you to a room, and then we can discuss this over some dinner." Maggie placed one hand on his back and motioned toward the stairs. Phillip grabbed his suitcase, shrugging away from her, but followed her up.

"What about *him*? Is he going home?" His tone sounded less derisive, but still laced with bitterness.

"He is home. Angel lives here."

"Lives here?"

"I'll explain everything after you get settled. We can go out to eat—just the two of us—or we can eat here." She opened the door to the nicest of the new guest rooms, decorated in pale blue and white with antique mahogany furniture. Turning, she looked up into his brown eyes, trying to ease his hurt. "I'd really like you to get to know him, but I know this has been a shock. I'll let you take a few moments to decide. I'll be downstairs." Phillip nodded, his mouth set in a firm line.

As Maggie closed the door, she heard Phillip say, "Come on, Dad. Pick up the damn phone…"

She found Angel cleaning up the Christmas decorations.

"You okay? Are we okay?" He stacked the boxes on the coffee table.

Maggie nodded, but then she shook her head no and stepped in to his open arm.

"Everything will be okay, baby. He's just shook up." Angel stroked her hair, and she snuggled in to his chest, listening to the steady beat of his heart.

"I'm such a lousy mother. I've hurt my son."

"I can leave."

"No. This isn't about you; it's *me*. And Brian. By staying in our pretense of a marriage, we hurt the only good thing between us. I'm sad and ashamed. And I guess I should've told him about us on the phone. I didn't expect him to show up like this."

"You're not a lousy mother. You did the best you knew how…"

He appeared lost in thought for a moment. He smiled down at her and kissed her forehead. "You were a good mother. I'm sure Phillip believes that deep down. He's just confused about us. Hell, *we're* confused about us. Cut him some slack."

Maggie nodded. "I offered to have dinner with him, just the two of us. Is that okay?"

"Of course. That's fine. I'll just grab a turkey sandwich and go to my room. I don't mind a bit."

"You're a nice person," she said with a quick kiss to his lips.

"I'm *Angel* Sinclair, remember? My brother is the demon."

"Demon Sinclair? I know that bastard." Phillip stopped halfway down the stairs.

Maggie pulled away from Angel's arms, alarmed by her son's confused face.

"Damien's my brother."

"Holy shit." Phillip bounded down the rest of the stairs.

"Phillip, stop with the language."

"Sorry, Mom. You do know who Demon Sinclair is, don't you?"

Maggie shook her head, though a niggling thought that the name *did* sound familiar rattled around in her head.

"Damien Sinclair is the divorce lawyer who represented Tiffany's ex-husband. He dragged Dad's name through the mud. He's an asshole."

Maggie frowned. "Yes, now I remember."

Phillip glared at Angel and pointed. "Your brother made my dad out to be some horrible prick. He and Tiffany had a terrible time of it during her divorce. She didn't get shit from her ex."

Angel shrugged. "I didn't know. My brother and I don't speak." He added, "But good for Damien. It doesn't sound like your father ever considered your mother's feelings in making his decisions."

Phillip's face flushed, and the change in his pocket jingled fast and furiously. Maggie promptly stepped in before he combusted.

"Angel, stop. What did you decide about dinner, Phillip? And how long will you be here?"

"We can eat here. I didn't fly down here to eat out in some lousy restaurant. I came to see you and eat your cooking. I told you, Tiffany can't cook worth a damn. I'm catching a flight in the morning so I can get back to school and finish a paper."

"I'll eat later. Enjoy your visit." Angel picked up the boxes to take back to the attic.

Phillip watched Angel leave, staring daggers at him. He shook his head. "You and him? Seriously, Mom? Is this some sort of midlife crisis? Couldn't you have just bought a red convertible like most moms?"

"Leftovers or a turkey sandwich?" Ignoring his hurtful comments, Maggie placed a hand on her son's shoulder, leading him into the kitchen.

"Both? On your homemade bread?"

The wistfulness in his voice made her heart ache for the little boy she missed.

"Of course." She patted his back before getting the bread and leftovers out of the refrigerator.

Phillip sank into a chair. He covered his eyes with his hands and took a deep breath. Finally, he looked up and asked, "Are you happy, Mom? Living here like this?"

Maggie took her time slicing the bread, considering her answer carefully. She wanted to be truthful with Phillip, without causing him more pain.

"Yes, I am. For the first time in a very long time. I'm excited about my new life, and Angel's a big part of it. He's interested in me, as a person, and has been a huge help getting this business up and running. I couldn't have done it without him, and I'm hopeful our relationship will continue to grow stronger.

"I planned to tell you about Angel at Christmas. I'm sorry. And while I'm apologizing, I'm sorry about the decisions your father and I made that hurt you. You mean everything to both of us." She vowed to be civil about Brian for Phillip's sake.

"I don't think Dad's happy."

Maggie paused and looked at Phillip. At one time this statement would've made her ecstatic. "Then I'm sorry for him."

"Tiffany nags him all the time. He acts like everything's okay, but I think he misses you."

More than likely, he only misses the doormat mentality. Good for Tiffany. Her opinion of the woman she despised went up a notch.

"Your father doesn't miss me. As you said, we weren't good together. All relationships have ups and downs, but ours just never recovered. The only successful thing we did was raise *you*. We're both very proud of you."

"Did you ever love him? And him you?"

She dug deep to find the memories, long buried under Brian's verbal abuse. Yes, she'd been crazy in love with him. He'd been handsome, attentive, and fun. But she'd often wondered if Brian had ever truly loved her, or if he'd simply been railroaded into marrying her.

"Yes, I did. There were some good times. It wasn't always bad," she admitted.

Phillip nodded and sat up a little straighter. Maggie was glad she could give him at least a small respite. He was her son, and she would protect him as much as humanly possible. If putting aside her anger toward his father helped him, she would do it. It was time to move on and not dwell in the past.

Chapter
Twelve

"I will, Mom. Stop." Phillip hugged her tighter than he had in a long time.

"I can't help it. I'll always worry about you. That's what moms do. Calling or texting me when you get home won't kill you." She stepped away, blinking back her tears.

"I know; I will. Look, I've got to go. I have to turn the rental car in at the airport before my flight."

"I know. You'll come here for Christmas?"

"Yeah, I'll split my time and do New Year's with Dad. How bad can Tiffany fuck up a ham?"

Maggie laughed and smacked him on the arm. "Language, young man. Be careful with your carry-on. I've got two loaves of bread packed in there."

"Thanks, Mom. You're the best."

Maggie looked up into her son's face, which so resembled his father's. "Your dad…I tried, Phillip. Truly."

He nodded. "Okay. I love you." He waved as he walked down the steps to his rental car and threw his suitcase in the backseat. Pausing, he looked down the driveway. Maggie turned to follow his gaze. Despite her misgivings, Angel was working on the new sign for the bed and breakfast. At least he was wearing his sling. He'd been thoughtful and made himself scarce so she could spend time with her son.

Phillip frowned for a moment, hands on his hips, then stared at the ground. After a moment, he squared his shoulders and strode toward Angel. When Maggie moved to follow, Angel looked up and shook his head as he waited. Nervous, she watched her son speak to Angel, with his hands in his pockets. Without a doubt, he was jiggling the change. The back of his neck flushed.

Angel kept his eyes trained on Phillip, nodding every so often. At the end of the conversation, he smiled and held out his good hand. Maggie held her breath until Phillip shook it. Turning on his heels, Phillip darted to the car, throwing her a quick wave as he backed out of the driveway.

Maggie blew him a kiss and wrung her hands, waiting on Angel. His breath billowed in the cold air, and she followed him into the house.

"What did he say to you? I'm sorry if he said something offensive. He's not thrilled with my choice, or his father's," she chattered, closing the front door.

"He's a good guy, Maggie, but he's confused, and that's understandable. He loves both of his parents. He feels torn, I bet—on some level, maybe even responsible." He winced and rubbed his sore shoulder.

Maggie gently massaged it. "Responsible? He didn't do anything. Tell me what he said. Do you want me to rewrap your wrist? I think you're doing too much too soon."

"That feels good. I'm fine. You know he isn't responsible, and hopefully Brian knows that. Deep down, I think Phillip knows it, too. But think about it, Maggie. When your father drank, did you feel like you could've done something to prevent it or make it better? Kids sometimes take the blame for things they don't understand."

"Hmm…You're right. I'd think if only I hadn't come home late, or if I'd done better in school, or made less noise…" She stepped around to face him and folded her arms. "But if you don't tell me what Phillip said to you, there will never be another pumpkin pie in this house."

"Threatening a pie ban is low." He kissed the top of her head. "Your son told me if I ever hurt you, he'd kick my ass all the way back to Georgia. I agreed. Now, that brat didn't eat all my pie, did he?"

Her guilt lifted, and she hugged him tight, planting an exuberant kiss on his mouth.

"I saved you a piece. And I'll make you another one if you want me to." She tucked her head under his chin and listened to his steady heartbeat. "And don't call my son a brat, even if he is sometimes."

Angel's chest rumbled with laughter. "It takes one to know one. Hey, I'm starving. I'm going to eat a bowl of cereal."

"No, I'll make you breakfast. Waffles okay? I have batter left. And a pot of coffee."

"Yum. Pancakes ribbed for my enjoyment."

Angel smiled against Maggie's hair, her laughter easing his anxiety. Phillip's visit had brought back the lines of worry around her eyes, and he was determined to erase them. He kissed her tenderly, savoring the taste of her lips.

"This is my favorite place to be," she whispered, molding her body into his.

"I prefer bed."

She snickered. "I meant in your arms. Bed sounds good. But first, breakfast." Holding his hand, she moved to the kitchen.

"I missed you last night. I think I need a 12-step meeting."

"I'll take you to one." She busied herself, getting the waffles ready.

"I'm teasing you. You're my new addiction. I can't get enough."

His phone rang, interrupting his thoughts of seduction by the fire.

He dug it out of his pocket and frowned.

"Aren't you going to answer it? Is it Emma? I have a loaf of bread for them if they're back home."

He wished it was Emma. *Dammit.* Angel let it ring three more times before reluctantly answering.

"Hello?"

"Are you in trouble?" Damien's clipped voice came across the line. Always direct and to the point, his brother skipped the niceties.

"No. Why?" He gave Maggie a small, reassuring smile. To say his brother could be condescending would be an understatement.

"Mom told me you called the other night. She's worried sick over you and hoped you'd call back at a reasonable hour. Goddammit, what the hell's wrong with you? Why would you call in the middle of the night unless you're in trouble or need money? You've always been such an inconsiderate little shit. Are you using again? Emmanuelle says no, but she's always protective of you."

Angel watched Maggie wiping down the counters. It wasn't hard to figure out she was lingering so she could eavesdrop. He sighed. *I will not use.*

"Emma hates being called that. I'm not using. I'm clean — not that I owe you any explanation."

Angel started drumming his fingers. Granted, Damien had helped him out of bad situations in the past. And when he'd been too fucked up on drugs to take care of himself, much less anyone else, Damien had helped Emma. But why was he in touch with her now? Was it to keep tabs on him? It was probably his father's doing. Damien was Dad's yes-man. Taking a deep breath, he reined in his anger. He really needed to work on that fuckin' ninth step.

"Then come home."

Angel snorted. "Come home to what? Dad's open arms? Yeah, right. Do you really believe I'd be greeted as the prodigal son?"

"Mom needs you. At least come see Mom." Damien's voice lowered, and Angel detected urgency in his tone. However, he suspected it was a ploy instrumented by his father.

"Yeah, Mom needs me so much she hung up on me the other night. Look, we have nothing to say. I'm fine. I need to go. I have things to do."

"Come home, Angel. Don't live with regrets. Mom doesn't look good. Something's going on that she's not talking about…"

Angel rolled his eyes, wishing Damien could see him doing it, just to piss him off. "When has she ever talked about *anything* unless it's her charity work? Maybe I'll come home around Christmas if you can tell me when Dad won't be there. Just let Emma know since you two are such big buddies now." He hung up.

Fuck. So much for working a step. He'd just reverted to reacting instead of thinking first. Damien was right. He shouldn't have
called his mother so late. *Shit, I really need to go home to see her. Or
at the very least call and apologize.* He scrubbed a hand over his face.
Damn, damn, damn. I need a meeting. The urge to check out roared
to life. He gritted his teeth. Would drugs ever *not* be his first thought
when stressed?

"You should go see your family. Take your driver's test, borrow
the truck, and go see them," Maggie urged.

"'*Et tu, Brute?*'"

"Family is important. And being a mother, I can understand how
much your mom misses you."

"Family doesn't have to be blood relations, Maggie. You're my
family. Emma's my family. Ken was my family. My mother hung up
on me. My so-called 'real' family doesn't want me, and they never
have." *Goddamn, I sound whiny.* He clenched his fist.

"Your mother hung up on you after you scared her to death by
calling in the middle of the night. My heart races triple time when
the phone rings late, fearing bad news. And if your family is so un-
interested in you, why did your brother track you down?"

The demons from his past continued to whisper an easy, mind-
numbing solution.

No! I choose to be clean.

He wanted to run. His palm itched with another solution. He
needed to write and reduce this anger and frustration building in
the pit of his stomach.

He always felt this fight-or-flight instinct when dealing with
his family.

The memory of his lowest, darkest moment taunted him in a
horrible flashback. Usually it only happened in his nightmares…The
feeling of helplessness, the grip on his neck…

Bile rose in the back of his throat. Inside, he was still that scared,
stupid little kid. Angel struggled to maintain control and not throw
something or put a fist through a wall. Now was not the time to
deal with the frightening, shameful recollection that had caused so
many of his relapses.

"I need to go out tonight," he bit out hoarsely. A cold sweat
beaded on his brow. His hands shook.

"O-*kay*." She looked sharply at him.

Wanting to set her mind at ease, he schooled his features and attempted a smile.

Her shoulders relaxed.

"That would be fun. We'll finish decorating for Christmas and then relax before things get hectic with the guests and holidays. Where do you want to go? We could go grab a bite to eat and maybe take in a movie, just as long as it isn't scary or gory," Maggie chattered, stirring the waffle batter.

For two seconds, he entertained the thought of pressing his hand onto the hot waffle iron. He'd be able to get pain pills…And the physical pain would mask the pain within…

Trapped. It was the only word to describe the way the panic welling up inside of him made him feel. He glanced at the clock. It was close to ten. Maybe Emma was home; he'd call her. "I'm, uh, going to call Emma and go to a meeting."

"I'll take you. Is it an open one?"

"No, but I need to talk to Emma." *Emma will understand. She's the only one who will.*

Maggie looked away, hurt visible on her face, and he berated himself.

"It isn't personal, Maggie. I just need to talk to her about Damien. She's been talking to him about me. This is family crap I need to deal with, okay?"

"Sure. Fine." The coolness of her voice indicated it was anything but fine. And a stony silence hung heavy in the room as she finished preparing his breakfast.

Angel accepted the plate of waffles. "Thank you. Maggie, I'm sorry. Holidays are hard for everyone, but especially for addicts. It's me, not you, I promise. Okay?"

"Are you ever going to open up and trust me? I know nothing about your family except that you don't like them. I'm sure I've met your brother. We were in the same circle, but I wasn't in Atlanta long."

"You haven't missed anything. I'm not being dishonest. I haven't seen my mom in over two years, my brother in somewhat longer, and I can't even remember the last time I saw my dad. My addiction put a rift between me and my family that may never heal. I wish you'd just accept me as I am now. The past is the past."

"If you can't remember the past, you're doomed to repeat it."

Angel shook his head and chuckled. "You're paraphrasing Santayana, the philosopher?"

"Am I?"

"Yeah, my dad used to tell me the same thing damn thing. I believe it was responsibility lecture 101."

"You're very smart. This is the most you've ever talked about your past. I don't even know when your birthday is." She sat next to him with her coffee.

"Was. It was two days ago. Mom didn't even remember…" He took an inordinate amount of time with his bite of waffle, swirling it in the syrup. "I'm anything but bright, and I barely passed high school. As a matter of fact, I probably didn't pass. My father *bought* me a diploma from the last private school I attended. It's amazing what a multimillion-dollar donation to the building fund will purchase for a kid in dummy classes."

Maggie shook her head. "That's a horrible name. Stop it. They're classes for children with different learning abilities, and it isn't anything to be ashamed of. You're not dumb. And why didn't you tell me Friday was your birthday? I would've done something special!"

"I can't do math. *At all.* I could read by age four, but at twenty-five, I still can't fuckin' tell time unless it's a digital clock. It's called dyscalculia." He shrugged. "And my birthday means nothing to me."

"Don't be so hard on yourself. You're bright, creative, a whiz at organization, and you have good common sense."

"Tell that to my dad." He got up to refill his coffee, wanting to change the subject. "Look, there really isn't much else to tell. After I eat, let's finish decorating the house. Maybe we can catch a nap or something later."

"Okay." She smiled, but her worried face said more than her words.

"Thanks for giving me a ride, Emma."

Angel could feel himself breathing again, even as his palms itched. Soon he'd find relief from the inner turmoil Damien's phone call had stirred. He'd helped Maggie finish the decorating, and while she had napped, curled into his body, he'd stared at the ceiling, planning.

"Angel, I can't keep doing this. David has the patience of Job, but he's starting to get concerned that there will be talk with you and me being seen together so much—even if it is for a good reason like NA." Emma glanced at him as she drove. "And he doesn't even know about the writing. You've already bombed the area. Why do you have to keep doing it? This truly is an addiction, a cross-addiction. Instead of a substance, you're writing graffiti. Is it the paint fumes?"

He chuckled. "We've been careful. You only stayed at the church the first meeting; you've dropped me off ever since. And you know I wear a respirator. No, I just gotta do it, Emma. It's like therapy for me. When I can't handle shit, I write. Call it urban intervention." He bounced his leg, itching to get out there. Emma was right. This was another addiction. One he wasn't ready to give up. Not yet.

"It's illegal. It's time to grow up, Angel."

Irritated, he mumbled, "Look, just drop me off, and I'll walk to NA. I'll get someone at the meeting to give me a ride home."

"I w-won't abandon you." Emma's voice tripped with emotion. "You saved my life once. Can't you see I'm trying to do the same for you?"

"I know, Emma. I just…One more, okay?" *Shit, this is an addiction.*

One more time…

Just once more…

I can quit at any time…

How many times had he said it?

He meant it.

This time.

Maybe.

Emma pulled over next to the abandoned building. "I'll circle the block."

"Go home, Emma. I mean it. Just go home. I'll walk to NA. I've got time, don't I?" He pulled on the black latex gloves.

"Time means nothing to you. I'm not leaving you. Now get the hell out of my car and do it. And make it beautiful." Emma stared straight ahead, her face grim.

He leaned over and kissed her cheek. "I always do."

Jumping out of the car with his backpack, he settled the respirator on his face and watched her drive off. As he shook the can, the sound of the ball swirling soothed his frayed nerves. Despite the adrenaline rush, he felt calm and at peace. He loved writing. It was his way to make his presence known. To be heard. To be somebody.

As soon as he found his spot, he fell into a rhythm, throwing up the outline of his message. *You matter,* followed by his tag. Thirty minutes passed, or maybe an hour, or maybe more. He didn't know and didn't care. Emma circled several times, and each time he motioned for her to go home. She finally pulled up and admitted David had called and was worried. Angel waved her on, and she drove off.

He went back to work, in the zone. It was almost like a drug-induced euphoria. Now more than ever, he was glad it wasn't his dominant arm that had been affected by his fall.

Then just as he finished his piece, red, blue, and white lights circled and highlighted it.

Fuck, fuck, fuck...

His survival instinct kicked in, and in a panic, he took off running. He ran as hard as he could, ignoring the screams for him to stop. Scaling one fence, he jumped over a garbage can and narrowly avoided being hit by a car. His shoulder and wrist burned. Someone pounded the pavement close behind him, but he knew better than to take the time to look. This wasn't his first run from the law.

"Stop!" A male voice commanded, again. "Hands up!"

Maggie. He couldn't do this to her.

It was time to accept responsibility for his actions. He stopped running and held up his hands, his hurt arm throbbing like hell. His pulse raced, and sweat poured down his face like a dope-sick addict at his first NA meeting. Panting for breath, he dropped to his knees, hands still up in surrender. Maggie's admonishment from earlier and his father's dire prediction taunted him: *Those who cannot remember the past are condemned to repeat it.*

Fuck, I'm screwed.

Chapter
Thirteen

"Thank you." Angel winced and buckled his seatbelt. His entire body hurt from his mad dash to escape and the less-than-gentle handling by the cop who had handcuffed him.

"Thank Emma. I was all for leaving you in jail," David Patterson replied. His mouth settled into a grim line, and his look darkened as he started the car. "You know, I don't really care how you mess up your life. That's *your* choice. But when you get *my* wife and the mother of *my* daughter involved, I draw the line."

Angel hung his head and nodded. "I'm sorry; it won't happen again. I promise. And thank you for talking to the cops and arranging the community service before I was booked. I know I got off easy."

"Too easy. But you matter to Emma." He sighed. "Why? Why would you do something so irresponsible? Emma's right. You're not all there in the head, are you?" David scowled.

"She said that?"

The betrayal felt like a kick in the gut, but he couldn't blame her. As Pine Bluff's finest had loaded him in the back of the police car, he'd caught a glimpse of her pale face, talking on her phone. Apparently, she'd changed her mind about leaving, circled back around to check on him, and witnessed him being brought down by the five-o.

"Okay, maybe not exactly like that," David admitted. "She said, and I quote, 'He's crazy as bat shit, brilliantly gifted, and passionate about writing.' Wouldn't it be called painting?"

"I call it writing. It's a form of self-expression. But some do call it painting."

"Or vandalism," David added with a pointed look.

"Or vandalism," Angel reluctantly agreed. "And let me reassure you, I'm not psycho or anything. I mean, Emma's safe with me."

"That I'm not so sure about," David replied.

They drove in silence to Maggie's. The closer they got, the more Angel's anxiety escalated. His leg bounced, and he wiped his damp palms on his jeans. *Will she kick me out? Dammit, I've really fucked up this time.* The only thing he hadn't done was relapse to shootin' heroin. He was so scared, he felt an urge to vomit.

"I'll call you next week to start your community service. I covered the cost of the stop signs, and you can either pay me back weekly or paint my house. You're also required to paint over your graffiti, and I want you to think about what you plan to say to my students. It needs to make an impact. And no bullshit, understand?"

Angel shot a surprised look at David and sighed. He'd gladly paint the man's house for everything he'd done for him. And talking to the kids wouldn't be too bad. Painting over his work would be harder.

"Okay." He still didn't think what he'd done was that bad. It wasn't like he'd bombed businesses or private residences. They were abandoned buildings, eyesores. And he'd written positive messages. All he wanted to do was make an impact. He wanted — no needed — to be heard. Well, maybe tagging the dumpster and stop signs had been wrong.

When they pulled up to the house, the front porchlight cast a diffuse glow into the yard. He knew Maggie was awake, waiting on him. He just didn't have a clue what her reaction was going to be.

He glanced over at David. "How upset was Maggie when Emma called and told her what happened?"

"She was shocked. If I were you, I'd prepare for the worst. This is serious, Angel. You need to think about everything you stand to lose."

Angel took a deep breath and shook David's hand. "Thanks again. I'll call you tomorrow." *What if I don't have a home tomorrow?* "Or at the very least, I'll be in touch — somehow."

David nodded, and Angel stepped out of the car. From experience, he knew this could go down several ways. She'd either be furious and scream about his stupidity, give him the silent treatment, cry about him wasting his life, or she'd simply kick him out of the house.

Worst-case scenario: all of the above.

He wondered if he should have asked David if he could stay with him and Emma tonight. But then again, maybe not. That would've been pushing his luck. David had put his job and reputation on the line by standing up for him at the station. It had surprised and humbled him, even if he'd only done it for Emma. He wondered if he'd ever have anyone do something like that for him.

Maggie.

She'd done it when she took on that asshole doctor. But now? He dreaded seeing the disappointment in her eyes.

It was cowardly, but he took his time walking up the driveway, psyching himself up to be prepared to pack his belongings. He didn't relish the thought of finding a bridge to sleep under.

No, it wasn't that. *It was Maggie.* He needed her and didn't want to leave. He vowed to change for her, if she'd only give him a chance. He meant it this time.

Opening the front door, he slipped into the house. He found her on the couch, sitting with her feet tucked beneath her, staring at the dying embers in the fireplace. Her nose was red, her eyes bright. The Christmas tree lights twinkled on and off, and ironically, Elvis sang softly about it not being Christmas without the one you love.

Angel bit his lip to keep from breaking down. He wanted to be with Maggie more than anything in this world. Not since he was a kid had he looked forward to a Christmas as much as this one. He'd even gone back to that hardware store and bought cookie cutters for her stocking, and he'd been working on a special present hidden in the back of his closet. His heart hammered like a strung-out meth-head, and fear gnawed at his gut. Unshed tears burned his eyes. He was about to lose the person who mattered most to him.

Goddamned fucking idiot.

He was about to lose *everything*.

She didn't look at him when he entered the room, but her breathing hitched. The arm resting across her lap tightened as if to shield herself. He stole softly to the couch where he sank to the floor next to her feet. He was prepared to grovel for forgiveness.

"Were you hurt? Are you hungry?"

Her soft questions of concern threw him. He looked up, confused. "No, ma'am."

"Don't ma'am me. I'm *not* your mother," she snapped, covering her face with her hands.

Pulling his knees to his chest, he wrapped his arms around them and stared into the dying fire, not wanting to witness the disillusionment sure to be written across her face. It was a look he'd seen countless times before, with his family.

"What *am* I to you, Angel?"

Without hesitating, he replied, "My lifeline."

Looking up, he saw incredible, heart-stopping sadness. He'd rather have seen disappointment. He could handle that; he'd done so for years. One tear tracked down her pale cheek.

"Why? Why would you do something so —"

"Stupid?" he interrupted.

He'd heard this lecture before, many times, and braced himself. He could probably quote it verbatim.

"I was going to say dangerous." She dashed away the tear.

"I don't know how to explain it." Resting his chin on his knees, he turned his gaze back to the fire. *How can I explain what it's like to be invisible? How writing is my way to be seen and heard?*

"Well, try. Your learning disability is in mathematics, not language." Her tone was sharp.

He glanced back at her, and she crossed her arms in front of her chest.

"I tag to show I exist —"

Her anger exploded, interrupting his explanation. "Haven't you ever heard the old adage: *fools' names like fools' faces are always seen in public places?*"

He jumped up and paced, irritated. "Too many fucking times to count from my parents. Are you going to listen to my explanation, or have you already passed judgment and sentenced me?"

Maggie sprang to her feet and faced him, her hands clenched into fists. "How dare you! You don't have the right to be angry! You're the one who did something wrong. Haven't you learned to take ownership of your mistakes in those damn 12-step meetings? It's vandalism! And senseless!"

He looked to the ceiling and made himself take a few deep breaths before responding. "That's your take on it. People have been writing on walls since the cavemen. The word graffiti comes from the Italian word *graffiare*. It means to scratch. I write because I have something to say. When I tag, it shows I exist, *that I matter*. I'm making a statement, and I make it beautiful. It's what I do. Plain and simple."

"You could journal to let those feelings out," she countered.

He snorted in derision. "You think I've haven't tried that? What's the point of a journal?" He sneered and finger quoted, "To explore your inner feelings." He stopped pacing and blew out an exasperated breath. *How do I explain this?*

Facing her, he pounded his chest with his hand. "I know what the fuck I'm feeling. I kept those feelings bottled up until I damn near exploded. *I want others to know. I need to be somebody! I need to be heard...*"

He gazed into her troubled face, looking for even a hint of understanding. He didn't find any.

"But it's a criminal activity, Angel."

He shrugged. "Truthfully? That's part of the draw. I'm also an adrenaline junkie. My endorphins are pretty well shot because of my drug addiction. Doing this cranks me up, gives me a rush. It's a high I can still access. *It makes me happy.*" Resorting to old habits, he'd answered flippantly. And in the process, he'd discounted her feelings. He regretted it as soon as he spoke.

"I see..." She blinked back more tears.

Angel struggled to rein in his frustration and kept his mouth shut, knowing if he lost his temper, it would make things worse. It was a full minute before she spoke again.

"I thought I made you happy. I guess that's my mistake."

Her voice had a frosted edge to it, but the pain in her eyes and quiver of her lower lip damn near killed him. Losing her was his new rock bottom. Life without Maggie would hold no meaning. He sank to his knees in front of her.

"No! You *do* make me happy, Maggie. With you, I'm happier than I've ever been in my entire, miserable life. God, I'm so sorry." He looked up into her eyes. "I know in everybody's eyes I've fucked up.

And maybe you're all right. But dammit, I'm trying. I have a *disease*, and if you break down the word, it describes how I feel. I'm at dis-ease most of the damn time. Writing helps relieve the symptoms. It allows me to zone out and just be in the moment. When I'm laying down those lines, nothing else matters.

"Recovery's fucking hard. This past eighteen months is the longest I've ever been clean. Since meeting you, my life has improved more than I ever thought possible. I never felt worthy of happiness until I met you. I mean, who wants to be with a junkie? No one except other poor bastards in the same boat.

"You're different, and it makes me want to be different, too. When I'm with you, I'm comfortable—for the first time ever. But every-thing with you is so new. I don't know how to do society's so-called normal. I'm still learning how to deal with shit without using, but I'm trying. Don't give up on me, please. I know I don't deserve it, but please, Maggie. Please forgive me. Just one more chance." *Spoken like a true addict.*

She huffed. He died a thousand times over, waiting for her answer.

"I'm trying to understand." She stared at the fire, as if she could find the answers in the dying flames. "Tell me what happened."

He wanted to see acceptance and acknowledgment on her face, but at least there was no condemnation. He took his time, knowing everything hinged on his explanation of what had happened tonight. It was the only way he could hope for a second chance.

"I'm lucky this is a small town, and David went to bat for me with the police. At least this time, the cop didn't pull a gun on me."

The color drained from her face. "You've had a gun pulled on you before? You could've been hurt."

Angel shrugged. "Multiple times. Also knives, switchblades, and tasers. I lived on the street. I've been mugged, robbed, hungry, and lonely. Despite my ridiculous name, I'm no angel. I've done shit to support my addiction that was illegal and reprehensible, but that's in the past. Anyway, David's missed his calling. He really should study to be a lawyer instead of a preacher. I didn't get booked. I agreed to do community service. I'm going to talk to his school and Sunday school class about the unpleasant aspects of my life, and I've got to paint over my work. And I'm going to pay David back for the stop signs he paid to replace or paint his house, whichever he decides."

She shook her head. "I've noticed the stop signs. I just thought it was kids…This is all well and good until you need that 'rush' again. Did you think about how your actions would impact those who care about you? David's a teacher, and Emma's his wife. This is a small town—you could've ruined his career, their lives." With a heavy sigh she added, "What about *me*, dammit?"

Angel sat down, wrapping his good arm around her. He felt a measure of reassurance when she didn't pull away. "Honestly? No, I didn't think first. I acted on impulse. But I'm going to do better, I promise. Don't cry, Maggie. Please don't fuckin' cry. I'm sorry."

She turned and buried her face in his shirt. "I can't bear the thought of you being arrested, or worse."

He froze as her words pierced the protective armor he kept his heart encased in. Maggie cared about *him*.

"I'll stop, I promise. For you, I'll stop."

Somehow, he'd try.

She shoved away from him and ran a hand across her glittering eyes. "I've heard this before from my father. I care for you, but I also know you can't stop for *me*. You have to stop for *yourself*. I don't know if I can do this again. I watched what being co-dependent did to my mother. And what ignoring warning signs did to me. I have to protect myself."

"Protect yourself?" He felt as if he'd taken a punch to his gut. "Maggie, I'd never hurt you."

"I don't mean physically. Sure, my dad got heavy-handed at times. But it was nothing compared to the mental toll. And Brian was never physical with me, but emotional abuse hurts, too."

Maggie ran from the room and slammed her door shut, leaving Angel alone. He sank to the couch and buried his face in his hands.

He was just like her father. Mick Maguire had been charismatic, passionate, and full of love, but when he drank, he was destructive. His binges were like tornados, destroying everything in their path, leaving only bits and pieces of his family's life behind, to be rebuilt from scratch. To escape her father, she'd married a man she thought was different.

Brian was self-controlled, cautious, and cold. But his controlling behavior had been just as damaging as her father's drinking. He had the same ability as her father to tear her fragile, battered ego to shreds. Brian just used different tactics. His weapon was language. It was why he was a brilliant lawyer.

Which was worse? Hard to say. The result had been the same: her heart left in tiny, broken shards, which she'd worked hard to piece back together. Could she risk going through that again?

Maybe she should've listened to her initial gut feeling that they would never work. Who had she been kidding? They were too different—their ages now seemed insignificant compared to their views on life and their backgrounds. *But he's not my father. He's clean.* And although they'd had their problems, he'd never treated her with anything but respect—unlike Brian. *He loves me.*

The sad fact was, she was falling in love with him, too. Still, her mind told her she had to let him go for her own self-preservation.

But her heart disagreed and begged her to fight for him.

Maggie heard the bedroom door open and felt the bed dip with his weight.

"Please. I want to be alone. Just go away." She buried her damp face in her arm.

"Would you at least look at me when you tell me to leave? Really, truly look at me?"

Rolling over, she took in his red-rimmed eyes. He brushed away her tears with the back of his fingers. He broke eye contact, and his throat bobbled.

"I can't do this. I'm not strong enough." She held onto the hand stroking her cheek and his beautiful face blurred. Looking at him, her mind wavered in favor of her heart. He looked as devastated as she felt.

"I disagree. You're the strongest woman I know." His brow furrowed as he appeared to struggle with his thoughts. "I'll leave if you tell me to. But I don't want to. I want to try to make this work. I meant what I said the other night; I love you."

"You're too young to know what love is—"

"Bullshit. That's fuckin' bullshit, Maggie. Don't pull the age card on me and think you can win with that argument. I may be stupid, but I know my own heart. And that heart belongs to you." He held up a hand. "I know. I know my language sucks. Sorry...

"When I fell off the ladder, it was the strangest feeling. It was like an analogy of my life. I've been free falling since I was ten and headed for disaster. It's exciting, but scary as shit. You know how you buffered my fall the other night? Well, meeting you has provided me a soft cushion for all this pain inside me. You're my safety net, Maggie. When I'm with you, I don't have to be as scared." He leaned forward and kissed her lips, managing to look both resigned and vulnerable.

Has anyone, aside from Emma, ever fought for him?

"Please, give me a chance. Give *us* a chance. I know myself well enough to know I can't promise a lot. But every damn day, I get up and say I won't use. And I mean it. I'll add no illegal writing, and I'll say it to *you*, too, if that's what you need from me. I'm far from perfect. Matter of fact, I'm as imperfect as they come, but I want to take care of you. I want to be your companion, your helpmate, your lover. I want to dry your tears when you're sad and laugh with you over stupid stuff. I don't have much to offer, but my heart is yours."

He kissed the tears from her face.

She sighed. And prayed she wasn't making the biggest mistake of her life.

"I forgive you, and I want those things, too. With you."

"Thank you. I won't fu—er, screw up again."

"I still think I want to be alone for a bit."

His face fell, but he nodded. "I understand." He stood, but paused at the doorway, staring back at her before closing the door behind him.

Maggie turned off her lamp and cried herself to sleep.

The next morning, Angel woke her with a gentle kiss. She opened her eyes to find he'd brought her breakfast in bed. She sat up and accepted the coffee and toast. Like a puppy who'd been kicked one time too many, he looked cautious but hopeful.

"Good morning, baby. Today I won't use or write illegally."

"Morning, and thank you. I believe you." She pushed her hair behind her ear. "Don't stare at me. I'm sure I'm a mess." She sighed. "I probably turned gray overnight. I need to put hair color on my grocery list."

"You told me to be honest, so yeah. You're kind of a mess. But you're my mess. Don't you dare color your hair—it's beautiful. You're the best thing that's ever happened to me. I love you, Maggie."

She wanted to say it back, but fear kept her silent. One day at a time…

The silence became awkward.

Elbows on knees, he buried his face in his hands. When he looked at her, his brow puckered. "You okay? Be honest."

"I forgive you, but I'm scared."

He looked startled. "Scared? Of me?"

"You said last night you weren't perfect. I'm not either. I've been betrayed before, and trust is hard for me. But I do want to try again, but you'll have to be patient with me. And don't put me on a pedestal; I don't like heights."

"Honesty, and no pedestals. Got it."

"I need to get up."

He stood and watched her slip into her robe. She made a beeline for the bathroom. When she returned, he was headed out the door.

"Where are you going?"

He turned. His lips curved in a small smile. "A shower. Hey, you know that honesty thing? Well, I could use help scrubbing my back. You know, because of my hurt shoulder and all." He gave her a semi-convincing wince but ended up snickering.

Maggie raised a skeptical brow. "I don't believe you're being totally honest right now."

"No?" His blue eyes simmered with desire and raked her from head to toe. "How's this for honesty?"

He stepped toward her, and before she could think, he dragged her to him and kissed her until she was sure she saw stars. His hands moved down her body, and his tongue explored her mouth, teasing and coaxing her to open to him. All thoughts of their differences and reasons they weren't good for each other vanished. Suddenly nothing mattered, as a primal need to be with him overtook her body. He loved her, and she just might be in love with him. It would be enough to overcome their differences. It had to be.

Maggie broke away and tugged his shirt over his head. He flinched. "You weren't kidding; you're in pain," she gasped.

"I'm fine, but I do need a shower. Come with me." He grabbed her hand, and she followed him to the bathroom where they finished taking off their clothes. He folded his; she dropped hers on the floor. He advanced toward her and backed her against the door. When he didn't pick her up, she worried about his shoulder.

"If I ask you something, will you tell me?"

"Yes."

"Tell me about your tattoos." She traced the writing above his heart. "I assume this is for Emma, you, and your friend Ken."

"Yep, we were the three amigos. You know about the wings on my back. This crown was when my crew declared me king."

"Crew? King?"

"Graffiti terms. Um, my cohorts in crime, so to speak, declared me top dog." He pointed at his bicep. "These numbers are the coordinates where Ken died…"

She kissed the numbers. "I have a small confession."

"Oh?" He stilled.

"Right after Emma called and told me you were at the police station, I headed out to be there."

"You did?"

"Yes, but I was so angry, I ended up changing my mind. Driving home, I swung through downtown and looked at your work."

"And?"

"You're very talented. And your messages *are* uplifting."

"Thanks. I sense there's a *but* in there."

She smiled. "I still don't agree with the delivery, but I'm trying to say I understand."

"Got it, boss."

She flicked his nipple ring, making him laugh before she continued with her exploration. "This is the serenity prayer."

"Yup."

He nipped her earlobe and one finger danced across her collarbone, making it hard for her to keep her eyes open, much less concentrate. Two could play this game. She tickled the outline of the image on his side and paused, discovering a long scar underneath the flames.

"Surgery? I like this one—a phoenix?"

"Knifing. And yes, a phoenix. It's how I felt once I was clean. A rebirth through fire."

"Dear God, you were stabbed?"

"A long time ago. New beginnings…" He touched his forehead to hers and looked her in the eye.

She swallowed her fear and smiled, nodding. "And this date?"

"The day I got clean. And someday I'll have your name on my skin. You're already under my skin, Maggie May." His erection pressed against her, and she gasped as his hands and lips roamed down her body.

Angel stopped her worries with another toe-curling kiss. Suddenly, he broke away and closed his eyes. His breathing was ragged as he hung his head, pressing his forehead against hers.

"Fuck."

"Okay," she agreed. She wrapped her arms around his neck. "Maybe the F word isn't so bad after all."

"Fuck, fuck, fuck," he ground out again.

"What's the matter? Is it your shoulder?"

"Protection. I don't have any. Do you?"

"Fuck. No."

He threw his head back and laughed long and hard. "I'm a bad influence on you."

Grabbing her hand, he pulled her into the hot, steamy shower and kissed her again as he began to smooth her bath gel over her skin.

"Maybe this isn't such a good idea. I could still get pregnant."

"I guess we'll just have to improvise. Did I mention that although I can't tell time, add, or subtract, I'm quite creative?" He sank to his knees before her.

Maggie looked down at him and held his face in her hands. "We'll be okay?"

Blue eyes filled with love met hers. "We'll work on communication; the trust will follow." With his arms wrapped around her waist, he closed his eyes and held her tight as the water cascaded down on them. "I promise, Maggie," he whispered over and over as he trailed kisses down her stomach.

Chapter
Fourteen

A week later, Angel reviewed his driver's test facts as he whitewashed over his writing. "No parking within fifteen feet of a fire hydrant. No passing on a solid line. A stop sign has eight sides." Angel smirked and paused in his painting. He knew that one well. He'd just had to replace six of the stop signs he'd "defaced" as part of his community service. Dipping the roller brush in the white paint, he continued reviewing. "Stop for school buses, yield to pedestrians, don't run over blind people. No texting and driving. *As if.*"

"Hi, Captain Angel. Whatcha doing?"

Angel turned to see Emma's daughter, Kenzie, and another little girl who looked to be about the same age. They licked their chocolate ice cream cones as they stared intently at him. Both had on crowns and wore pink hoodies over their princess dresses. Standing behind them was a man with a sandy blond hair, wearing sunglasses and eating his own cone.

"Hiya, Princess Kenzie. Who's your friend?"

"Angela. She's my bestest friend."

"Hmm, did you try to steal my name, Angela?"

Angela's blue-violet eyes narrowed. "No. It's *my* name. Angel is a dumb name for a boy."

He laughed. "I totally agree. But I had it first."

"Don't say that. My daddy will whoop your butt!"

"Hey, don't be getting me involved in your fights," her father chided. Turning to Angel, he asked, "Do you always talk out loud to yourself when working?"

"Nah, not usually. But it's driving me nuts to use boring white paint, so I'm distracting myself and studying for my driver's test." He held out his hand to shake. "Angel Sinclair."

"Dylan McAthie, Angela's father—the one who's 'gonna whoop your butt.'" He laughed as they shook hands. "It's a shame to cover that up. It was a piece of art."

"Thanks. I agree." Angel stopped painting. "Wait, did you say Dylan McAthie?"

"That's me."

Dylan McAthie had been lead guitarist for Angel's favorite band, Crucified, Dead and Buried. These days he was in huge demand for studio work.

He looked at Dylan, embarrassed not to have recognized him and star struck at the same time. "Wow—I don't know what to say. You're famous. I mean, your music is the shit."

"He's not famous; he's just *Daddy*." Angela rolled her eyes and licked her cone. "And you said a bad word."

"*My* daddy says Dylan's full of himself," Kenzie added with a knowing nod.

Dylan laughed and shrugged. "Gee, thanks, girls. It's hard to be a hero in your own home." He motioned with his cone toward Angel's piece, now half-covered in white paint. "So you work for the city?"

Angel sighed. "No, I'm the writer who got busted throwing it up. Painting over it is part of my community service." He nodded toward the white paint. "It sucks ass."

The little girls' snickering and shoulder nudging reminded him of his need to watch his language and set a good example.

"I, er, mean it was wrong of me to vandalize this property."

"Too bad. I really liked it." Dylan stepped closer to the wall and cocked his head to the side, studying the portion that hadn't been covered.

Angel grinned with pride. "Thanks."

"Daddy laughed when my baby brother, Rory, used markers on the dining room wall," Angela reported. "Mommy didn't think it was funny, and they both got in trouble."

Dylan smirked and winked at Angel. "Mommy made a valid point. Rory was wrong to color on the walls, just like it was wrong for Angel to write on public buildings without permission."

Angel was both amazed and amused by Dylan McAthie being all dad-like as he spoke to his precocious daughter. It was so off-the-charts different from the way the media always portrayed him.

Dylan turned his attention back to him. "Listen, you got a sketch-book or something I could look at? If so, we live next to David and Emma. Drop it by sometime. I'd like to check it out. I'm working on a friend's album, and we've been knocking around ideas that involve graffiti for the cover. Maybe you could help us."

Angel's mouth dropped, and his brows shot up. "You're shittin' me!" Too late, he remembered the kids. "Sorry. Language like that is wrong, and I'm in big trouble for using it."

Dylan's blue eyes twinkled. "Right. Bad language is a no-no, girls. And no, I'm not kidding about being interested. If I'm not home, leave it with my wife, Jen. I'll let her know to expect you. Angel Sinclair, right?"

Angel nodded, still dumbfounded that Dylan McAthie wanted to look at his work.

"Okay, well...Carry on. I've got to get the two princesses back home and pretend like we ate something healthy for lunch before their mothers get back from Christmas shopping."

"Hey, just tell them ice cream is milk, one of the major food groups." Angel gave them a wave and went back to work, whistling.

Two days later, Angel burst in the back door, waving the paper copy of his driver's license. "I did it, Maggie," he yelled.

"Shhh, the Stapletons are here. Our first guests." Her green eyes sparkled and a smile lit her face as she moved toward the oven with a potholder in one hand.

Angel grinned, and his heart did a somersault of joy. Since getting busted, they'd been talking more, and their relationship had shifted back from cautious to easy. *And now she'd said* "our." Grabbing her by the waist and hand, he gave her a resounding kiss on the lips and twirled her in a quick dance around the kitchen.

"We have a lot to celebrate." He placed the copy of his license in her hand. "I did it. I passed my driver's test. Emma took me, and I passed." He couldn't stop grinning like a fool.

"Of course you passed. I never had any doubts." She smiled at him and reached up to flick the white paint off his cheek. "How much did you get done on your community service?"

"All the stop signs are replaced, and four out of five walls are painted. I still need to talk to David's students and his Sunday school class. Will I have to get a suit or something for that?" He rubbed his neck, thinking about a tie.

"I wouldn't think so. You'll make more of an impact dressed like you normally do. You'll be more relatable. It's called street cred, right?"

He laughed and admired her ass as she took cookies out of the oven. Her dark skirt hugged her hips, and the emerald green blouse enhanced her eyes. She wore her dark hair down, but off her face, showing off the gray streak, just the way he liked it.

"You look beautiful," he whispered in her ear, giving her a quick kiss on the neck. He shrugged out of his hoodie and hung it up. Pushing up his sleeves, he whistled as he washed his hands. "Hey, I have something else to tell you—"

The spatula hit the floor. At her cry of pain, he spun around, thinking she'd burned herself.

"Get out! Get out of my house, *now,*" she whispered hoarsely, her eyes narrowed.

"What? Maggie—"

"Get out!" She screamed this time, pointing to the door.

"Shh, baby. The guests…What the hell's wrong with you?" he whispered. Drying his hands, he looked down at his arms where her eyes were focused. Both arms were bruised to hell and back, but she'd jumped to conclusions before he'd had a chance to tell her why. His heart sank to the pit of his stomach, and anger stirred. *She doesn't trust me one damn bit.*

"Get out. I hope the high you got from shooting up your drugs was worth it. I'll send the money I owe you through Emma. Be gone in thirty minutes." She threw the cookies on the plate, her breath coming out in angry spurts, her cheeks reddening by the minute.

"Look, it isn't…I didn't…"

Spinning on her heels, she grabbed her coat and stormed out, slamming the back door behind her. Angel heard laughter from the top of the stairs. Swearing under his breath, he rolled down his sleeves and went to check on the guests.

An older couple strolled down the stairs, holding hands, and he forced a smile for them.

"Hi, I'm Angel." He held out his hand to the white-haired gentleman with the neat, white moustache.

"Bill Stapleton, and this is my wife, Edwina." Bill smiled as they shook hands.

"Ma'am," Angel nodded an acknowledgment.

Her blue eyes sparkled with fun. "You look like a natty dread angel."

Angel laughed. "Bob Marley fan?"

"Of course. Bill and I are old hippies. We met at Woodstock."

"I'd love to hear that story. Um, Ms. Robertson has stepped out for a moment. Is there anything I can get you? There's a fresh pot of coffee and a kettle of hot water for tea in the kitchen." He threw another log on the fire.

"We're fine, thank you. We'll be content cuddling and looking at the fire. We're celebrating our wedding anniversary this weekend." Edwina tucked her hand in her husband's arm and smiled up at him like a newlywed.

"Congratulations, that's great. I'll make myself scarce, and I believe Maggie, er, Ms. Robertson will have dinner ready around six."

Flashing the couple an envious look, he left to find Maggie. This couple had been together more years than he could count. The way things stood now, he and Maggie weren't going to make it another thirty minutes unless he could convince her he was clean. Following the path to the dock, he prayed she'd calmed down enough to listen.

Illuminated by the dim dusk-to-dawn light, the dock beckoned to Maggie, offering a quiet refuge from the storm raging within her. The bruised track marks on Angel's arms had scared her and sent her running. She had to get away, refusing to let him see her self-worth once more shattered into a million pieces. Where did you draw the line between being supportive and being co-dependent? At yesterday's Nar-Anon meeting, she'd felt oh-so smug about not needing to be there. Was Angel's insistence she go because he'd relapsed already? Had it been his way to prepare her?

Broken heart. The term used to seem trite and cliché. When she and Brian finally divorced, the feeling had been one of relief. Maggie now realized it wasn't trite, or cliché. The excruciating pain in her chest was testament to a very real phenomenon.

How many times had she watched her mother suffer her father's relapses? She refused to be her mom. Leaning against the railing of the dock, she listened to the water lap at the shore. An owl hooted in the distance, and she could smell the smoke from her chimney. It was tranquil—a direct contrast to her tumultuous emotions. The ultimatum had been made, and she had to stand by it, no matter how badly it hurt.

She swore under her breath at the sound of crunching leaves behind her. Of course he'd come after her. God forbid he leave as requested. No, make that *demanded.* She knew what would happen next. The profuse apologies and promises it would never happen again. She'd been on this merry-go-round too many times to count. Her father had relapsed, apologized, and sworn to do better. Mama would believe him, losing more and more of her self-respect until all that remained was a shell of a woman by the time her father died. Maggie steeled her heart and turned to face him.

"Baby, it isn't what you think." He stood a few feet away from her, his hands in the pocket of his hoodie. The muted light cast shadows across his face, and she turned away from him. It was impossible to remain strong while looking at him.

"Go." Her voice remained firm, despite her trembling. Crossing her arms in front of her chest, she stared out over the inky water, wishing she could jump in and sink to the bottom. Death might be preferable to the pain of his betrayal.

"I don't have any veins left—"

"Obviously." She moved to walk past him, back toward the house. Her guests might need something. She didn't need to lose business in addition to her heart.

He grabbed her by the shoulders, and she attempted to shrug away.

"Let me go," she snapped, feeling like a trapped animal.

"Maggie, I didn't do this. It's not what you think."

The fingers gripping her shoulders were the same fingers that made her shiver with their gentle caresses. Ice ran through her veins.

Angel gave her slight shake. "Please listen to me." Desperation tinged his voice.

A sneer formed on her lips. "You didn't do this? Wonderful, who helped you? Some other loser from NA?" Too late, she realized she sounded like her ex, hitting below the belt. Ashamed, she looked away.

Angel dropped his hands and stepped away from her, holding his hands up in surrender. "No one helped me. I didn't use. Dammit, would you please let me explain…" Measured puffs of cold air moved between them. "I went to the goddamned health department for my blood test."

"W-What?"

"I go every six months to be tested for HIV and Hep C. I'm clean, but I still get checked. My sponsor recommended it. Because I don't have any veins left, it took the nurse four goddamned tries to get the draw. I did this for you! You have no idea how hard it is, seeing the rig…" He closed his eyes and shook his head.

Turning away, he swore, "Fuck it. I'm outta here. I'm done. I get it—you don't trust me. I understand that, but dammit, you could've at least listened to me first." Pulling a sheet of paper out of his back pocket, he threw it on the ground. Without another word, he turned and trudged back toward the house, his hands stuffed in his pockets, his head hung low.

Maggie caught the paper just before it blew into the lake. It was a note on letterhead from the local health department, with his name and today's date and time stamped on it. He'd even had the nurse sign underneath the written verification that she'd stuck him four times. Just as he'd said.

Dear Lord, what have I done? I'm no better than his family. "Angel! Wait!"

He turned and waited on her. Running up the hill, she threw herself against him, wrapping her arms around his neck. "Oh God, I'm so sorry. I'm so very sorry. Please forgive me."

He sighed. "It's as much my fault as yours. I should've told you I had the appointment. Truthfully, I didn't because I wasn't sure I'd have the balls to go through with it. Sometimes it takes me a few tries to actually get it done. Seeing needles is a huge trigger. I'm working the program, I promise." He held her tight as she clung to his neck.

"You are. I'm sorry I jumped to conclusions. I'm totally at fault."

"It's okay. Thank you." He rubbed her back.

"This isn't going to be easy, is it?" she asked in a hushed voice as she snuggled into his embrace, inhaling the scent of clean soap and fire on his hoodie.

"Nothing worth fighting for is." He pulled away and gave her a kiss on the forehead. "Let's go talk to the Stapletons and see how they've managed to put up with each other since Woodstock. Maybe we'll learn something." They walked toward the house holding hands.

"Good grief, if we're together that long I'll be—"

"Forever *thirty-nine* to me," he finished for her.

"Smart answer," she said with a chuckle. "Angel?"

"Yes?"

"Your willingness to forgive me and understand my trust issues… I've never had this in my life before. I'm grateful you're a strong man. We'll make this work."

Angel gave her a quick kiss as they entered the kitchen. "Yes, we will. Go freshen up in my bathroom. I'll start getting stuff ready. The Stapletons are in the living area enjoying the fire."

When she returned, Angel had his back to her, tossing the salad. She wrapped her arms around his blue flannel shirt and rested her cheek on his back.

"We're okay, aren't we?" Her voice faltered. She desperately needed to hear his reassurance.

"We get stronger every time we work through something like this. Hell, yeah."

His confidence brought a smile to her lips. She kissed his back and went to the oven to get the roast. While the meat rested, she lit the candles and made sure everything was ready for a romantic evening for her guests. Pausing at the doorway to the living area, envy and longing rushed through her when she saw the couple cuddling in front of the fire.

Mrs. Stapleton pulled away and laughed. "My goodness, I feel like a teenager caught making out with my boyfriend." She slapped her husband's hand away with a teasing smile.

Maggie smiled and announced that dinner was ready. She put on some soft music and watched as Mr. Stapleton took his wife in his arms and spun her around the room before escorting her to the table. Had she ever been that much in love? Yes, maybe when she first met Brian, but his verbal abuse had worn away her feelings like water eroding a rock—slowly but surely.

She walked into the kitchen, and her eyes met Angel's across the room. He winked, and a lazy smile spread across his face, making her incredibly happy.

Is this love or lust? Or the delightful combination of both? She prayed it was both.

"Won't you be joining us for dinner?" Mrs. Stapleton asked as Maggie poured the wine and Angel served the salad.

"No, ma'am. I don't think you two need chaperones," Angel teased.

Everyone laughed. She and Angel excused themselves and returned to the kitchen. The moment the door closed behind her, she found herself pushed back against the kitchen counter. He silenced her squeal of surprise with his mouth and helped her up on the counter.

"Your shoulder…"

"Not worried about it. I have other things to concentrate on."

He stood between her legs, as his wicked tongue explored her mouth and his hands crept under her blouse. Scared of being caught, she shoved them away, giggling. He pinched her nipples hard and growled. She moaned with a primal, powerful need for him.

"A lifetime of forever, that's what I want…Promise me, Maggie. We can do this."

She saw his vulnerability and hopes laid out for her to accept or reject.

"I promise." And she meant it. She wanted a future with Angel.

"I promise, too." He smiled and returned to kissing her.

Chapter
Fifteen

"This is nice," Angel rasped in Maggie's ear.

He pulled her closer, his arm around her waist, his thumb rubbing the underside of her breast.

"Mmmm-hmmm," she replied, sounding not quite awake as she snuggled in deeper, her hand over his.

He growled in her ear and poked her with his hard on.

"I thought we were sleeping in this morning."

The guests had left two days ago, and since then he'd enjoyed proving to her the advantages to being in love with a younger man.

"I can't help it. You know I love your ass. Things come up," he snickered as he rose to one elbow and kissed her neck. "I love you, Margaret Mary Maguire Robertson."

"Angel Won't-Tell-Me-His-Middle-Name Sinclair...Why won't you tell me what it is? That should be part of our honesty deal."

"My middle name is stupid, and I don't use it. My parents were cruel and should have been prosecuted for what they did to me. Maybe I'll get my brother to sue them for me." He kissed her shoulder and gave it a playful bite. Slowly, with the intent to drive her insane with need, he trailed kisses down her warm, soft skin.

"If you promise not to stop, I'll never ask your middle name again," she moaned.

Chuckling, he cupped her full breast, and with his thumb flicked her nipple until it pebbled. Unable to resist its lure, he took it in his mouth, teasing with his teeth and tongue.

"Deal." His lips moved lower, and he nipped her hip while his hands smoothed across her soft skin. He flipped her over and gave her butt a playful swat. God, how he loved her ass.

The phone rang, and they groaned simultaneously.

"Let it ring," he whispered.

"I can't. Something's wrong. It's seven in the morning." Maggie reached for the phone, only to discover it wasn't on the bedside table.

"Phillip's on Eastern Time. It would be eight there, inconsiderate cockblocker," Angel grumbled.

Maggie finally found the phone under the bed. She looked at the caller ID and frowned. "It's an Atlanta area code, but not Brian's number…"

Annoyed, he grabbed the phone and barked, "Hello?"

"Angel, you need to come home." Damien's voice cracked with emotion.

The hair on the back of Angel's neck stood on end. His brother was known for his icy demeanor, the epitome of self-control.

"What's wrong?" Now fully awake, he sat on the side of the bed. He tried to still his racing thoughts as he searched for his underwear on the floor.

"It's Mom. She's really sick and asking for you. We didn't realize how serious this was. They were going to do surgery and fix it. We thought she'd be fine…"

"Really sick? What do you mean, 'really sick'? How did you get this number?" The knot of dread lodged in his stomach moved up to his throat.

"You weren't answering your phone. Emmanuelle gave it to me. The surgeon said it was too late. Nothing can be done. Mom's home now. Hospice is here." A loud sigh echoed across the line. "Mom's dying, Angel."

Angel remained silent, his mind trying to process his brother's words. *Mom's dying?* "W-What did you just say? You're wrong; she's just sick." Fear wrapped itself around his heart, squeezing like a vise. Surely at any moment he'd wake from this nightmare. How could life be perfect one moment and with two words dissipate into nothing?

Damien's lying. It's a ploy to get me home. It can't be true.

"It's ovarian cancer, stage IV. She doesn't have long, and she's asking for you. Please, Angel. Come home. For her."

"Shit." He pinched the bridge of his nose. "Shit, shit, shit."

"I can come get you if you need me to."

"No. I, uh, I'll be there in a few hours." He hung up, unable to move or to think.

"What's the matter? Who's sick?" Maggie sat up, frowning.

He leaned his elbows on his knees and covered his face. It took him a few seconds to be able to speak. "My mom's dying. I need to go home. Fuck, I shouldn't have stayed away so long. This can't be happening."

"Oh, Angel…" She pressed a kiss to his forehead and put her arms around him.

Frozen and unable to move, he raised his head and watched Maggie pull on her robe. She darted to her closet, grabbing a suitcase that she threw on the bed next to him. "Go shower and get the things you need. We can be on the road in less than thirty minutes. I'll get Emma and David to take care of things here."

Angel nodded, still not moving. Maggie stood between his legs. Wrapping his arms around her waist, he buried his face in her stomach, drawing strength from her support. She kissed him on top of his head and wiggled from his grasp.

"Angel. We need to go."

In a daze, he left to get ready.

After they'd driven in silence for over three hours, and despite her trepidation, Angel took over to drive the last fifty miles. He was a very good, cautious driver. Maggie stared in amazement at the homes they passed, at least the ones she could see behind their gated walls.

"You live in this area?"

"No. My family does." His sardonic smile spoke volumes, and his driving slowed to a snail's pace. She could feel the anxiety emanating from his taut body.

"Your family is rich?" She had suspected his family might be upper-middle class, but she'd never expected to find he grew up in a gated community.

"Disgustingly so."

The questions continued to rack up in her mind. Angel slowed to turn in to a driveway shrouded by a canopy of trees. The house wasn't visible down the long drive. Pausing at the gate, he pressed the button for the intercom instead of punching in the code.

"It's Angel." The ornate gate creaked opened. He drove slowly down the shadowed drive, overhung by large oak trees. His mouth was set in a straight line, his eyes as bleak as a January morning. Maggie reached out to squeeze his leg, and he took her hand in his.

"Why didn't you tell me?" she asked quietly. "Is this why you've insisted on being so underpaid for your work? Because you have money?"

Old fears crept in, and she wished they could turn back. Was it because of her history of marrying above herself? *Was he afraid I'd want his money?*

He shrugged. "I never saw the need to talk about it. This hasn't been my life for a long time, if it ever was. And no, *I* don't have money; my family has money. Money is a trigger, so I like our agreement the way it is. I don't need much, and truth be told, I'd work for you for nothing, because I love you."

The driveway seemed to weave through the oak trees forever until the huge, Tudor-style house loomed in front of them. A loud squawk drew her gaze from the estate, and she swiveled to look behind them.

"Were those peacocks?"

"Yep."

Maggie took in the red brick monstrosity in front of her, feeling like Dorothy in the land of Oz. "How big is it?"

"Eighteen thousand square feet. It has nine bedrooms and eleven baths. More room than two people need."

"Don't you mean four? My truck's going to look very out of place here."

"It isn't my home. I don't belong here. And Damien lives downtown; I think…I really don't know. And who gives a shit if your truck looks out of place?" Turning off the ignition, Angel closed his eyes and laid his head against the steering wheel. "I don't want to do this."

"I know." She leaned over and kissed his cheek. When he opened his eyes, the hopelessness she witnessed tore at her heart.

"Thanks for coming. I want Mom to meet you before..." His voice trailed off as he looked out the window. She watched him swallow and blink back tears as he blew out a ragged breath.

"You can do this. You're clean. I'm sure your family will be happy to see you. And I'm here for you."

"I doubt all of them will be. Maybe Mom..." With a bleak nod, he came around to open her door. Looking around, she now understood where he'd learned his impeccable manners. How had he ended up homeless? She could understand while he was using, but he'd been clean for over eighteen months...

Taking Angel's hand, she stepped out of the truck and looked up when the front door opened, revealing an older gentleman dressed in a dark suit.

Angel escorted her to the door, his hand firm on her lower back.

"Angel!" The man spoke with a distinct British accent. His gray hair gave him a distinguished look. His smiled widened into a grin and his blue eyes sparkled with what looked like genuine affection. *Is this the man who kicked his son out of the house?*

"Taylor." Angel acknowledged him with a handshake, but the gentleman quickly pulled him into a bear hug. Angel rolled his eyes at Maggie, but he returned the hug before pulling away, looking a bit uncomfortable. "Maggie, this is John Taylor, our estate manager. He's been with my family forever. Mom or Dad will try to tell you otherwise, but Taylor's the one who runs this place. Taylor, this is Maggie Robertson, my girlfriend."

Taylor gave them both a warm smile. "Don't you mean Elise runs the place?" He nodded at Maggie and whispered, "Elise is my wife. She manages the Sinclair household and is the *real* boss."

He took Angel and Maggie's coats in one arm and shook Maggie's hand, smiling. "Indeed, it's a pleasure to meet you, Ms. Robertson. If there is anything you need, just ask." He motioned for Angel and Maggie to enter.

Elise? The woman Angel had wanted to marry works for his family? Maggie blinked, and her heart stuttered.

Angel didn't act the least bit concerned. Did this man know Angel had been interested in his wife?

"Angel, you *will* be staying here, I presume?"

"Th-Thank you, Mr. Taylor," Maggie replied. She gripped Angel's hand, silently praying he'd say no.

"Just Taylor is fine, or John, if you prefer."

"I'm not sure yet," Angel replied. "I'll let you know. Regardless, only one room will be necessary."

"No! Two rooms." Maggie's face flushed hot with embarrassment.

Angel shot her a disappointed look. "Two rooms. But make sure they're next to each other."

"Very good, sir." Taylor made no attempt to hide his smile before leaving the room.

"Elise is here?" Maggie whispered. "And I'm your girlfriend?" she whispered to Angel.

"Of course Elise is here. She and Taylor have a house at the edge of the property. What did you want me to say? This is Maggie, my fuckbuddy? My boss with benefits? Or perhaps, this be Maggie, my booty call. Nope. Wait, I've got it. Taylor, this is Maggie. She's my home skillet," he whispered back, with the first hint of a smile since the phone call this morning.

"Home skillet?"

"Or I could've just said, Taylor, meet Maggie, *my old lady.*"

Glaring, she punched him in the arm. He laughed.

"That's *not* funny—" Maggie stopped to stare at the opulence before her.

She'd thought she was used to dealing with the upper class. Brian's family had money and lived in a nice home in Connecticut. In Boston, she and Brian had lived near Beacon Hill before moving to an expensive townhouse just outside of Atlanta. But nothing in her experience compared to the lavishness of the Sinclair home.

An enormous crystal chandelier hung over an antique marble table in the center of the foyer with a huge, fragrant floral arrangement on it. Behind the table, a carved cherry staircase curved upward. The sun peeking through the stained-glass window on the landing cast a rainbow onto the hardwood floor, accented with Aubusson rugs. Gilt-framed paintings of pastoral scenes lined the walls. It made Pine Bluff seem like a different country.

A handsome, dark-haired man in a pair of black jeans and a starched white shirt descended the stairs, buttoning his cuffs. His eyes appeared black. He had a strong, clean-shaven jaw, and his short, damp hair was combed, but the natural wave wasn't quite contained. A small furrow in his brow was the only indication something was wrong. He moved with the grace of a powerful panther, without any wasted movement.

Maggie recognized the infamous Damien "Demon" Sinclair from various fundraisers in the past. Brian had never formally introduced her, but she distantly recalled Tiffany, of all people, gossiping that he was a "player."

Angel placed a hand on the small of her back. Whether it was to bolster her confidence or his, Maggie wasn't sure.

"I'm glad you're here. Mom wants to see you." Damien stood in front of Angel and glanced over at Maggie. A slight lift of an eyebrow signaled his curiosity.

"Maggie, this is my brother, Damien. Damien, this is Maggie Robertson."

Damien cocked his head to the side and gave her a puzzled frown. "Maggie Robertson, you look familiar… Wait—you're Brian Robertson's wife."

"Ex-wife. Tiffany is the current Mrs. Robertson." Maggie shook the hand he offered.

"Yes, I know Tiffany *Robertson* well. I represented her ex-husband." Damien's eyes crinkled, and one corner of his mouth curved upward.

"Yes, so I've heard. My son says she's a terrible cook, but I'm fairly certain we both know that isn't why Brian married her." *Did I leave my filter in Pine Bluff?*

Damien chuckled. "I like you, Maggie. And trust me, Brian got what he deserved, in the courtroom and out of it. I don't believe he always thinks before acting or speaking."

"Not with the head on his shoulders, *obviously*." This time she clapped a hand over her mouth.

Angel chuckled, but Damien threw back his head and laughed outright.

"You said it, not me. As a matter of fact, you should've hired *me* as your divorce attorney. He got off way too easy with your settlement. It would have been a pleasure nailing his balls to the wall twice."

Maggie nodded, not surprised Damien knew the details of her divorce. With Brian's cronies, she'd found lawyers to be worse gossips than their bored housewives. "I wasn't concerned about money. I just wanted out of the marriage."

"Are you done flirting with my girlfriend? Tell me about Mom. Why didn't you tell me at Thanksgiving she was sick?"

Damien's face fell. "I'm not flirting with your girlfriend. I didn't tell you about Mom because I didn't know how ill she was. She hid it from us. And if you recall, I asked you to come home and told you Mom didn't look well. I thought she was just run down and dieting again. I had no idea…"

He stopped and shook his head, his grief now apparent. "You know Mom; she never complains. She didn't go to the doctor until it was too late. It's an aggressive cancer, and she's refused all treatment except for comfort measures. She's now under hospice care. Dad's not dealing well, at all." He drew Angel into a hug and slapped him on the back. "I'm glad you're here. Mom's been asking for you. You sure you're okay?" He stepped back, seeming to search Angel's face for answers.

Angel shrugged away, clearly uncomfortable. "Despite what you and Dad think, I'm not stupid. I know that's code for *am I using*. The answer is no. I'm clean. Does Dad know I'm here? I can't imagine he'll be thrilled to have his loser son home. Now that I think about it, I think it best we get a motel room." Angel's voice sounded bitter.

"Yes, I told Dad you were coming. And you're not getting a motel room. This is a big house. You need to be *here*, for Mom. I'm staying, too."

Angel's bravado crumpled, and he glanced up the staircase. "H-How long?"

"Days at the most. She's refusing to eat and has advanced directives refusing any heroics. Her lucidity comes and goes. Today's a pretty good day. She's more alert than yesterday. The nurses are keeping her comfortable and said she should eventually just fade on out…" Damien averted his eyes.

Angel turned to Maggie and croaked, "I need—"

"Go to your mother. Perhaps you can point me in the direction of the kitchen for a cup of coffee?"

Damien nodded. "We can go to the library. I'll have Taylor bring us coffee and some of Elise's scones."

Oh, great.

Chapter
Sixteen

Angel crept up the staircase, uncertain what he'd find behind his mother's door. Nostalgia brought him a memory of sliding down this very banister at age six. The terror of flying out of control into the air before he'd hit his head and passed out was similar to the crushing anxiety he felt now. How he wished Elise and Taylor could kiss his fears away like they had in the ER after his concussion. His parents had been out of town and hadn't bothered to cut their trip short after his injury.

Maybe Mom will have some opiates to take the edge off.

Just one would do the trick.

She'd never miss it...

He collapsed on the step, sickened by the thought, knowing there was a time not too long ago when he'd willingly have stolen his dying mother's meds. *Fuck, that didn't take long.* Inhaling a deep breath, he let it out through pursed lips, pushing the thoughts away.

I'm clean.

I'm not alone.

I have my higher power.

I have Maggie's love and support.

I choose to not use today.

When he felt stronger, he stood. Reaching the top of the staircase, he paused for a moment. Despite his effort to remain calm, his hand shook as he reached for the doorknob. The soft strains of Vivaldi drifted through the closed door, and he leaned his forehead against it, listening for a moment.

Then he turned the knob and entered his mother's room. Sunlight streamed through the large windows. White. Everything in the room was white. The walls, the curtains, the duvet, even the roses on the bedside table were void of color. His mother—once so full of life—was still as death, looking tiny and frail in the oversized bed, her skin the color of alabaster. It was as if color no longer belonged in her fading life.

Taylor and Elise's daughter, Harley, sat on the side of the bed, massaging his mother's colorless hand. She turned when Angel came in and gave him a sad smile as she tossed her flaxen braid over her shoulder. She wore a faded Harvard sweatshirt that had once been Damien's and a pair of jeans.

"Mrs. Sinclair, Angel's here." She stood and gave him a gentle hug.

Over her shoulder, his mother gazed at him silently. Purple pain circled her dark eyes. He held Harley a little tighter, using her as a buffer between him and the overwhelming sorrow enveloping the room.

"Hey, Harley. I didn't know you were back."

"I just got here yesterday. Mamma called me, and I was between jobs, so I'm moving back home for a bit to help. I'm so sorry," she whispered.

"I'm not deaf," his mother snapped. Although she'd been an American citizen for years, her Romanian accent was always more pronounced when she grew angry.

Angel frowned and mouthed *sorry* to Harley. He'd never understood why his mother was so standoffish to her. She'd grown up with them. Hell, her parents were more like parents to him than his own.

"Jumping Jehoshaphat, your Dad's gonna stroke when he sees your hair!" Harley giggled, softly.

"If I'm lucky, maybe the stroke will affect his vocal chords."

"I'll leave you two alone and bring you a cup of coffee. Do you still drink it black? And a protein shake for Mrs. S." She slipped under his arm and out of the room before he could reply.

"Don't bother. I don't want it nor need you." His mother glared after the young woman.

He approached and sank to the side of his mother's bed before his legs crumpled beneath him. Her pale, gaunt face was so different from what he remembered. A tiny smile curved her dry lips. She'd always been thin, having suffered from an eating disorder for most of her life, but now she appeared downright fragile. He doubted she weighed more than seventy-five pounds. Her black hair was almost completely gray now and thinner. Instead of her usual tastefully coifed French chignon, it was styled in a long braid.

Angel leaned over and kissed her soft, parchment-like cheek, inhaling the familiar scent of her French perfume. She reached up and cupped his face in her cold hand, peering at him with eyes full of pain and love.

"My darling Angel, my sweet boy. You're here. Am I dreaming?" Her voice quivered, and he placed his hand over hers on his cheek. He smiled down at her, unable to speak, unable to see as her face swam before his eyes.

It was difficult, but he managed to swallow the lump in his throat. "More like a nightmare than a dream, but yes, I'm really here."

"Don't cry, son. Everything will be okay."

"How can you say that? Nothing will ever be okay…M-Mom, I'm sorry," he choked. He laid his head down on her fragile chest and wept like he hadn't wept since he was a terrified ten year old. His heart felt heavy with the pain he had caused her.

She stroked his face. "You're here. That's all that matters to me."

She whisper-sang a lullaby from his childhood, and pain exploded in his chest. He was both heartbroken and relieved when she stopped.

She gently pulled one of his dreads. "Your father *will* have a conniption fit over your hair." She gave a soft laugh. "I hope I get to see it."

Angel sat up, wiped his eyes, and attempted a smile. "Gee, thanks, Mom."

"It looks like it did the summer you went to camp and didn't comb your hair for two months. Do you remember?"

Angel nodded and grinned. "You were hell with that comb getting the tangles out. Then Dad marched me to the kitchen and had Elise buzz it all off anyway to teach me a lesson."

His mother squeezed his hand. "Don't let him buzz cut it again. After seeing your beautiful blond hair lying on the floor, I went to my room and cried. Although I do prefer your waves to this tangled mess," she chided.

"You cried over my hair?" Angel had rarely seen his mother cry, unless it was when she played the piano. And only if she thought she was alone.

She nodded. Her sad, pinched face fell. "He tried, you know."

"Who tried?"

"Your father. Don't blame him too much when I'm gone." She gazed at him with a sorrowful smile and patted his cheek. "I don't know if I like this facial hair, hiding my beautiful boy's face." She laughed and ran an icy, bony finger over his moustache and beard.

"I look twelve without it," Angel replied with a smile. He looked away, not wanting to make promises he couldn't keep regarding his father. He dug in his jeans pocket. "I have a present for you."

"You know I love presents," she winced a little and glanced at the IV machine that clicked every so often, infusing into a vein in her skeletal chest.

"It's okay. Don't hurt because of me…" Angel reached out and punched the button for her, pushing the thoughts of the narcotic and needles from his mind. He could do this for his mother's sake. His tears started again, and he dashed them away with the heel of his hand. "Never hurt again because of me, Mom."

Pulling the key ring from his pocket, he placed it in her hand, closing her blue-veined fist around it. Her rings spun around her bony fingers. With his thumb, he rubbed his favorite, the emerald. He'd done the same thing when he was a little boy on the rare occasions she'd put him to bed.

"What is it?" she asked as she tried to read the keychain. "I don't have my reading glasses."

Angel grinned and murmured, "Just like Maggie. She can never find her glasses, either." He found the glasses on her bedside table and helped her place them on her face. "It's my eighteen-months clean key tag from NA."

She held it in her fist. "This is the best gift you've ever given me. Now who is Maggie?"

"I want you to meet her. She's the best thing to ever happen to me. I want to marry her, if she'll have me." He smiled even as tears trekked down his cheek. "I'm in love, Mom."

"I want to meet this girl who has ensnared one of my elusive sons. I'd given up on you and Damien ever settling down. Although Damien has been with Lauren for a while now. The woman's attractive, but she has no passion. He'll be bored to death with that cold fish."

"I wouldn't blame you for giving up on me. I'm the loser son, unlike your first-born."

"Shush, don't say that. You're not a loser. You were merely lost. You're my fair-haired Angel, my gift from heaven. And Damien is only number one in birth order. Although he acts a little cold and formal, he's a good man with a big heart. I love you both, you know. The heart doesn't divide with love. It expands. You need to learn that lesson. Don't be like Sebastian." She paused and stared off into space, drifting into a narcotic haze as her physical pain began to subside.

"I want you to meet Maggie. I'll go get her, okay?"

"I'd like that."

Harley entered the room with a tray and placed it on the bedside table. Maggie had followed and stood in the doorway with Damien. Angel went to her and clasped her hand, squeezing it tight while he drew her into his mother's room.

"Mom, this is Maggie Robertson, the love of my life."

"Hello, Mrs. Sinclair," she said, but she hung back, casting an uncertain glance at Angel.

"You may address me as Nadya. Mrs. Sinclair is how the help address me."

Angel flinched and glanced at Harley's red cheeks. His mother's condescending attitude toward those who worked for their family had always bothered him. She always made sure everyone knew his or her place. Harley left the room with her head held high. Damien followed her, hopefully to smooth things over.

"I want to speak to Maggie alone." Although weak, her imperious voice demanded obedience.

Angel looked at Maggie with apprehension. She nodded and gave him a small smile before biting her lip.

Kissing his mother on the cheek, he whispered, "Be nice. She's important to me."

"I'm always nice, Angel. Don't be impertinent. Go. We need to get to know one another. And don't let that busybody nurse or Harley in until I summon them."

Angel gave his mother another kiss on the cheek, his eyes filling with tears once more. Squeezing Maggie's hand, he grabbed his coffee from the tray and left.

Maggie approached the oversized bed with hesitant steps.

"Come closer. Despite what my son thinks, I won't bite." Nadya motioned to her, much like a queen beckoning a royal subject.

Maggie wondered about her slight accent. Her dark eyes, so very much like Damien's, gazed at her with the intensity of a scientist examining a germ under a microscope.

Maggie stood by the bed and held the frail hand offered to her.

"I'm…I…" Maggie fumbled for words.

"Sit down, dear. Don't stand on ceremony. I don't have time for that anymore. Let's chat." She reached for a glass of water with a straw in it.

Maggie helped her get a sip and perched on the side of her bed.

"I'm dying." Angel's mother said. "I do not want things sugarcoated, and I don't want to waste time on small talk. I want to know everything about you, and I need to know if my son is truly okay." She gazed at the NA key tag in her other hand and kissed it.

"Yes, he's doing very well. He has over eighteen months clean and is conscientious about going to his meetings."

"Do you love him?" Her piercing eyes bore into Maggie, appearing to assess her every nuance, past whatever words she might answer.

"I…" Maggie moved her hands to under her thighs to keep from squirming like a teenager. She nodded.

"You're older than he is."

Nodding, she stared at the white rose arrangement on the bedside table. "Fourteen years older, to be precise. My son is six years younger than Angel."

"This bothers you—the age difference." Nadya's soft voice was surprisingly kind.

Maggie met her unwavering gaze. "I would be lying if I said it didn't."

His mother smiled and patted her leg. "It may seem insurmountable now, but when you are eighty-four and he's seventy, it won't seem like much. You'll both be old and crotchety."

Maggie's eyebrows lifted, and she relaxed a bit, chuckling. "I hope that's true."

"I'm going to give you some advice from a woman who has lived a bit longer than you have."

"I'm listening."

"Angel's a lot like his father. He's restless, creative, and passionate — and very self-destructive. You need to help him learn how to channel his spirit so he can fly without crashing. It takes a strong woman to love a man like that. I was not..." She sighed and appeared lost in her memories. "You must be tough enough to be the soft knoll where he can land without hurting himself, *or you*. Otherwise, you will lose him. He will smash against the rocks and shatter, breaking your heart in the process. If you are the woman who can do this for my son, you have my blessing."

"Thank you." She didn't know what else to say.

"Please...take care of him. I didn't do a very good job." A tear slipped from the corner of her eye.

Taking a tissue, Maggie wiped it away, not really understanding what Angel's mother meant. From the few things Angel had said, he didn't sound anything like his father. Nadya's eyes clouded with her suffering and the narcotics.

"As parents, we always worry about our failures. But your son is amazing. He's kind, creative, determined, and on the right track now. You have nothing to worry about. And I promise I'll take care of him," Maggie replied.

"Thank you. I'm tired now and want to rest. Take that disgusting drink Harley brought me away. I don't think it will make much difference now. If I'm going to eat something before I die, I'd rather it be chocolate. The nurse can sit with me while I rest a bit. It's why we pay her."

Nadya closed her eyes, and Maggie realized she'd just been dismissed.

She left the room, mulling over the things Nadya had shared with her. She found the nurse sitting outside the door reading. Giving Maggie a friendly nod, she went to check on her patient.

Unsure where to go, Maggie headed downstairs to find Angel. Maybe he was in the library. Maggie approached the heavy carved wooden door that was halfway closed and paused when she heard voices.

"You're the best, Elise. I've missed you."

Maggie heard true affection in Angel's voice. It made her pause, but she willed herself not to jump to any conclusions.

"*Gutten min.*" A female chuckled.

Not wanting to get caught eavesdropping, Maggie dashed into the next room, closing the door behind her. Squeezing her eyes tight, she pressed against the door. *What is Angel's relationship with Elise?*

Chapter
Seventeen

"**W**ho are *you?*" a weary male voice asked.

Maggie jumped and turned around. A handsome, older man sat with his feet propped up on a massive desk, his head resting on one hand. Deep creases furrowed his brow. He covered his eyes for a moment before wiping them. It seemed she'd wandered into his study.

"I'm terribly sorry. I'm afraid I got lost. I'm Maggie Robertson. I'm with Angel."

"Ah, the prodigal son returns to witness his mother's death. How noble of him." Bitterness laced his voice. "He hasn't graced us with his presence in years, and he broke his mother's heart. I'm sure he thinks he can earn forgiveness by waltzing in here as his mother lies on her deathbed. Nadya may forgive him. I will not."

Lowering his feet to the floor, he clasped his hands on the massive desk. "He's always been a selfish, irresponsible, undisciplined, spoiled brat who only cared about himself and his pleasure. Tell me, Ms. Robertson, why is he really here? Does he hope to get an inheritance?"

Maggie gasped and stepped forward. "I know you're under a great deal of stress. You can't possibly mean what you just said, sir."

"I meant every damn word. I'm his father."

"Then I don't think you know your son very well. He is the strongest, bravest, kindest man I know. He's here because he loves his mother. He didn't come asking for anything—"

The door behind her flung open and slammed against the wall. "Maggie, don't argue with him. It isn't worth it."

She turned to find Angel in the doorway, his arms crossed over his chest. He leaned against the doorframe, glaring at his father. "Maggie, this is my father, Sebastian Sinclair. Dad, this is Maggie Robertson."

Sebastian flew to his feet, and his fist slammed down on his desk hard enough to topple a book to the floor. "Why are you here? Where have you been?"

Angel stepped into the study, his face emotionless. "Don't worry, Dad. You won't have to suffer my presence for long. I'm here for *Mom*, not *you*."

Maggie flinched at the hatred in the air. "Please, both of you. Tempers are on edge because of the situation. Everyone needs to calm down, take a deep breath, and be civil."

"This is none of your damn business," Sebastian ground out.

Angel pushed Maggie behind him, facing off with his father over the desk. She worried he'd act on the anger emanating from his body.

"Never, *ever* speak to her like that again. I won't think twice about knocking you on your ass, old man." His hands curled into fists.

His father snorted and rolled his eyes. "Get a suit, and cut your damn hair before your mother's funeral. Or so help me, I'll do it myself. You've brought enough shame and scandal to this family. You will at least look presentable and honor your mother's memory for once in your miserable life."

"Geezus, Dad. Shut the hell up. She's not dead yet," Angel cried, jerking away from the desk.

Sebastian took a deep breath. When he looked up, his bloodshot eyes were filled with grief. "It's just a matter of time, son. You should have been here sooner. You broke her heart, and for that, I don't know if I can ever forgive you."

He stood and brushed past them, slamming the heavy door in his wake. The framed paintings on the wall tilted, and antagonism hung heavy in the room.

Maggie stood horrified, unable to speak for a moment. This level of cruelty made her fights with Brian seem mild by comparison.

Angel stuffed his fists in his pockets and wandered to the window. His Adam's apple bobbed as he stared into the rose garden.

"Not today, not today, not today," he whispered.

Maggie walked over and wrapped her arms around his stiff, unyielding body, laying her head against his chest. "I'm so sorry."

All the questions about Elise and her own insecurity faded away. He was hurting, and needed some compassion after the horrible things his father had said.

"He's right, you know." Angel pulled his hands out of his pockets and stroked her hair. "I broke her heart." He took a long, shuddering breath and rested his chin on top of her head.

The door opened, and Damien entered the room. Without saying a word, he closed it behind him. Letting out a deep sigh, he waited a moment before speaking, as if weighing his words.

"I'm sorry. I overheard…Look, Angel, Dad's a wreck. Don't take anything he says to heart. No one is thinking clearly or reacting rationally at the moment."

Maggie gave Angel a quick squeeze.

"That's bullshit, and you know it," Angel's voice was expressionless. "He hates me. He's *always* hated me." He pinched the bridge of his nose. "Dad's right. I need to get a suit. And a tie. I don't even know where to buy them."

"We'll do that later. Stay here with Mom. Don't leave," Damien ordered in a hushed voice. "She needs you. Dad needs you."

Angel huffed his disbelief. "Dad needs no one. He's the fucking almighty Sebastian Damien Sinclair, lord of all—master of his kingdom."

"That's not true. Just let it go, for Mom's sake. I'm going to go sit with her for a while." Damien turned on his heels and left the room, shutting the door behind him.

Maggie looked up at Angel, who scowled at the door. He clenched and unclenched his fists as he began to pace. "I gotta get out of here. I'm going to go find a meeting, and I'll be back."

"Do you want me to go with you?"

"No."

The curt refusal stung. Instantly insecure, Maggie stood with her arms crossed in front of her chest. "How will you get there? Do you need to use my truck?"

If he did, she'd call a cab. She didn't belong in this house. As much as she wanted to be here for Angel, she had questions—a lot of them now that she was face-to-face with his past.

"I…Shit, I don't know. I can't think—this house is suffocating me. I can't fuckin' breathe!" He held his chest and stopped pacing. Rubbing his eyes, he bit out, "I'm sorry, I'm sorry. Let's just get out of here. I shouldn't have brought you into this pit of toxic dysfunction." He grabbed her hand and pulled her toward the door.

They ran into Damien in the foyer with a mug of hot chocolate.

"Where are you going?" he demanded. "You can't leave, Angel."

Angel dropped Maggie's hand and took a deep breath before answering.

"I'm going for a walk. I just need a few minutes to process all of this…Mom…" He closed his eyes, let the air out of his lungs, and whispered hoarsely, "I'm not leaving…I just—fuck it." He threw up his hands and headed out the front door. The wild, unsettled look in his eyes sent a shiver down Maggie's spine.

Maggie turned to Damien. "I'm scared this has been too much for him."

The look in Damien's eyes confirmed her fears.

He nodded toward the door. "I know. Go. Make sure he doesn't do anything stupid."

Maggie ran after Angel but stopped when she saw him talking to Taylor in the yard. Taylor put a hand on Angel's shoulder, and together they walked toward the large garage, which was the size of a moderate home. Eight doors opened, one by one. After a moment, Taylor strolled back to stand next to Maggie.

"I don't think he needs to leave," she offered hesitantly. "He's too upset to drive. What if he relapses?"

"He won't be driving, Ms. Robertson. I've merely offered him an outlet for his pain."

Maggie gave Taylor a skeptical look. A gray Lexus SUV backed out of the garage. Angel stopped, got out of the car, and went back into the garage. Next was a Rolls Royce. The process repeated six more times. A red Harley Davidson roared to life, and Angel appeared on the back of it, a wide grin on his face. He revved the motor and waggled his brows at them before cutting it off.

"Whoa now, careful with that one, Angel," Taylor shouted in his clipped British accent.

Angel laughed, giving him a thumbs up.

"That one is mine," Taylor admitted. "Would you like some tea?"

"No, thank you." She glanced worriedly toward the garage, wondering what Angel was doing.

Taylor nodded and returned to the house.

Maggie walked toward the garage. Her head pounded, and her stomach cramped. This was a lousy time to be hormonal. Peeping in, she watched with horror and fascination as Angel shook a spray can rhythmically. His back was to her as he surveyed the blank wall in front of him. Perching against the hood of the black BMW, she watched as Angel laid down his lines on the wall. He appeared to be in a trance-like state, oblivious to her presence. No wonder he'd been caught in Pine Bluff. It was a wonder he hadn't been caught more often. She shivered from the cold.

"Go get your coat." Angel didn't turn around as he continued to work.

"I didn't think you knew I was here. Your father will be furious when he sees this. What about your promise?"

"Taylor gave me permission. I always know when you're around. I can sense it. You're part of me — the part that matters. You're my blank wall. The cap to my can."

She laughed. "Thanks, I think."

"What? I thought that shit sounded deep."

He paused and cocked his head to the side, studying his artwork. "You're my heart and my love. My father is never happy with me. I might as well contribute one more item to his list of Angel's failings. I am, after all, the fallen angel." He turned and gave her a wry smile. "You're freezing. Go get your coat, baby."

His heart and love? Her heart tripped over itself. "Shouldn't you be wearing a respirator or something?"

Angel turned toward her. The air changed, and electricity snapped between them. His blue eyes burned with danger, longing, and need. If she could have backed away, she would have, but her back was pressed to the BMW. He slammed the spray can down on the hood of the car.

Grabbing her, he pulled her to his chest and slanted his mouth to hers. His tongue forced her lips open to his searing kiss. There was nothing tender about it — a kiss of anger and passionate possession. Maggie resisted for a moment, afraid someone in the house would see them.

But all rational reasoning left her as the kiss intensified. Her legs felt weak, her heart thundered in her chest, and she gripped his biceps with her nails. At the sound of brisk steps, she jumped and pushed away.

"Oops. Whoa, uh, hi, Angel…" Harley's face flushed. Her eyes were bright as she stared at them. She opened the door to the BMW and placed the umbrella she'd been carrying inside.

"Gee, Harley, thanks for the cockblock." Angel laughed when Maggie smacked his arm.

Harley blew her bangs out of her eyes and grinned. "Mamma sent me to return the umbrella to the car; blame her. Sorry for the interruption…Carry on!" With a quick turn, she hurried down the path toward a house on the back edge of the property.

"Do you love her?" Maggie's voice wavered, and she shivered, crossing her arms in front of her chest.

Angel dragged his gaze back to her. "Who, Harley? Well yeah, of course. She's like a sister to me. She and her brothers, Keats and Byron, grew up with us."

Maggie examined the ground. "I meant her mother."

"Elise?" He drew back, looking confused.

She nodded. "Isn't she the Elise you told me about? The woman you proposed to? I heard her call you something earlier." She looked up. "I didn't mean to eavesdrop. I was walking by…"

It started as a smirk. Then a chuckle. By the time he was done, he was leaning against the car laughing.

Maggie turned to march toward the house, but he caught her and drew her to him. "Baby, I was teasing you when I said that about Elise — I can't believe you even remember. She and Taylor are like parents to me. More so than my own, actually."

"That's it?"

He snickered. "Promise. When she was younger, she looked a lot like Harley. I fell madly in love with her blond hair, accent, and cookies. As a lonely four year old, I told her I wanted to marry her. I gave her a ring from a bubble gum machine. Even so, she turned me down."

She groaned and hid her embarrassment in his chest. An overwhelming sense of relief flooded through her body. Was there something inherently wrong with her that she couldn't stop worrying *ever*? Was she too damaged to ever believe him?

"We good, baby?"

"I'm a bit hormonal," she mumbled against his chest, ashamed. "And I'm worried about you."

"I love how you worry about me," he breathed into her ear, holding her cocooned in his arms. "Don't leave me."

"I'm not going anywhere." She stood on her tiptoes and kissed him, wrapping her arms around his neck, enjoying the dance of their tongues and the warmth of Angel's hands when they moved under her sweater up her back.

They jumped apart again when they heard a quiet, "Ahem." Taylor stood with their coats over his arms and two steaming cups of coffee. His blue eyes twinkled as he smiled at them. "Perhaps you don't need these to warm up."

Blushing, they shrugged into their coats and thanked him for the coffee.

Taylor looked at Angel's work on the back wall and raised one eyebrow. "Oh, this ought to be better than New Year's Eve fireworks." He chuckled as he left them alone.

"Angel!"

Angel rubbed the weariness from his eyes as he closed the door behind him. He braced himself as his father raced up the stairs, bellowing his name. It brought back many unpleasant memories.

Sighing, Angel waited in the hallway for the blistering rant sure to follow. It had been a long three days. Last night he'd sat by his mother's bed, watching her shallow breathing, praying she'd wake up just one more time—and in the next breath praying she wouldn't, that her suffering would end. He'd just crawled, exhausted, into bed a little over an hour ago.

"*Fuck cancer?*" his father roared, his face red with anger. "You not only defaced my garage, you wrote an obscenity on it? Goddamn it, Angel. Do you ever think?"

"Nope, I never think. I'm too *stupid* to think, remember? We've had this conversation, multiple times. Are you getting senile in your old age?" Angel goaded. "And quit yelling. You're going to disturb Mom and the rest of the house. It's early, Dad."

His father's face went from red to a deep purple. Angel felt a momentary pang of regret. Dad was under enough stress with Mom dying, not to mention the return of his wayward, addict son. He needed to make amends, not taunt his old man. *God, I'm such a dick.*

"I-I'm sorry." Angel turned to go back to bed, but froze when his father grabbed him and spun him around. Immediately, his guard went up. He raised his fists, ready to fight, snarling a warning. "Back off and never touch me again."

His father dropped his arm and stood with his hands on his hips, taking deep, heavy breaths. Angel shifted nervously. He hated his father's scrutiny. It never went well.

"Look at you. You disgust me. You don't even look like a Sinclair. You certainly don't act like one. Does your mother know about the piercings and tattoos? Didn't I tell you to get a damn haircut?"

Angel glowered at his father and snapped, "Mom likes my hair, and no, she doesn't know about the tats or the piercings. What does it matter, Dad? It's my body. I can do whatever the hell I want with it. You don't have a say over my life. You haven't since you threw me out of the house."

"You little shit, that was *my* garage wall you defaced, and you're my son. You'll do as I say."

The door to his mother's room opened, and the lamp from the nightstand cast long, dark shadows. Unshaven, Damien ran a hand through his hair as he emerged. The ice-cold stare he leveled at the commotion in the hall was surely the same look he used when grilling people on the witness stand. With a deliberate movement, he pulled the door closed behind him. Maggie's door opened, and Angel felt her presence behind him.

"Must we have World War III out here at seven in the morning?" Damien whispered harshly. "Look, you've disturbed Maggie and the nurse. Just shut up, both of you."

"How is your mother this morning? I was headed to the office for an hour or so when I saw the crap your brother put on my garage wall."

Disbelief crossed Damien's tired face. "She's in a coma, Dad. She hasn't been awake since the day after Angel arrived. You know this.

Her breathing is labored, and her heart rate is slow and erratic. The nurse doesn't think she has much time left. You need to be here, not at the damn office, for Christ's sake."

For a moment, his father simply stared at Damien. Then it was like watching a movie in slow motion. He slumped against the wall. Covering his eyes, his shoulders shook, but he remained silent. Angel had never seen his father cry before. He appeared old and broken, far different from the vital, authoritative figure he was used to.

"Dad, look, I'm sorry about the garage. I'll paint over it. I planned to do that anyway. I was just letting off some steam."

He reached out, but his father shrugged away from him, refusing his aid, his comfort…his love. *Why am I surprised?*

A memory of sitting in his father's lap — scribbling on a legal pad with different colored pens — came to mind. He'd been around five years old, back when his father had at least tolerated him, perhaps even loved him. It had been a long time ago.

Angel watched his father slowly compose himself. His eyes remained red-rimmed in his haggard face, his lips thinned. Brushing past Angel, he entered his wife's bedroom, followed by Damien.

Angel gave Maggie a quick hug and a kiss on her forehead. "Go back to bed, baby. I'll be there in a few minutes."

She hesitated for a moment, worry in her eyes. But after giving him a kiss on the cheek, she left him alone in the hall, closing her door behind her.

Angel stepped into his mother's room. She remained lifeless, lying on her back with the covers drawn up to her chin, her eyes open but unseeing, her breaths shallow and ragged. The gentle kiss his father placed on her hand was almost more than he could bear. He couldn't remember his father ever being this tender with her.

"Get out, all of you," Sebastian choked, sinking to the bed beside her still body. Gathering his wife in his arms, he held her to his chest, softly stroking her braid. "And shut the goddamned door."

The air was heavy with impending death. Angel took a deep breath to ease the feeling of suffocation. The click of the narcotic dripping into his mother was alluring, and the demon of his addiction whispered of a way out of the pain. He followed Damien and the nurse into the hall, closing the door on temptation. Looking at the nurse, he raised an eyebrow, unable to ask the question.

"Not much longer," she confirmed softly.

Damien nodded. "Go get some coffee and take a break." He looked at Angel with pain-filled eyes — eyes like their mother's.

But before Angel could reach out to him, Damien turned and walked away, shutting the door to his bedroom to be alone with his grief.

Standing in the hall, a devastating need to flee overcame him. He wanted out of here. He envisioned his safe place. Home. In Pine Bluff. He wanted to make love to Maggie by the serene lake and pretend nothing was wrong.

That his mother wasn't dying…

That his father didn't hate him…

That he wasn't a worthless son…

That he wasn't a fucked-up addict.

Angel opened the door to Maggie's room and closed it, leaning against it for a moment. She had refused to stay in his room with him, saying it was disrespectful. He hadn't pressed the issue, not wanting to upset her or his father any more than he already had. But he needed her. He needed her to ground him before he gave in to the urge to use drugs to numb the pain.

When his eyes found her, the desire to use receded, and he smiled. *I will not use today.*

She sat waiting for him on the side of the bed, wearing those silly purple flannel pajamas with the white bunnies on them.

God, I love her more than anything. Not today, heroin. You don't win today.

Not saying a word, Maggie held out her hand, and he collapsed on the floor at her feet, burying his face in her lap. She held him, stroking his back.

"You can do this. I know it's hard, but you're strong enough," she whispered.

He nodded, breathing in the scent of vanilla and Maggie, a comforting combination he now associated with love and acceptance. The need to be closer had him on his feet, pushing her back onto the bed as he crawled next to her, holding her.

"I love you, Maggie."

Her lips brushed his cheek.

"You feeling better?"

He stroked her jaw with the back of his fingertips and gave her a chaste kiss. She'd been plagued with terrible cramps, and the emotional strain of being in this dysfunctional house hadn't helped. Her cheeks turned the color of one of his mother's hothouse roses. "I'm fine now. I love you, too."

He peered at her face. "That's the first time you've ever said that to me. Do you mean it? I mean, this isn't like a sympathy fuck or anything, is it?"

"No. I love you." She pulled one of his dreads.

He chuckled. "I know, my language sucks." He rolled to his back and covered his eyes with his arm. "When I'm with you, I'm still."

"Still?"

"On the inside. I don't know how to explain. Inside, my soul has been fragmented, like broken glass on pavement—sharp, painful. Since I met you, it's become softer, more like a dandelion scattered in the wind. But now, even with this shit with my mom and my dysfunctional family, I feel more together. I'm the broken toy, and you're the glue holding me together…" He lowered his arm, wondering if she was trying to keep from busting a gut laughing at him. He knew he wasn't a poet, but damn, that sounded like a trip on X.

She pecked his lips and smiled. "You're not scattered or broken."

He laughed. "I'm also not very romantic. I'll just leave it at *I love you*."

She kissed him again, deeper, exploring his mouth, but stilled when the quiet strains of a violin could be heard from a distance.

"Who's playing?" she whispered as they listened to the mournful music.

"Damien. He's on the roof."

Maggie sat up and pushed her hair out of her face. "He's what?"

"Crazy, I know. He's on the roof playing the violin." At her continued look of skepticism, he stood and held out his hand. "I'm serious. Come. I'll show you."

Maggie shoved her feet in her slippers, grabbed her coat, and followed him. He stopped by his room and grabbed a sweatshirt, slipping into his shoes before leading her downstairs toward the kitchen with its tantalizing smell of coffee and baked goods.

"Good morning, Angel, Ms. Robertson." Taylor greeted them with a nod.

"Please, just Maggie."

"*God morgen,* Maggie. Are you going to see our fiddler on the roof?" Elise asked with a shake of her head. Her Norwegian accent was as comforting as the smell of her cinnamon rolls. "He will kill himself one day, foolish boy."

Taylor nodded in agreement as he drank a cup of coffee in the spacious kitchen. Neither seemed concerned that Damien was on the roof of this three-story mansion. Angel tugged her toward the back door. She gave a plaintive whimper toward the coffee pot and pouted.

"We'll be back in a few minutes for your coffee fix. You need to see this."

They stepped out into the cold morning, the sound of the violin louder as it filtered from above them. Shielding their eyes against the sunrise, they looked up, and Harley walked over to join them.

"What is he playing?" Tears filled Maggie's eyes as they listened to the haunting music.

"'Méditation' from the opera *Thaïs* by Massenat," Angel answered. "It's one of Mom's favorites."

"But why on the roof?"

"Because he can," Harley replied, openly crying.

Damien balanced on the shingles, playing with quiet emotion.

"He hates playing in public or for people. The only time he ever did was when Mom made him. He played the fiddler in his high school production of *Fiddler on the Roof.* He told her he would only do it if she'd allow him to practice on the roof. Dad was furious, but Mom let him." Angel smiled at the memory. Things hadn't always been difficult between him and his brother. "He's playing for Mom."

Damien finished the piece and lowered his violin. He stood with his eyes closed for a moment before hurling the instrument and bow to the ground. Then he turned and climbed back into his bedroom window.

Picking up the broken violin pieces, Harley slowly walked toward her parents' house on the edge of the property.

"This is all so surreal." Maggie shivered.

"I would've said fucked up, but you hate the F word." He smiled sadly and wrapped his arm around her shoulders. "Come on. Let's go get some coffee and give the illusion of being normal. It's the Sinclair way."

A few hours later, his mother took one last shallow breath and was gone. Angel stood behind his father next to Damien. His older brother patted him on the shoulder.

It was as if he'd blinked and she disappeared. The nurse left them alone to say their goodbyes. No one said a word. It seemed like a dream. He watched as his father kissed her wedding band. The uncharacteristic, loving moment confused and angered him. Dad had been a cold prick toward his mother for as long as he could remember—until she was dying.

His dad left the room, looking like he'd aged ten years.

"I'm sorry, Mom." He covered his face and broke down crying. *Who am I to judge Dad? I broke her heart.* So many regrets, so many things left unsaid. He'd put his mother through hell. He'd stalled on working that damn ninth step because of what? Pride? Anger? None of that mattered now.

Damien hugged him for a moment but pulled away when the nurse entered. Although his dark eyes shone with unshed tears, not one fell.

The nurse quietly told Damien she'd notified the appropriate people. Then she left again.

"Angel…I know this is hard, but we need to help Dad."

Angel huffed his displeasure. *What I need is a hit—Fuck!* He broke out in a cold sweat.

"Are you okay?"

The question pissed him off. "Sure, I'm great. Mom's dead." He clenched his fists and gritted his teeth. He knew he was being irrational. But the urge to use consumed him.

"Exactly. Dad needs us. Just put aside your differences for now. Take the high road."

Maggie slipped into the room. Immediately, she rushed to him, wrapping her arms around him.

He didn't hug her back. He didn't deserve her. His mother was dead, and he wanted to slam drugs. His tears of grief turned to shame. He tried to pull away, but she wouldn't let go.

Damien turned and walked out, without saying a word.

"What can I do?" Maggie asked softly, brushing the tears off his face.

He shook his head and tried to get a handle on his emotions. Damien was right. He needed to be strong. But he knew his limitations. When he could speak, he whispered, "I'm calling Randy and going to a meeting."

After his NA meeting, Angel walked out with his sponsor, looking for Maggie. The session had helped him off the ledge, and Randy had told him to call day or night. But instead of Maggie, his brother sat on a bench, looking lost in thought.

"Oh great. I wanted you to meet Maggie, not my brother."

Randy slapped a hand on his shoulder. "It's all good, man. I'll meet her at the funeral."

Damien stood, rubbing his hands together. His breath was visible in the frigid air. Angel wondered how long he'd been here.

"Randy, this is my brother, Damien. Damien, Randy's my sponsor. Where's Maggie?"

The two men shook hands.

"I texted her and asked if I could pick you up," Damien explained.

"Nice to meet you, Damien. I'll see ya, Angel. Call if you need me." Randy gave him a bear hug and left.

"Thanks, will do." He turned his attention back to Damien.

"And she said yes?"

"Yes. She's at a Nar-Anon meeting." He walked with Angel toward his car.

Angel nodded. "Good. I'm glad." He wasn't sure how he felt about being alone with his overbearing brother, but he understood Maggie's need for support. On the way to the meeting, he'd confessed he was having some scary-ass thoughts about using.

Damien unlocked his Jag. "About Dad—"

"Look, I just came from a meeting. Mom just died. I can't. Not now. Please, drop it." *Denial, a poor way of coping with hurt...Great way to work the program...I need another damn meeting...*

They got in the car and Damien pulled out, his face dark. It was the look Angel expected from his older brother.

"At least don't provoke him for the next few days. This has been hard on him."

Angel snorted. "He didn't particularly seem to give a shit about her until the end." *Stop it; you're not helping. You can only control your feelings, what you think and what you do…*

"Neither did you," Damien retorted.

The blow landed square on his guilt, and he flinched. *Well played, shame. Well played.* "You're right. And I'm sorry."

"I'm sorry, too." His brother reached out and clasped his shoulder. "Really, I am. I'm proud of you for being clean."

Angel closed his eyes, not answering. Silently he repeated his mantra: *not today, not today, not today…*

Maggie returned from her meeting and found Angel and his brother in the den. Damien silently communicated his worry and left.

"You okay?" she asked.

"For now," Angel replied. He stared pensively at the fire. "Is it your turn for babysitting duty?"

"We care; that's all."

He sighed but didn't say a word.

The rest of the day, she kept an eye on him, trying not to be blatant about it. Everyone in the house did, except his father, who refused to come out of his study. Mid-afternoon, she found Angel pacing in the garden, his dog-eared NA book open on the cold cement bench next to his sketch book and markers.

"Elise sent some hot chocolate." She offered the warm mug to him. "Where's your coat?"

He blinked and looked around as if just seeing her. "I guess inside."

"Is there anything I can do?"

He shrugged, sipping the hot chocolate. "Work your program, and I'll work mine, and hopefully, we'll be okay."

She swallowed and said what needed to be said. "If you relapse, I won't stay — unless you seek treatment."

He smiled and brushed a strand of hair off her face. "Fair enough, Ms. Nar-Anon." He kissed her forehead. "And I'm not going to. Not today. I'm going to go make amends and whitewash over the writing in the garage."

"Okay, I'll go take a nap."

He left, and Maggie sighed, feeling out of place, unsure of her role. She wasn't family, but she was more than a friend, at least to Angel. After seeing if Elise needed any help, she walked toward the staircase and paused. The door to Sebastian's study was ajar, and she overheard her name.

"This Maggie's obviously with him for what she perceives to be his bank roll, why else?"

"Dad—" Damien sounded tired.

She bit her lip to keep from crying out and slipped away, not wanting to hear anything else. This wasn't the first time an irate father had accused her of being a gold-digger. *At least this time I'm not pregnant.* She ran upstairs, closed her door, and sank onto her bed. She wished she'd never come here. Closing her eyes, she tried to find a measure of peace in this discord.

A few hours later, she washed her face and reluctantly made her way to the dining room. Perusing the pastoral scene in the huge gilded frame, she wrinkled her nose. It was rather like a bad wreck on the interstate. She couldn't help but stare at it and wonder. In her mind, the hunting scene was inappropriate for the dining area, even if there was minimal blood on the dead pheasants. The painting was like an allegory for this family: pleasant at first glance, until you truly looked at it.

She wandered around the huge table—it could easily seat twenty people. At one end, a place had been set for four, but no one else had appeared yet. She rather hoped she'd be eating alone, unsure if she could stomach being in the same room with Sebastian.

Harley entered and placed a basket of rolls on the table. "Angel's still in the garage. He said he's not hungry." She bit her lip. "Um, I know I'm supposed to be silent and unseen, but I wanted you to know I've checked on him a couple of times, and he's okay."

Maggie smiled. "Thank you, Harley. I appreciate it. You're a good friend to him."

"You're welcome."

Damien entered the room, rolling up the sleeves of his starched white shirt.

"Where's Angel?" he asked.

He had to be the most perfunctory person she'd ever met. Harley hung around for a minute, blushing. When he didn't acknowledge her, her face fell, and she quietly slipped out, leaving them alone. *What an ass.*

He raised an eyebrow, waiting on her answer. Maggie found his unwavering gaze disconcerting and made a conscious effort not to fidget.

"Harley said he's still painting the garage. He might just paint over the graffiti, only to throw another one up and paint it again. Painting, writing, whatever you want to call it, relieves his stress."

Damien's brows furrowed. "Oh, for Christ's sake. Will he ever grow up and settle down?"

"I hope not."

"Why? Don't you want him to be a responsible, productive man? Someone who can provide for you, care for you? Surely you'll tire of being Wendy to his Peter Pan."

Damien pulled her chair out for her. Despite her misgivings, she sat, placing her napkin in her lap as she weighed how to answer him. The Angel she knew was not the conflicted, drug-using kid brother he remembered.

"I see a different person than you and your father. I know his addiction and past actions color your viewpoint. But the Angel I know *is* responsible. He's clean and working a recovery program. We both are, as you saw this morning. Thanksgiving night, he fell and sprained his wrist and dislocated his shoulder. He refused all pain medications.

"Together, I think we can work hard and make a go of my bed and breakfast. He's also had a job offer to do some artwork for Dylan McAthie. He's really excited about the prospect. Have you seen his work? He's truly gifted."

"He's always been artistic," Damien conceded. "But he's also impetuous and immature. He needs to grow up and get a real job."

She fiddled with the fork, moving it to line up perfectly with the plate. "He has a job. He works for me. I've had the workaholic husband. I'm willing to try something new. I don't care what you think of me, but I wish you'd consider getting to know your brother before passing judgment."

"You love him." Damien studied her as if she was on his witness stand.

"I'm not discussing my feelings with you." Meeting his gaze with her own, she raised her chin in a small show of defiance. She was determined Damien Sinclair would not make her feel inferior. She may have been a small-town, Midwestern girl growing up, but being married to Brian had taught her well how to hide her insecurities when dealing with the upper crust.

"Do you want to remarry?"

"Again, I don't see where that is any of your business," she snapped.

Damien's eyes darted to the doorway. He was silent as Elise served them their dinner.

Maggie knew why. *Snob.* Never let the *help* know your problems. Brian's family had been the same way. If they only knew just how much those who worked for them did know…

After Elise left the room he commented, "You haven't seen him when he's out of control. It's disturbing, infuriating, and sad. He's stolen, probably sold drugs, and done God knows what else to feed his addiction. Sure, he'll clean his act up for a while, but it never lasts. And unfortunately, I don't foresee this ending well. You haven't seen him lying unconscious in his own puke, a needle in his arm. I thought he was dead…I'm just worried."

"Of course. I am, too. But he's clean now. Tomorrow we plan to go shopping to buy him a suit and tie." She took a bite of the perfectly prepared roast beef with fresh horseradish. The bitter flavor was nothing compared to her thoughts.

Why did Damien mention marriage? Is he of the same opinion as his father? Does he not think I'm good enough for the Sinclair family? Old insecurities crept forward, and she lost her appetite.

"I'll give you my credit card and the name of my tailor." Damien looked uncomfortable as he shoved his food around on his plate.

Maggie paused before taking another bite and looked at Damien. "That won't be necessary. He'll buy his own suit. I don't think he wants to be beholden to his family. Despite what you may think, he has some pride."

"Fine. His clothes are the least of my worries. Maggie…" He put down his fork and pushed his plate away. "I'm worried about you, too. Angel's never handled stress well. In the past, he's been reckless and self-destructive. Take my advice. And know it isn't done to hurt my brother, but rather to protect you. Get out, Maggie. Get out while you can. You seem like a nice person, and God knows Brian put you through enough hell for one lifetime. You don't deserve the rollercoaster ride my brother will put you through."

Maggie shoved her plate back. *"How dare you?"* She took a moment to steady herself before continuing. It had been a long time since she'd felt such self-righteous anger. "How dare you speak to me like this? You don't know me. You speak about your brother like he's gum on the bottom of your shoe. No, I haven't seen him in the throes of his addiction, but that's not who he is. You no longer know your brother. The man I love is working hard to beat this disease. What I find amazing is the fact that Angel survived this family at all. I'd probably be on drugs too, if I had to live with all of you. If I choose to go on this 'rollercoaster ride' with Angel, it's our business. Not yours. Not your father's."

"I didn't mean—"

She interrupted him. "All he wants from his family is love and acceptance. Did he make mistakes? Yes. Should he be accountable for them? Yes. But should he have to pay for them the rest of his life and grovel to people who don't give a damn about him? *Hell no.*"

She stood and threw her napkin on the table.

"I've lost my appetite. Enjoy your meal." She stalked out of the room, holding her head high as she prayed with everything within her that Damien wasn't right.

Chapter
Eighteen

Angel stood back and surveyed the white walls. He'd repainted the entire damn garage. Yet again, he'd bent to his father's bidding, hoping for some measure of acceptance, knowing deep down it would never happen.

The garage door opened, and a blast of cold air raised goose bumps across his skin. He turned as Maggie rushed in. Her eyes were bright, her cheeks flushed. Instantly he knew something was wrong.

Before he could speak, she launched herself into his arms and hid her face in his shirt.

"Baby, what's wrong?" He held her tight, stroking her soft hair.

She took a shuddering breath, and his concern escalated.

"Talk. You're kinda scaring me."

"Nothing. I'm fine. No, I'm not. I just need a minute." She kissed his neck, his lips, and his forehead. "We have to get out of here. Immediately after the funeral."

Angel held her at arm's length. "What happened? Did someone say something to you? Did my father offend you?" He gripped her arms tighter than he meant to, and she winced. He loosened his grip.

"I just…I totally understand why you left this toxic environment." She blew out a breath and looked at the ground. "I'm sorry. I'm emotional and being silly. Ignore me."

She attempted to pull away, but he held her fast. *She came to me. She needs me.* He wanted to shout the rooftop down.

Cupping her face in his hands, he kissed her, his lips smiling against her mouth. "Ignore you? No chance in hell. Marry me, Maggie."

She inhaled sharply. "It's too soon." Her eyes looked like a trapped animal's.

But he pushed his case. "So?" He shook his head. "When has time ever meant anything to me? Marry me. I love you. I think I have since the day I met you." He kissed her forehead and flashed a smile he hoped would ease her doubt.

"Angel, don't be ridiculous—" Her eyebrows rose, and her mouth popped open when he dropped to one knee and held her hand.

"Margaret Mary Maguire Robertson, would you do me the honor of being my wife?" He kissed her left ring finger.

The pounding in his chest escalated as she hesitated. He hadn't planned on proposing today. But he couldn't imagine his life without Maggie in it. Seemed like the right thing to do.

Looking up into her panic-stricken eyes, he now had second thoughts.

"You c-can't be serious," Maggie stammered, startled by the depth of emotion in his clear blue eyes. It terrified her.

The conversation she'd overheard between his father and brother, and the one she'd just had with Damien had been a hard dose of reality. Although she loved Angel, she'd failed at one marriage born of recklessness already. She didn't want or need another—especially if his family thought she was after his money. And yet, here he was on bended knee, proposing...

"Serious as a heart attack, *ma'am*," he replied with a wicked grin.

She pulled one of his dreads. "Please don't joke..." *He's just doing this to rebel, lash out at his overbearing father.*

Angel wrapped his arms around her waist and laid his head on her stomach, holding her tight. "I'm not kidding, Maggie. Marry me. I want you. I need you." He gazed up at her with love and hope.

"You're my peaceful spot in the shit storm. With you, I'm me, for the first time ever. I'm not flowery with words. I love you, baby."

"Oh, Angel." She held his cheeks in her hands, praying he'd understand. The last thing she wanted was to break his heart. "I know you think you mean it at this moment. There's something about death that sparks a primal need to feel as if life is worth living, but we're still getting to know each other. Now isn't the time to be making any life-altering decisions."

"You don't love me?"

The stricken look on his face made her want to cry.

"I *do* love you."

She loved him so much it scared her. But what if she lost him? Or worse, what if she lost herself, like she had in her first marriage? They were still getting to know one another. She didn't know his middle name.

He rested his forehead against her waist. "Then why won't you marry me?" He stood and pulled away from her. "Is it because I don't have a job? I'll get a damn job. Somehow, I'll find a way to support us. I'm ready to settle down, form roots." He began to pace. "Dylan seems really interested in my black book. And I want to discuss an idea with David about doing classes for troubled kids, using art as an outlet. Hell, I'll see about a job with the city. I've proven I'm pretty good at whitewashing and sign replacement.

"I promise, Maggie, I won't let you starve. Plus, I'll keep helping you with the bed and breakfast. You need to add that back deck—I've got some really kickass ideas for it. And you should add a hot tub." He nodded. "Yes, we definitely need a hot tub. I know we can make this work…" He stopped pacing and stared at her when she didn't reply.

Fear blocked her airway for a moment. "Angel, I-I can't."

"Why? Why the hell not, if you love me?" he shouted.

"You're emotional right now. Your mother just died. We're in an environment in which neither one of us is entirely comfortable. I need time to think about this. I'm older than you, and I have my son to consider. What would your family think?" *And I refuse to be accused of being a gold-digger…again.*

"You know how much I care about what my family thinks. My mother is gone, and she's the only one whose opinion mattered to me. I'm sick of you throwing out our age difference. I don't give a fuck that you're older than me. And I'm not marrying your *son*; I want to marry *you*." He threw his arms out.

She went to him and hugged him, gazing into his stormy eyes. "He's my son. You never marry just the person; families are involved. I love him and would want to talk to him about this. I'm not saying no; I'm saying not now, okay? You're overwrought, and I'm tired. We'll revisit this when we get home, after the holidays."

She kissed him. This would give him time to reconsider, when they were away from the emotions and dysfunction of his family. And it would give her time to think.

He hung his head. "I'm not good enough. You're afraid I'm going to relapse."

"No. I admit the thought of you relapsing is scary, but that's not it. And never think you're not good enough. You are."

Angel nodded. "Okay." He still looked as if she'd told him *no*, instead of *wait*.

"I'm not saying no. I'm saying I'm not ready to make that big of a decision *yet*."

A glimmer of hope lit his face. His lips found hers, his tongue exploring her mouth as his hands moved up under her sweater. "I love you so damn much it hurts. God, Maggie. I need you. Don't leave me. Promise you'll never leave me."

"I'm more concerned that you might get restless and bored and leave me. I need you too, and I'm not going anywhere," she whispered as she inched his sweatshirt up.

"I won't get bored, and I'm done running." He tore off his sweatshirt and threw it on the floor, yanking her sweater over her head in turn. Their heavy breathing was the only sound in the garage as they stared at one another for a few seconds.

Maggie reached behind her, unsnapped her bra and let it fall to the ground. "Now, Angel. I need you now."

His lips curved in a seductive smile. "I know just the place."

He backed her against his father's BMW Z4 until she lay across the hood. The combination of cold metal at her back and a burning need for Angel left her nipples puckered into hard peaks. Goose bumps spread across her skin. Drawing one into his mouth, he nibbled and sucked as his hands divested her of her pants and underwear. He pulled her legs up over his shoulders and kissed the inside of her thigh, nipping it with his teeth.

"A-Angel," she gasped. "What if someone comes in here?"

He grinned. "Kinda makes it more fun, that edge of danger." He winked, and his tongue flicked her clitoris until her mind quit protesting.

When he came up for air, she stuttered, "I-I don't do this sort of thing, I mean, have sex in weird places...ah..."

Ignoring her, his mouth continued to work its magic.

"Oh my...I guess...I do now...Don't stop," she panted.

His wicked tongue delved deep inside her and then back to circle round and round until she was close...so close...Her body shook, and she sucked in oxygen like she'd just run the Boston Marathon. He slid one, then two fingers inside. His eyes were dark and full of hunger as he watched her, holding her gaze with his own. He pumped and licked, building the tension within her until he found the sweet spot that sent her hurling over the edge. He silenced her release with a passionate kiss as she lay beneath him, trembling with the aftershock. She tasted herself on his lips and smiled against his mouth.

"You are indeed a wicked, fallen angel," she whispered.

"Indeed." He reached in his back pocket for a condom. In no time, he had his belt unbuckled and jeans unzipped. He trailed kisses back down her chest, stopping to lick her belly button.

He stood to unroll the condom onto his erection and whispered, "Follow me to heaven."

"Heaven, hell, I don't care. Take me with you. I want to ride the rollercoaster."

Maggie woke up wrapped in Angel's arms. He'd begged her not to leave him last night, and she'd stayed. He rubbed circles on her back and kissed the top of her head when she stirred.

"Morning," she whispered, sleepy and replete from their love-making last night.

"Marry me, Maggie."

"Trying to take advantage of my un-caffeinated state is unfair and underhanded. And, my answer remains not yet. I don't know your middle name." She yawned, stretched, and pulled one of his dreads for good measure.

"How about I reveal it at our wedding?"

She shook her head. "Tell me more about your tattoos. Did you design any of them?"

"Just the wings on my back. That one was an impulse decision and my first one."

She laughed. "Go big or go home?"

He rolled on top of her and nudged his erection between her legs. "My big will take you home," he teased.

"And the dragon?"

"My addiction. It's always with me. Sometimes it slumbers, other times it's angry. Regardless, I have to be conscious that it's present and dangerous."

She fingered the semicolon below his track mark scars. "This one is my favorite. Your story is far from over."

He murmured against her lips. "I want to tattoo your name as my happily ever after."

"Tattoos are awfully permanent."

"That's the point. You're my permanent, my forever."

His rough face scrubbed across her cheek. "I, uh, I've made a decision. I'm going to cut my hair."

Maggie worked her way out from beneath him, shocked. "I'm not quite awake. Did you just say you're going to cut your hair?"

He sat up on the side of the bed and pulled on a pair of navy pajama pants. "Yeah."

"But you said your mom liked your hair," she protested.

Angel shrugged. "I don't think she really cared for the dreads. She just didn't want me to shave my head. It's time. I'm no longer homeless, and maybe it will make Dad happy." He rubbed his eyes. "Or at least take some of the stress off him. You know…if I conform and act like a Sinclair heir."

"But, Angel —" *Sinclair heir…Gold-digger…*

"And maybe if I settle down, cut my hair, and get a nine-to-five job, my girl will marry me." A heartrending grin spread across his face as he leaned in and kissed her lips.

"Maybe your girl loves you just the way you are and needs to take time before rushing into another commitment." Maggie cupped his scruffy cheek in her hand.

"I'm gonna go downstairs. Get moving so we can go buy that damn monkey suit and noose."

Maggie laughed. "Okay. I'll be down after I shower."

Angel drifted toward the smell of coffee and bacon and found Elise in the kitchen with Harley. Elise nodded and accepted the kiss he bestowed on her cheek while he snatched a piece of bacon off the plate in her hand.

She smacked him with the spatula. "*Slem gutt.*"

He chuckled. "Hey, Harley, can you and Elise do me a favor later this morning?"

Harley looked over her shoulder as she put the orange juice back in the refrigerator. With a graceful ballet spin, she turned, tossed her foot up onto the counter, and did a stretch. "Sure. What do you need?"

"Harley Blake! Get your foot off my counter, and clean it," her mother fussed, shaking her head and muttering in Norwegian. "And you need to put a shirt over your bra."

Harley rolled her eyes behind her mother's back. "Sorry, Mamma. Don't get your knickers in a wad. This isn't a bra. I just did a yoga class. And how come you're not fussing at Angel to put some clothes on?" She stuck her tongue out at him as she wiped down the counter and blew her bangs out of her eyes.

Angel snickered. Having parents from two different countries and being raised in America, Harley and her two brothers always had an interesting way of turning a phrase.

"I have on clothes. I want you to cut my hair."

"What?" Harley's dark blue eyes widened.

"*Hva?*" Elise echoed with a frown. "You cannot shave your head. Your mamma loved your hair."

"No, no, just a haircut. I'm doing it for Dad." He snatched another piece of bacon from the plate and laughed when she again fussed at him in Norwegian.

"Did you just cuss at me, Elise?" He pretended to duck for cover when she went off on another tear and shook the spatula at him.

The back door opened, and a statuesque brunette with languid doe eyes walked in with Damien. Dressed in a tan, designer wrap dress, she clung to his brother's arm as if afraid he would disappear. Damien appeared oblivious to her smug look of ownership. He glanced at Harley, who stared daggers at the woman.

"Lauren, you remember my brother, Angel. Angel, Lauren Cuthbert."

Lauren held out a perfectly manicured hand to Angel. "It's been a while. I'm Damien's *girlfriend*," she purred.

Angel shook it, but winked at Harley—who made a gagging face. Elise shook her head and gave Harley a stern glare, which made it even more entertaining. Lauren seemed to be studiously ignoring both women. She wore her snobbery like a Girl Scout badge of honor.

"Nice to see you again, Laurie," he goaded.

"You've been gone quite some time. Traveling, I believe?" The bitch responded, sending a chill of distrust up his back.

Angel could well imagine the stories she'd heard about him.

Lauren's smile never reached her eyes as she continued in an oh-so-sincere voice. "I was terribly sorry to hear about your mother's death. I'm here for all of you, if you need me." She gripped Damien's arm with her fake nails.

"Good morning, Elise. Harley. Breakfast smells wonderful, but a toaster tart would've sufficed for me," Damien commented with a twinkle in his eye.

"Sufficed? Who the fuck talks like that?" Angel dug.

"*Ja* and it will be when I am dead and gone you get such a breakfast from my kitchen, *søt gutt!*" Elise scooped perfect, fluffy scrambled eggs onto a platter. "And watch your language, *slem gutt.*"

"Hey, how come he gets called sweet boy and I'm a naughty boy?" Angel grabbed another slice of bacon.

"Because he doesn't steal the food; he asks." Elise patted Angel's cheek with a smile, just as she used to when he was six.

"Once we're married, I'll make sure he eats nothing but healthy food," Lauren asserted.

"I'll have dementia and be in the nursing home if I ever marry, so it won't matter what I eat, now, will it?" Damien replied without missing a beat, wrestling out of Lauren's grip. He pulled Harley's braid as he passed.

Harley blushed and giggled. Annoyance likely would've creased Lauren's brow, if it were able to move. Angel wondered just how much Botox one face could hold.

Lauren's narrowed gaze widened when Maggie walked in. Wearing jeans and a red sweater, her face was clean, without any makeup, and her hair pulled up in a haphazard ponytail. She looked natural and beautiful, much more so than the fake Lauren. Maggie stepped back, color draining from her face as she caught sight of Lauren.

Angel threw an arm around Maggie's shoulders and kissed his favorite gray streak at her temple. "Looks like you fell for the wrong Sinclair, Lauren. I'm the one wanting to get married, but Maggie's dragging her feet."

Maggie's blush matched her sweater, and the kitchen fell silent.

"Oh, I see." Lauren's eyes darted between him and Maggie. After an awkward moment, she held out her hand. "Hello, Maggie. I haven't seen you in quite a while — not since you and Brian divorced. When you resigned from the charity benefit for the underprivileged, it left us in quite a lurch. Luckily, Tiffany stepped up to take your place. She's a new, energetic addition to the board." Her voice was all sweetness and light.

Maggie raised one eyebrow and returned the fake smile. "I'm sure Tiffany brings many talents to the board. I'm just not sure all of them will be fully appreciated by the married women. You know Tiffany, Damien. Wouldn't you agree?"

Damien's mouth quirked, and his eyes crinkled. "I just hope she isn't spreading herself too thin with all of her extracurricular activities."

Lauren pulled in a sharp breath, narrowing her eyes like a hawk viewing a mouse. "I can see it's been a while since you've been to the hairdresser. I could call and see if mine can fit you in before the funeral for a color and cut." She patted her own perfectly styled, dyed Junior League bob.

"Whoa. Don't you dare, Maggie. I love your hair the way it is. There's nothing more refreshing than *natural* beauty," Angel noted.

"Sheath the claws, Lauren," Damien murmured.

Harley scurried from the room, snickering.

"Breakfast is ready in the dining room," Elise announced. As she turned away, Angel heard her mutter, "For those not already too full of themselves."

Chapter
Nineteen

The sound of Beck's "Devil's Haircut" drew Maggie to the bathroom door. She knocked. "Angel? I'm home."

"Don't come in yet," Harley shouted. "I'm almost done."

Maggie had picked up Angel's suit on her way back from her appointment with her old gynecologist. Never having been one to use Brian's name for favors, she'd done so today, and they'd managed to work her in to see the overbooked doctor.

"Okay." Maggie smoothed her black pencil skirt and adjusted the ruffle of her red blouse. She thought red inappropriate for a viewing, but Angel insisted his mother would have loved it. According to him, red had been Nadya's favorite color. She couldn't wait to see his hair and tell him the reason for her errand today.

From behind the closed door, Angel exclaimed, "Holy shit, Harley."

The sound of a smack and fast-paced Norwegian came from behind the door. Maggie laughed, feeling antsy.

"Ouch! Sorry, Elise. It's gonna take some time to get used to it, but it looks great. Thanks."

He stepped out of the bathroom wearing a pair of low riding jeans. Maggie took a second to admire the delicious V of his hipbones and slowly made her way up to his hair. She gasped and clapped at the difference. With his dreads and beard, Angel had oozed street sexiness. Now he looked like a romance cover model. His short blond hair fell a bit longer on top, and his face was clean shaven. She jumped from the bed and circled around him, running a hand through his hair and over his cheek.

"You're beautiful."

He blushed and rolled his eyes. "Ugh, don't call me beautiful." He ran a hand through his hair. "It feels weird, but good, even if I do look twelve. Do you think Dad will approve?"

"He better! That was a lot of work," Harley piped in from behind him with a wide smile.

Elise nodded. "His mamma would have loved it. It's too bad it had to be so short on the sides, but the top is nice."

"We'll leave you to worship your Adonis," Harley teased. "But don't forget the viewing is in an hour." The women closed the door behind them.

Maggie hummed appreciatively in the back of her throat. Angel's eyes lit with desire, and his lips curved. He picked her up and laid her down on the bed. Warm kisses trailed up her neck to the sensitive spot behind her ear. When his hand moved to shove up her skirt, she stopped him.

"No, you need to get ready, and I can't right now."

He stopped and looked down at her with concern. "You okay? Girlie time is over. Garage sex proved that. We could try the pool house this time." He waggled his brows.

She snickered. "Girlie time? I'm fine. I had an appointment with my doctor today."

"Doctor? What? Baby, are you sick?" The fear in his eyes made her smile, and she rubbed the backs of her fingers up his smooth cheek.

"Not sick. But I'm out of commission for a day or so..."

"Why? What's wrong?" He kissed her fingertips. She was amazed at his ability to focus on her as if she were his entire world. *How did I get so lucky?*

"I, uh, had my blood work updated — you know, since I have no idea what Brian had been up to — and, well, I had an IUD inserted. Merry early Christmas."

A seductive smile spread across his face. "Yeah? Bareback riding, nice! This will be a first for me. Best. Christmas. Ever." He winked at her. "I can't wait to get home."

It was her turn to blush, and she gave him a quick kiss. "Me, too. Now get ready. We need to go, my love."

"Marry me."

Maggie laughed. "No. Not now. Go!"

He sighed dramatically and rolled off her. "I can be very persistent, and I won't stop until you say yes. I'm not like Damien. I *want* to be married." He shucked off his jeans and headed back to the bathroom for a quick shower. "You love me. I love you. I don't see what the problem is," he grumbled.

"I'm putting a moratorium on any marriage discussion until after the new year."

"You can, but I'm not agreeing. I'm going to ask you every day until I wear you down and you say yes just to shut me the hell up."

In a few minutes he returned, dressed in charcoal gray pants and buttoning his white shirt. Looking in the mirror, he frowned. "Jesus H. Christ. I look like a fuckin' lawyer."

He ruffled the longer portion of his hair, mussing it somewhat. He rolled his eyes. "Dad will love it."

Maggie laughed and peered around him into the mirror. "A lawyer? Never. You don't have that cutthroat look in your eyes."

He fumbled for a couple of minutes, attempting to knot his tie, until she took mercy and did it for him. She laughed when he held the end up and stuck his tongue out as if being hung.

"You only have to dress up for two days. You can go back to jeans and tees after the funeral," she reassured him with a pat on his chest.

His face fell at the mention of the funeral. He shoved his hands in his pockets and stared at the floor, looking lost.

Maggie folded him in her arms and held him. "I love you."

He nodded and smiled as he wrapped a lock of her hair around his finger. "Marry me?" With a quiet laugh, she shook her head.

Nearly twenty-four hours later, the limousine pulled into the driveway, and Angel glanced over at his father, leaning on the armrest, his eyes covered with his hand. Both his dad and brother had been aloof and cold during the viewing last night—and at the funeral and the graveside service today. Sinclair men were expected to keep their emotions under wraps, more so in public.

He'd tried to abide by the unspoken rule, but when they'd lowered his mother's coffin into the ground, he'd been unable to contain his grief. The finality of knowing he'd never see his mom again, hear her call his name or play the piano, overwhelmed him. He had so much more he needed to tell her, to apologize for. The tears had rolled down his face as he held Maggie's hand, drawing comfort from having her there beside him.

Even now she held his hand, rubbing soothing circles with her thumb.

"We're here, Dad," Damien commented quietly as the limo stopped in front of the house.

"Yes. Right. Thank you." Sebastian rubbed his eyes and glanced at Angel with annoyance. "Try to hold it together, Angel. And for God's sake, run upstairs and comb your hair."

Earlier, he'd voiced approval of the haircut, but suggested it should have been shorter on top. Angel wasn't surprised. According to his father, he hadn't done anything right since he was five years old. His father stepped out of the limo, buttoned his jacket, and entered the house without looking back.

Lauren gave Angel a smirk before following Damien. She was playing the part of grieving daughter-in-law-wannabe beautifully, complete with an over-the-top black hat with a veil and designer black dress. He glanced over at Maggie, who, in her simple black dress, looked a hundred times more beautiful than Lauren.

She wore her hair up in some sort of twist thing that accented the streak of gray he loved. He couldn't wait to watch her take it down. There was something inherently sexy about a woman taking her hair down and running her hands through to loosen it, especially when the woman was his Maggie.

"I think you look fine," she muttered, glaring at the front door. "And if that bitch makes one more passive-aggressive comment, I'm going to scratch her eyes out!"

"You go, tiger. I know for a fact your nails can do damage. My back can testify." He chuckled when her cheeks flushed pink as he helped her from the limo.

Cars pulled up behind them in slow succession. Guests walked over to greet them and offer comfort. Personally, Angel wished they'd all leave them the hell alone to grieve in private. He wanted nothing more than to get out of his suit, into his jeans, and go home to Pine Bluff. The situation eased, and his stress lessened when Emma and David's daughter, Kenzie, jumped out of the car, followed by her beleaguered parents.

"Mama! Angel lives in a castle. There are even peacocks!" She squealed when she saw Angel and ran to him. "Make me fly, Angel."

He threw her in the air, caught her, and smiled happily when she hugged his neck. Her harried parents ran to collect her with profuse apologies. Maggie stood beside him, a comforting hand on his lower back.

"She's not bothering anything. As a matter of fact, I needed that hug," Angel assured Emma and David.

"We're going to head home, Angel. We're very sorry for your loss, and we'll pray for you and your family," David offered as he shook his hand.

"Unless you want us to stay," Emma added quickly. She rose on tiptoe to give him a peck on his cheek. Worried hazel eyes met his.

"No, go home. I wish Maggie and I could go with you," Angel answered.

"I miss your pirate hair." Kenzie scowled at him, wrinkling her button nose.

"Aye, lassie. But sometimes we pirates have to go in disguise to get away with more mischief and mayhem," Angel replied.

Kenzie kissed him goodbye as he handed her back to her mother. The Pattersons left with a wave and a promise to check on their home.

"You're good with kids," Maggie said as they walked to the house.

"Probably because I've never grown up," he admitted, peering at her from under his lashes. She laughed.

Randy came up and shook his hand. He'd trimmed his graying beard and wore a sport coat, but no tie. With his hair in a ponytail, he looked as out of place as Angel felt. But he was a calming presence.

"Maggie, this is Randy, my sponsor. Randy, this is Maggie."

"Nice to meet you." Maggie and Randy shook hands.

"You comin' in?" Angel asked, hopefully.

Randy grimaced. "If you insist, but I'd rather not. I'm outta my league with all these fat cats."

Angel laughed. "Me, too. Thanks for coming."

"Anything for you. Call me anytime." Randy hugged him and shook Maggie's hand again before leaving.

Maggie smiled. "I like him."

"He keeps me honest." Angel sighed and looked at the front door. "I guess we have to go make nice."

"We can do it." Maggie squeezed his hand as they walked through the front door.

He nodded a polite greeting to those offering condolences. His father stood in the foyer speaking to some of his cronies. Damien, too. He felt out of place, only recognizing a few of the mourners. The entire thing felt more like a cocktail party than a funeral. His mother would've been in her element.

They weaved through the people to the dining area where Harley and Elise were serving food and drinks. He frowned as Maggie shook her head and declined their offerings. Her face appeared pale and pinched. Angel took her hand and led her into the music room. He closed the door behind them and looked around with a heavy heart. In this room he missed his mother the most, and he turned his back on her grand piano. But at least they were alone.

"Are you okay?"

"I'm fine; are you?" she replied with a wan smile.

"No, not really, but I'll make it. I've resolved not to relapse and use today. You know what they say—one day at a time." He frowned at her. "You don't look well, baby." He searched her face for the answer, and she lowered her eyes.

"I'm still having a few cramps from the IUD placement," she muttered. "And some of Brian's colleagues are here...I just need some ibuprofen."

"Go get some from my bathroom and lie down if you need to. You aren't expected to do the meet and greet. We'll leave early in the morning and go home, okay? I want to be home for Christmas."

She smiled at him. "I love that you call it home."

"It is home. Marry me?"

Shaking her head, she smiled and backed toward the door. "No. Now go make polite conversation with your father's business associates and friends. I'm going to take you up on the offer to lie down."

"I could go with you…"

"No, your family needs you. I'll be back in a bit; just give me thirty minutes." She gave him a quick kiss and left him alone.

Angel walked to the piano and sat down. The haunting smell of his mother's perfume still lingered in the room. He had so many regrets. With his head resting on his arm on top of the piano, he willed his tears to subside. God, what he would do right now to numb his feelings. At the height of his addiction, this would have been the perfect excuse to use. *Not today. I will not use today…* Taking his index finger, he pressed middle C on the keyboard softly over and over.

Sitting up, he loosened his tie and unbuttoned the top button of his shirt. He stretched and began to softly play "Moonlight Sonata." The memory of his mother's face when she played this piece encouraged him to continue. He remembered her sitting next to him, helping him with the correct placement of his fingers. The memory of her frustration at his inability to read music, and her joy when she realized he could play by ear, brought a sad smile to his face.

This one's for you, Mom.

He jumped when the door to the music room slammed open and shut.

"Stop!" His father's face was flushed and his eyes glassy from what Angel suspected was one too many glasses of scotch.

He continued to play. He didn't give a damn if it pissed his father off—this was for his mother.

"Did you hear me? I said *stop*."

"I think the entire neighborhood heard you," Angel replied, still playing.

His father strode to the piano and grabbed his right wrist in his ironclad fist. Angel jumped up and faced his father, his own temper sparking dangerously.

"Get your fuckin' hand off me, or so help me I'll knock your ass on the ground. No one—and I mean no one—ever touches me without my *permission*."

"I'll do whatever the hell I please. This is my goddamned house, and I never want to hear that music played again," his father ground out, releasing his wrist with disgust.

"Why? Why this piece? Why did Mom cry every damn time she played it? What did you do to her?"

"*What did I do to her?*" he roared. The vein on his red forehead popped out. "How dare *you* speak to *me* like that?"

The door opened, and his father ceased his tirade. Damien stepped in and closed it softly behind him. "What the hell? Can't you two get along for a few more hours until people leave?"

"I don't have to get along with him at all. I'm going to go get Maggie, and we're leaving. And mark my words, Dad, *I'll never be back*. Not even for *your* fuckin' funeral." He was tired of being his father's disappointment and felt no remorse for his words. His mother was dead, and a part of him had died with her.

"You're just like *him*. God knows I tried, but it's apparent genetics wins over nurturing," his father replied bitterly.

Damien hissed in a sharp breath and snapped, "Shut up, Dad. Not now, for Christ's sake."

"What the hell are you talking about?" Angel asked. His gaze narrowed as he noted the silent, pained looks passing between them.

"You're not a Sinclair, Angel. You are not my biological son. You're just like your despicable, worthless father. He was a goddamned musician who seduced your mother, broke her heart, and left me to pick up the pieces before killing himself with drugs—"

"Dad, stop! Good God, what's wrong with you?" Damien placed a firm hand on Angel's shoulder as he glared at their father.

Angel shrugged away and looked back and forth between his brother and the man he had known as Dad all of his life. A dull roaring in his ears grew louder as his reality spun like a top out of control. He braced against the piano to steady himself.

Run! The answer is out there, a solution to the pain...

He closed his eyes and struggled. Time seemed to stand still as everything became devastatingly clear—why his father had never accepted him, why he didn't look like anyone else in the family, why he'd always felt like an outsider. The breath he'd been holding whooshed out like a deflated balloon. He sank to the piano bench, no longer angry or upset. There was no longer any reason to be either. Angel Sinclair had ceased to exist. His entire life was a lie.

He felt completely and utterly alone, more lost and abandoned than he'd ever felt in his life. In the space of a few days, he'd lost both of his parents.

I will not use today…

Damien sighed. "I'll be back. I'm going to go ask everyone to leave. Angel, please stay put. We all need to talk. Promise me."

Angel barely nodded as he watched his brother leave. He dropped his gaze to the floor, taking a moment to collect himself before looking at the man he called Dad. When he could speak without falling apart, he raised his eyes, shocked to see tears streaming down his father's face.

"Who the fuck am I?" he asked him in a hoarse whisper.

Chapter
Twenty

Maggie sat up confused when she heard knocking at the door. "Come in," she called after a moment. Shoving her hair out of her face, she glanced at the clock on the nightstand. It was a little after four in the afternoon. *Good grief, I must have slept for almost an hour.* She blinked when Damien entered the room, his tie loosened, looking flustered and unsure of himself. Fear wormed its way into her heart.

"I apologize for bothering you, but Angel needs you."

"What's wrong?" She slipped off the bed and shoved her feet back into her heels as she tried to smooth her bed-mussed hair with her fingers. Giving up, she pulled the pins out and finger-combed it.

"It's Dad. He's, well...Just come with me. I'm worried about my brother."

She followed him down the stairs into the study, where Angel sat on a chair, his elbows resting on his knees, head down, while his father paced back and forth.

"Angel?" Maggie ran to him and placed a hand on his shoulder. He looked up at her with red, swollen eyes and didn't say a word before looking back at the floor. "What's going on?" She turned an accusatory look at Sebastian, who ignored her as he continued to pace back and forth, drinking his scotch.

"Dad, haven't you had enough to drink? Why don't we all sit down and discuss this like rational adults," Damien interjected.

"I want to know what the hell is going on here!" Maggie's hand rested on Angel's back as she waited for an answer.

Angel looked up at her and smiled. "I'm not Angel Sebastian Sinclair."

Not understanding, her brow rose with surprise. "Your middle name is Sebastian?"

"Yeah, and my initials spell ASS." Angel barked a laugh. "Did you do that on purpose, Dad? Do I even call you Dad?"

Sebastian stopped pacing and gave Angel a stricken look. "Of course. I'm still your father. Not by blood, but my name is on your birth certificate. I raised you, and I do love you, you know."

Angel snorted. "You've got to be fuckin' kidding me. You love me? How the hell would I know? You've never been there for me."

"That's not true, Angel," Damien protested. "Mom and Dad were always there for you. I think your addiction has given you an altered view of our childhood."

Angel shot out of his chair and faced his brother. Maggie stepped back. Fury washed over his face, and he spoke through gritted teeth. "Shut the fuck up. You haven't got a clue, Damien. He—" Angel gestured wildly toward his father. "He was *not* there when I needed him most."

"You little ingrate. Who the hell do you think kept rescuing you when you were in trouble, until the counselor said it was time to let you hit bottom?" Sebastian slammed his glass of scotch down on the table.

"You weren't there for me when I was ten and being bullied," Angel ground out. Agitated, he held up a hand for Maggie to stay back. He closed his eyes.

Rubbing his brow, Sebastian muttered, "Grow up, Angel. I told you to suck it up and deal with it. Just like I did with Damien when he came home whining about something that happened at school. Sometimes you just have to deal with situations—and I mean deal with them appropriately, not with illegal substances or by defacing public property." With a sigh, Sebastian poured some more scotch and drank. Maggie turned toward Angel and winced at the shell-shocked look on his face.

Something was wrong.

Something was terribly wrong…

The dull roaring in his ears became deafening. A wash of red and then black temporarily blinded him, and he couldn't breathe. He loosened his tie and unbuttoned his collar. *Where has all the oxygen gone?*

"Breathe, Angel." Maggie's soothing voice grounded him.

He gulped air like a drowning victim until he could think. He glared at his father and hissed, "Grow up?"

Blazing fury, such as he'd never experienced before, boiled through his veins like liquid lava. His body shook with the need to expel his anger. "*God damn you to hell!* Is being raped how you define growing up? Just how the fuck do you deal with that *appropriately* at age *ten?* Tell me, Dad, 'cause I'd sure as fuck like to know."

Silence reigned, and the color drained from his father's face. He staggered into his desk chair as if he'd been struck.

Angel wondered for a brief second if he'd actually hit his father. No, he was too far away. But he'd wanted to.

"W-What?" His father's hand shook as he placed the glass of scotch on his desk, almost spilling it in the process.

Angel rounded the desk and bent over his father, caging him in the chair. "That bully, the one I came to you about—the one you told me to '*suck it up and deal with*'—he sexually assaulted me when I was ten years old behind the dugout at the little league field, multiple times."

I will not use today. I choose to remain sober.

Grief-stricken eyes met his as his father's alcohol-soaked brain processed his words. The color drained from his face, and Angel enjoyed witnessing his pain. He watched his father's throat bob three times.

Finally he choked out, "Why didn't you ever say anything? I thought it was just school antics. Nothing serious…"

"Would it have mattered? Would you have cared? Why didn't I say anything? Are you fucking kidding me?" He pushed away, picked up an expensive glass paperweight from his father's desk, and hurled it against the marble fireplace, taking a small measure of satisfaction at the look of fear that crossed everyone's faces.

He whipped around, pointing his index finger into his father's chest. "I didn't say anything because *you* told me not to *whine. You* told me to *deal* with it. Because I was fucking *ashamed, scared,* and *traumatized.* Because I didn't want to disappoint *you, Dad.*" Angel's voice rose and then dropped as his anger sputtered like a fizzled firecracker.

Exhaustion overwhelmed him. He had revealed his deepest, darkest, most shameful secret, and he wanted to puke. He shrugged away from Maggie and stormed over to the window that looked out on his mother's rose garden.

The air in the study was heavy and stifling. *God, I just want to disappear, take this pain away.*

Scotch was readily available. Heroin beckoned.

The craving encroached and wrapped around his resolve to stay clean, like a noose around his neck. He struggled to catch his breath…

Just one hit will do the trick…No need to suffer…All this will disappear…

His eyes locked on Maggie's. He saw no condemnation, no pity—only love and acceptance. Her silent plea to hold on gave him his lifeline, his reason for living, and he stepped away from the lies his addicted brain spoke. *I will not use today.*

"Why didn't you ever tell your therapist?" Sebastian asked quietly.

His father's voice pulled him back another step from the darkness into the present.

"Because I didn't want you to be ashamed of me. I'm a sick, co-dependent bastard who only wanted your approval, your support… your goddamned nonexistent love. I didn't want to disgust you or Mom. I thought it was my fault. I was afraid you wouldn't love me anymore. Or love me less. Or differently. I don't know. I was ten years old; what was I supposed to do? The guy was older, twice my size…He threatened to hurt me worse if I told…"

Angel swallowed convulsively as he unloaded his secrets. "I prayed he would die. I prayed every damn day I would die. When neither one happened, I kept my mouth shut. And after suffering for years, I couldn't take it anymore. I numbed it with drugs. That's what addicts do. We turn the pain and self-loathing inward and deal any way we can. I used prescription opiates and then heroin. You know the rest…"

"Angel…" His Dad shook his head over and over. "I never knew. I had no idea. I just thought you were acting out, being rebellious and out of control. Dear God, the pain you must have suffered…"

He rubbed the heels of his hands into his eyes and whispered, "I'm so sorry, son."

Angel shrugged and continued to stare out the window. *Just one hit will do the trick.* He closed his eyes and began to list the things he would lose. *Maggie, my self-respect, a home, Maggie, my sobriety, my self-worth, Maggie...*

"You may not believe me, but I do love you, Angel. I've failed you as your father, and I take full responsibility for it. We'll get you some therapy. We can fix this somehow...I only hope someday you can forgive me."

Angel turned to look at his father, too weary to think and emotionally empty. "I don't know, Dad. I just don't know. I have to get out of here. I need to fuckin' breathe."

Throwing the French doors open, he stepped into his mother's rose garden and started walking. He craved a hit so badly he could virtually feel the rush. He stopped, bent over, and took some deep breaths, trying to channel the pain, to concentrate on what truly mattered in his miserable life. *Maggie. Me. I matter.* He refused to give in to his disease. *I choose to stay clean. I will not use today.*

Calmer and more in control, he took a deep breath and exhaled. He wanted to write, to get his feelings out there, to express the depth of his pain without the risk of exposing his vulnerability. His father's revelation and the verbalization of the horror he'd suffered as a child had left him untethered.

"Angel?" Maggie called from behind him.

He didn't turn around. He wasn't ready to talk. He needed a moment. And he trusted she'd be here when he returned. That in itself was liberating. *She loves me.*

Angel shrugged out of his coat and took off running. He pushed his body, running as fast and as hard as he could—away from the pain of his memories and toward a physical pain he could relate to. His legs began to burn, and blood coursed through his body with a fiery rage. His body protested, and he screamed, welcoming the pain. *Pain is good. Pain means I'm not numb.* He ran until he could no longer think, and his lungs could not work fast enough to get the oxygen to his brain. At last a tiny burst of endorphin kicked in, easing the suffering. He fell to his knees, vomiting. It was cathartic in so many ways.

Drenched in sweat, he rolled onto his back, sucking air into his deprived lungs. It took a few minutes before he could breathe without sounding like a wheezing church organ.

He concentrated on being in the moment, noting his surroundings. The sky was now orange, the air cold enough he could see his breath. Beside him a wild dandelion swayed. He wondered how it had survived the weather and his father's lawn crew. And then it came to him. He was like this innocuous weed—surviving against the odds.

I'm alive. I'm clean. He laughed until he cried, sounding like a crazy man. He sat up and picked the white puff, dispersing the seeds and his fears, shame, and anger into the wind.

Crawling to his feet, he stood and looked back at his childhood home. The lights outside flicked on, lighting the path. He didn't want to go back there. A sense of overwhelming sadness permeated that house. It always had.

Only the thought of Maggie kept him from walking down the driveway and away from his personal hell. He'd promised her he was done running. She was his saving grace, the one filament of hope. He would stay strong and not give in. Angel trudged up the driveway toward the cold mansion that was no longer his home—if it ever had been.

He found her in the garden, wearing the jacket he'd discarded, waiting for him. Her beautiful eyes beckoned him to return from his dark thoughts, to come home.

She was his home.

He sprinted toward her and pulled her against his chest. With his arms around her, her face pressed against his pounding heart, he drew in her strength. Peace replaced his uncertainties and apprehension. He loved this woman.

"I'm here for you," she murmured into his chest. "If you want to leave, I'll leave with you. If you want to hear what your father has to say, I'll stay with you. Whatever you decide, I am here because I love you. Together, we can get through this. It wasn't your fault. You were just a child. You're not alone. You'll never be alone again."

He held her, accepting her love and strength. "I love you," he murmured. He fisted his hands in her soft hair and, closing his eyes, whispered raggedly, "Who am I? I don't fucking know who I am anymore. Maybe I never did. Maybe that's been my problem…"

"You're Angel Sinclair." She pulled away a little and smiled up at him. "Angel *Sebastian* Sinclair."

He smiled wanly. "I hate my name."

"You can always change it to Goldilocks."

He laughed. And it felt good. The pain lightened a bit because this woman standing in the cold night air loved him and was willing to share his burden.

"I could, but it wouldn't solve anything, would it?"

"No."

Angel glanced back to the house. "I need to talk to my dad, don't I?"

"That's your choice." She brushed his hair out of his eyes.

"I can do this. I can do anything with you by my side." *I choose to be clean. I choose to live. I choose to be the man Maggie needs me to be.*

He straightened his shoulders. His fingers shook as he buttoned his shirt. Maggie helped him retie his tie.

Taking her hand in his, he stepped toward his past, confident in his future.

"Sit down, Angel. We need to talk, and I promise to tell you everything. Do you want Maggie in on this conversation?" His dad looked as if he'd aged twenty years in the last two hours.

"Of course. *She's my family.*"

Angel ran a hand through his damp hair and gulped a bottle of water. He'd taken a quick shower, brushed his teeth, and changed clothes. Feeling more like himself in his jeans and a long-sleeved T-shirt, he braced himself for his father's words. When his father winced and nodded, Angel halfway regretted his jab.

His father moved to his desk chair and sat down with a weary sigh. "Your father was a concert pianist. Your mother met him when he played at a charitable event she'd organized. I loved your mother—I always have. But I was ambitious and focused on my career, resulting in me being unaware of and inattentive to her needs. She fell madly and deeply in love with him. I daresay he might have been the love of her life."

Pain lingered in the deep lines around his eyes, and he swallowed a few times before continuing. "You were the result of their affair. Your mother planned to leave me, but the coward left the country when he found out she was pregnant. He died from an overdose a month later, leaving your mother devastated and inconsolable."

He took a deep breath, and his voice was barely audible. "My beautiful Nadya was going to leave me for a man who used her and cast her aside like trash. His actions were reprehensible. Your mother was my true love…my sweet gypsy girl…" Unabashed, his dad wiped the tears from his eyes. He chuckled. "She hated me calling her that. She preferred *Romani…*"

Angel had never seen his father this emotional before, and a quick glance at Damien confirmed he hadn't either.

"We decided to try to make our marriage work. I forgave her indiscretion, and I was by her side during a difficult pregnancy and birth. You were never an easy child, Angel; you even came into the world on your own terms, a week late. As you grew older, you looked like *him*, you had the same temperament, and your mother adored you. I confess, I prayed you would look like her, and I found it difficult when you didn't. You were a constant reminder of my failings as a husband…But son, I did, and still do, love you…" Guilt lined his face when he looked up at Angel.

"When you started school, we found out you had a learning disability. I never wanted you to use it as a crutch. This, plus your stubbornness, and the genetic predisposition for excess I knew you'd inherited from your father, made me lean on you. And yes, I was hard. I didn't want you to go down that road. I couldn't bear for my Nadya to go through the pain of losing someone again."

Angel turned and looked at his father. "Why didn't you just tell me? Why the secrecy? Why did that song make Mom cry? All my life I thought you hated me." Angel stopped and amended, "No, that isn't true. Just my teenaged years."

"They were difficult years, yes. I realize now I should have told you. Unfortunately, hindsight is always twenty-twenty." His father ran his hand over his desk. "That piece had special meaning to your mother and *him*. I believe he played it for her when they first met."

Angel rubbed his eyes. "This is too much to take in at the moment. I want to go home. *Home with Maggie.* I need time to think. I need to write, attend a meeting…"

"Angel, there's a reason I'm bringing all of this up now. Admittedly my timing is wrong, but I was going to tell you this tomorrow anyway." Sebastian pulled a folder from his top desk drawer.

"Your mother has left you some money. However, it is somewhat tied up to protect your assets. Damien has to review your spending — for your protection — until you turn thirty. However, if you relapse, you will forfeit the money. It will either go to your heirs in a trust fund, managed by Damien, or if there are no heirs, it will be donated to charity. You will be allowed input as to the charities you favor. Until you are thirty, you can access the money only through Damien. If you don't blow it, you could live off the interest comfortably for the rest of your life. I admit I was against this with your drug history, but your mother wanted to take care of you."

He sighed. "She loved you, Angel." He smiled sadly. "But it's apparent all those sessions on co-dependency she forced me to attend didn't quite sink in with her. Damien and our accountant can sit down and explain the details tomorrow. Quite frankly, I'm exhausted and need some time alone." His father stood and walked toward the door, his steps slow and deliberate. He stopped and turned, facing them.

"For the record, I love both of my sons."

After he left, a heavy silence weighed on the room.

"Let's go." Angel held his hand out to Maggie.

"When do you want to go over this paperwork?" Damien asked rubbing his brow.

"I don't. I don't want the money. I don't know. I just…I just want to go home."

The thought of that much money terrified him. He'd known too many addicts who relapsed after coming into money. It was too much temptation, even with the safeguards in place. His heart pounded.

"Angel, don't make any rash decisions —"

"You knew, didn't you?" Angel glared at his brother, furious at the betrayal.

"About the money?"

"No, you fuckin' asshole. About me, Mom, and Dad," he spat out.

"Yes."

"How long have you known?" Angel's voice broke.

Damien frowned and shook his head as he picked up the folder. "We can discuss this later—"

"How long, goddammit?"

"I overheard Mom and Dad fighting about it when I was fifteen. You were nine."

"Why didn't you tell me?" Damien's silence all these years sliced through him like a knife.

"Because Dad is our father, whether you like it or not, and because I didn't want to hurt you. It wasn't my place to tell you. My God, you were just a kid, Angel." He let out a deep breath and picked up his father's scotch, finishing it.

"I'll be in touch. I'm going home." Angel grabbed Maggie's hand and hurried out of the room.

Angel stormed up the stairs, forcing Maggie to run to keep up with him. When they reached his room, he slammed the door behind them. Under his breath he repeated *I will not use* as he paced.

"Angel, I'm sorry." She didn't know what else to say. If she was having difficulty processing all of this, she could only imagine the torment he felt.

"I don't want to talk about it. I just want to pack and leave, okay?"

"It's getting late. We should stay tonight. We can even find a meeting if you need it. And we can find you some counseling when we get home. Do you need to call Randy?"

"No. I'm not staying another night under this roof. If you don't want to leave, I'll walk home. I want out of here."

"Okay. Give me fifteen minutes." She gave his hand a squeeze and left him to go to her room.

As she packed, she wept—for the little boy who had been brutalized, for the man she loved, and for the family destroyed by lies and betrayal.

Chapter
Twenty-One

Maggie turned into her driveway, and some of her heaviness lifted. They were home. Angel had slept most of the way, clearly exhausted by the previous week. It was late, but the stars shone brightly over the house, and Emma had left the porch light on for them after Maggie phoned her to say they were headed home.

Turning off the truck, she leaned over and kissed Angel's cheek. He stirred and smiled at her, his eyes hooded with sleep.

"Sorry, I should have helped drive," he mumbled with a stretch and a loud yawn.

"It's fine. Let's go inside and go to bed. We can unpack tomorrow."

"Okay." Reaching over, he held her hand for a moment before kissing it. "Thank you. Thank you for bringing me home." He unbuckled his seatbelt and stood, stretching. Dragging their suitcases from the truck, he trudged behind her into the house.

"We need a dog, Maggie. Someone to greet us when we get home."

Maggie laughed. "Maybe you're right. But not a puppy. I don't want everything chewed to pieces."

"The only chewing that will be done is me on you." The sinful smile he offered made her heart skip a beat and her nether regions tingle.

A dog. A life together…It sounded wonderful, but one day at a time. Tonight, she would simply relish being chewed on by the man she loved. Together they'd try to forget the sorrow of the past week.

Maggie locked the front door and turned out the lights. Angel dropped the suitcases in the living area and pulled her to him. His hands wrapped in her hair and he kissed her with a savage possession. They began shucking their clothes as they made their way to her bedroom, kissing, fondling, not saying a word. Heavy breathing and an occasional moan infused the air between them.

Down to their underwear, Angel picked her up and carried her to bed, his lips searing hers as he unfastened her bra and slung it to the floor. He collapsed on top of her, planting kisses down her neck. Greedy hands kneaded and stroked her skin until she was sure she would burst into flames. His warm breath skittered across her stomach as his fingers hooked into her panties.

"Angel, we can't. Not yet…" She breathed with a sigh, her hands fisted in his hair as his tongue teased her belly button. He stopped his descent and took a deep, shuddering breath, his head resting on her stomach.

"Sorry," he whispered with his eyes closed. He brought their joined hands to his lips. "I just need you to hold me."

Maggie stirred underneath him until he rolled over on his back, and she stretched her body on top of his. He gazed up at her, and she brushed a blond strand out of his eyes. Leaning into him, she kissed the rough stubble on his jaw.

"You need to shave," she whispered with a smile, nipping his earlobe.

"Yes, ma'am. Now?"

His smile eased her worry. She was determined to make him forget his pain, at least for a little while. "No, I'm not letting you out of this bed. Don't make me get the rope," she replied with a husky voice. Flicking one nipple ring with her tongue, she smiled with satisfaction when he groaned and his erection against her stomach grew even harder.

"I plan to torture you." She smiled.

"Oh yeah? Do tell."

"Just tell?" She bit his neck. "Or would you rather I show you?"

His throat bobbled. "Fuck me."

"Sadly, that option is off the table. But I have other plans for you. Relax and don't think about anything. Just stay in the moment, Angel. Let me help you."

His eyes crinkled and a grin crept across his face as her lips swept down his chest, and she yanked his boxers down.

She laughed softly as her lips enveloped his cock.

"Marry me, Maggie," he gasped.

Where's Angel? Maggie sat up and glanced at the clock.

His side of the bed was cold, and it was after nine in the morning. Good grief, she never slept this late. She slipped into her robe and slippers, intent on finding Angel and some much-needed coffee. In the kitchen, she found a half pot of coffee and an empty mug in the sink, but Angel was nowhere to be found. A knot of worry formed in her stomach. Maggie wondered if it would always be this way, the fear of him relapsing perpetually dancing along the sideline of her mind.

She heard the truck pull up, and her shoulders relaxed when Angel stepped out with a couple of bags of groceries. He smiled and gave a wave when he saw her standing at the back door.

"Morning, lazybones," he teased as he brushed by her, giving her a quick kiss. "I went to an early meeting and stopped to pick up a few things. I didn't want to wake you, so I racked a few bucks from your wallet. Here's the change and receipt." His hair was pleasingly unkempt, and his day-old beard stubble only added to his appeal. She reached up and pulled him in closer for a real kiss.

"That's fine. You don't have to account for every dime you spend. And would you like to set up an account at the bank and get a debit card?"

"Maybe…Soon. Not yet, okay?"

"Okay. When you're ready." She tousled his hair. "I loved your dreads, but I truly love your shorter hair," she murmured in his ear as she nuzzled his neck.

"Yeah? I have to admit, it does feel good when you do that. Although pulling on the dreads when you were in the throes of ecstasy was pretty damn good, too."

Heat rose in her cheeks, and he laughed as he put the groceries on the table. "Not to mention, it will be much easier to wash this out after we play with our food." He held up a can of whipped cream with a smirk.

"The folks at the grocery store must think we eat an awful lot of pie." Maggie commented as she put the groceries away.

"Oh, I don't think so. Unless…" He snorted and stifled a laugh.

Maggie raised a questioning eyebrow.

"Unless it's magpie."

She rolled her eyes. "That was bad."

They both laughed, the mood between them lighter.

"Angel, if, um, you need to write, you're welcome to the inside of the garage. I mean, I know it isn't the same, but I'm giving you permission. And I won't even make you paint over it when you're done." She smiled, hoping he would, too.

Angel poured them each a cup of coffee and sat in the chair, pulling her into his lap. He sighed as he buried his face into her robe.

"Thank you. I'm good for the moment, but maybe…" He hummed with contentment. "God it's good to be home." He managed to open her robe, exposing one breast. She caught her breath as he licked circles around the hard nipple and then tugged with his teeth.

"Are you okay?" She cupped his cheek and turned his face up to hers.

"Getting there. I spoke to a guy about being my local sponsor this morning."

"That's good. I'm so sorry you went through such hell as a child."

He sighed. "Living on the street wasn't easy. I was mugged a couple of times, shot at, and knifed. I've been arrested. I've been beat up in jail. But that was nothing compared to what that asshole did to me. Nothing was as degrading as that, even lying in my own vomit with a needle stuck in my arm. But I survived. I'll be okay…" He smiled. "I *am* okay."

She kissed him. "Yes, you are. You're a brave man, Angel Sebastian Sinclair."

His upper lip twitched. "That's Goldilocks to you."

She giggled and hugged him tight.

He held her for a moment. "I've been thinking a lot this morning. The money Mom left us will complete your wish list for the bed and breakfast, plus anything else you want. You mentioned an account—we could have a joint one."

She stiffened in his arms and exhaled a sharp, "No."

"No?" He captured her nipple in his mouth again, and an involuntary moan escaped her lips while she half-heartedly pushed him to stop.

"I don't want you to use your money on me or my business." Maggie pulled her robe closed and hopped off his lap to refresh her coffee, keeping her back to him.

"It's *our* money. Why are you pulling away from me? I love you. You love me. You know I want to marry you; why wouldn't I help you with your business? Won't we be working together?" She heard the puzzlement in his voice and turned to face him.

"I won't use your money. I can't. I'm not going to discuss this any further." She stirred sugar into her coffee and resumed staring out the window with her back to him.

"Wait just a minute—you're the one always saying we need to talk. I don't understand. It's *our* money. I don't want the money. As a matter of fact, I could care less about it, but if you can use it—"

Maggie whirled around and faced him. "What part of *no* don't you understand?" She slammed her coffee cup down on the counter.

Angel sprang to his feet. "I'm not your child. Don't take that tone with me."

"Then quit acting like one."

He reeled back as if struck and sucked in an angry breath. His blue eyes blazed as he grabbed his coat. "I'm going to cool off before I say something I regret."

"Angel!"

He turned back to face her, his face set in stone. "What?"

"Where are you going?" she demanded.

"I just fuckin' told you—to cool off. I'm going for a fuckin' walk. Jesus H. Christ. You know, I expect this from my family—I put them through hell with my addiction. But you? Have I given you reason to think I'm going to relapse? What did I just get through?

You were there! Are you ever going to trust me? I'm not going to use," he snapped.

"In a couple of hours, I'm going to borrow your truck. I'll be back after I talk to the assembly at David's school as part of my community service. If the cops are there, I'll ask them to put a goddamned ankle bracelet on me if that will make you feel better."

Heat flushed her face. "Fine. We'll talk when you get home."

"Whatever." He slammed out the door.

Maggie sank into the chair. *What just happened?* They'd had misunderstandings, but this was their first real fight. *I wasn't honest with him. I didn't explain why the money pushes my buttons.* And she'd implied she didn't trust him when he left.

Angel had a valid point. She had to do better. She *would* do better.

Angel sat in Maggie's truck in the high school parking lot and exhaled a deep breath. He'd done it. He'd told his story to the school assembly. Without going into too much detail, he'd talked about his struggles as a child with a learning disability, bullying, and how drugs had not been the answer to his problems. Sharing the pain and shame of his addiction and the impact it had made not only on his life, but also his family's, had been difficult, but liberating.

By baring his vulnerabilities, he hoped he'd connected with kids who might be facing similar difficulties. He'd been surprised and humbled when they gave him a standing ovation. David told him his speech had been both powerful and influential, and the school wanted to talk to him about more assemblies. It was crazy. Angel had no idea what he'd even said. He'd simply spoken from his heart.

He wished Maggie had been there. *What the hell is going on with her?* He had no doubt she loved him. But was love enough? Were her insecurities too much for them to overcome?

Somehow he had to convince her they were meant to be to-gether, forever. He wanted to take care of her in every way, and that included financially. He wanted to settle down. *Weird.* He'd spent a third of his life running away, and now he wanted roots. Life really did go in circles.

Maggie was everything to him, and he truly believed it was real, not just co-dependency. Well, maybe it was. Kind of…Could love ever not be somewhat co-dependent? She was part of him. He needed her as surely as he needed water for his thirst, food for his hunger, and air to breathe. She completed him, filling in the gaps of his imperfections. All he wanted was to love her, care for her, comfort her, and laugh with her for the rest of his life.

How could he convince her? Driving past the wall he'd recently whitewashed, he felt the familiar itch to write. *Dammit, I promised…* He slammed on the brakes, and the car behind him leaned on the horn. Laughing out loud, he hit the steering wheel as his idea took hold. It was perfect and just might work. Utilizing his recently renewed parallel parking skills, he maneuvered into a space in front of City Hall.

The phone rang, and Maggie sighed. She'd already been interrupted once by Phillip letting her know when he'd arrive for Christmas — just four days away now. He'd expressed sympathy for Angel's loss, and she had high hopes this visit would be better than the last. She wiped her flour-dusted hands on a dishtowel and checked the caller ID before answering the phone.

"Damien." She kept her voice cool as she tucked the phone under her ear with her shoulder and went back to kneading her bread.

"Hello, Maggie. I trust you made it home without any problems?"

Maggie wondered if the man ever relaxed and let his guard down, then remembered the anguish on his face when he'd played the violin on the roof. She tempered her tone. "Yes, everything was fine. I'm sorry, but Angel isn't home at the moment."

"He really needs to keep minutes on his damn phone." Damien chuckled with half-hearted annoyance.

Maggie relaxed a bit and smiled in return. "I agree. He's getting a new one for Christmas — don't tell."

"Your secret is safe with me. I was stuck in a meeting and missed his call earlier. He spoke to my secretary about needing a significant amount of money and plans to build? I just wanted to touch base and see what this is about…" Damien's voice trailed off into an uncomfortable silence.

Typical lawyer, feeling me out for information. But the doubt in Damien's voice sent a chill down her spine. Angel had said he didn't want the money. What was he doing with it? Did this have to do with her business after she'd expressly told him no? She put a break on her wayward thoughts, refusing to jump to conclusions.

"I'm not sure. As I said, he isn't home at the moment. I'll have him call you."

"Okay." There was a pause at the other end of the phone and a sigh. "I owe you an apology. I'm sorry I came across as an ass when you were here. It was a stressful time, to say the least. I wanted to tell you this before you left, but I knew Angel was overwhelmed and needed to go. I think you're good for him, and I hope things will work out for the two of you. I sincerely hope you'll be part of the family. It's just that now with this money—"

Maggie interrupted him. It wasn't like she was stupid. She'd been married to a lawyer. "Thank you, Damien. I totally understand your concerns. I love Angel, not his money. I don't give a damn about his money. I loved him when I thought he was homeless. *If* we ever decide to marry, I'll be happy to sign a pre-nup."

"It isn't that I don't trust you, Maggie. I'm a lawyer; I don't trust *anyone.*"

Maggie smiled. "That's one of the casualties of your job—trust…"

Suddenly, the reasons for her worries and fears became crystal clear. Lack of trust was also a casualty of being the daughter of an alcoholic and a divorcée with a cheating ex. It had nothing to do with Angel. *Her* issues were the hang up, not his…

"I'm sorry," she told Damien. "I'm in the middle of making bread and really need to go."

"Okay, have Angel call me. And Merry Christmas if I don't talk to you before then."

"Thank you. Same to you. Bye." She hung up and finished kneading the bread while she formulated her plan for the evening.

Walking in the back door, Angel's stomach growled loud and long. He sniffed with appreciation as he hung up his hoodie. The lingering smell of homemade bread intensified his hunger pangs. A pot of vegetable soup simmered on the stove. Sneaking to the doorway, he paused and listened before hurrying back to sneak a taste. Tempted to snitch a slice of bread, he refrained, knowing he'd catch hell if he did. It was a little after five. The sound of a log shifting in the fireplace moved him toward the living area to check on the wood supply.

The lights were off, and the Christmas tree lights twinkled, but they paled in comparison to the alluring woman lighting the candles on the coffee table. Soft classical music played in the background, and when Maggie straightened up, the firelight outlined her luscious silhouette in her sheer white gown.

"Whoa, did Santa come early?" His breath hitched, and his dick hardened. He'd never seen her look more beautiful. "I, uh, thought you were mad at me."

Maggie's smile was one of pure seduction as she ran a hand through her glorious hair. "Do I look like Santa?" she purred. "And I thought I was mad at you, too. Turns out I was wrong. I was mad at myself, and I'm sorry."

"Oh? For?"

She came closer and looked him in the face. "Not giving you one hundred percent, the way you have me. For not trusting you. I took a long, hard look at myself and realized I have issues I need to work on as hard as you work on your recovery. I'm in this for the long run, Angel. And I trust you. Also, your brother called. He wants you to call him back."

"Thank you. Your trust means everything to me. I will do my damnedest to never have you worry about my recovery. This stuff between us? We'll figure it out—promise. I couldn't wait to get home and tell you about my day. I feel like some TV family dork.

"I had this idea I wanted to run past you and Damien, but I ran out of minutes. Talking to those kids got me thinking. There's nothing to do around here *except* get in trouble. I mean, all this town has is one diner and a bar that technically they shouldn't be allowed in. I want to donate some of my inheritance and build a park. There would be a section for little kids—you know, swings and stuff—plus a walking path around the entire thing, maybe a pond with ducks and goldfish and shit. And a place to skateboard, and best of all, a wall!"

"A wall?"

"Yep, a great big, long-ass blank wall of concrete for graffiti!"

She laughed. "I think it's a great idea."

"You do?"

"Yes."

He grabbed her and gave her an exuberant kiss. "Great! That's why I called Damien. I'll have to clear everything with him and get him to draft the proposal and deal with the legal shit."

She walked her fingers up his arm and brushed the back of her hand along his jaw. "Now, back to another question you never answered." She spun around. "Do I look like Santa?"

He whistled his appreciation. "Not even close. More like a present. And I love unwrapping presents." He slid his hands up and down her arms before fingering the spaghetti straps of her gown. "You're so beautiful, baby," he murmured, tilting her face up to his and kissing her soft lips.

"What, this old thing?" Maggie teased as she drew away from him. "I can go change into my frog flannel pajamas and reading glasses if you'd like." Her green eyes sparkled.

"You look beautiful in anything you wear and in nothing at all. But this—" He pulled her into his arms and nuzzled her neck, brushing soft butterfly kisses across her collarbone. She purred when he worked his way up to the spot behind her ear. "This is wicked good. I love the way you smell, the way you feel." He walked around to the pillows she'd laid on the floor in front of the fire. Lifting his brows, he grinned. "Ms. Robertson, are you trying to seduce me?"

"Why, yes, I believe I am."

She pulled the hem of his T-shirt, lifting it over his head. His thermal shirt was next, and when she pressed her lips to his chest and raked her nails down his back, he fell to his knees. He wrapped his arms around her hips and buried his face in her waist. Taking both of her hands in his, he held them, kissing each finger. He looked up at her and gave her a hopeful smile.

"I'm on my knees begging. Margaret Mary Maguire Robertson, you're the whipped cream on my pie. The paint in my paint can. I can't imagine my life without you. You color my world and bring light to my darkness. I love the way you care for me, love me, nag me, and make me laugh. I love your silly frog pajamas and the way you can never find your glasses when they're on top of your head. You make the best goddamned pumpkin pie in the world, but nothing tastes better with whipped cream than you. I need you. I crave you. You're my sweet addiction, and quite simply my fuckin' everything. *'Just' Maggie*. Marry me. Please?"

Maggie knelt before him with a smile and wrapped her arms around his neck. "I thought the plan was to revisit this after the new year?"

"That was your plan. I swore to ask you every day."

Maggie kissed him and smiled against his lips. "You're incorrigible. You know that, right?"

"Yes, ma'am."

With a playful growl, he pulled her on top of him. Gazing up into her eyes, he wanted to drown in their mossy depths. He chewed on his bottom lip and waited for her answer. She moved ever so slowly toward his face. He closed his eyes, suddenly feeling vulnerable. He braced for her rejection.

"Maybe," she whispered as she leaned forward and dusted his closed eyelids with whisper-soft kisses.

Angel's eyes flew open, and a grin spread across his face. "Holy shit. Did you just say maybe?"

"Yes, but we still have a lot to talk about, and I'm not saying one-hundred-percent yes. I'd want to sign a pre-nup. I won't be accused of marrying you for your money. When you mentioned using the money for the bed and breakfast, I had a knee-jerk reaction. Brian's family always thought I trapped him into marriage by getting pregnant on purpose. And I need to talk to Phillip in person —"

"Hush, baby. You said maybe. You didn't say no. I'm good with that. I'm young, remember? I got all the time in the world." Cradling her face in his hands, he kissed her lips, his tongue teasing her mouth. He sat up, and she straddled his lap, her arms wrapping around his neck. He couldn't quit grinning. "You really said maybe?"

"Maybe," she teased and then nodded. "Truthfully, I'm terrified about remarrying, but I do love you. I don't want to ruin what we have."

Lowering his lashes, he let out an exaggerated sigh of resignation. "Okay. I'll be patient. But just so you know, I want you to marry me,

Maggie. Not just shack up and be your boy toy. I want you to make an honest man of me."

Maggie laughed. "Worried about your reputation?" She pinched his nose and kissed his forehead.

"Well, yeah. Have you seen the way those women look at me at Hudson's Grocery? Like I'm cheap or something," he teased back.

"Gosh, it couldn't possibly be because you're devastatingly handsome and make lewd suggestions about food items, could it?"

Maggie nibbled his ear, and he sighed, happy to be enveloped in her arms.

"Mmmm, whipped cream..." He nuzzled her neck and smiled when she giggled. Life didn't have many perfect moments, but being in the arms of the woman he loved and hearing her carefree laughter definitely ranked as one of them.

She'd marry him sooner or later. Tomorrow he'd start working on making it happen sooner.

Chapter
Twenty-Two

For three days, he'd walked a tight line between guilt and excitement. He'd been lying to Maggie, telling her he was working with Dylan McAthie on the album cover, though they hadn't started on that project quite yet. Whistling, he walked in the back door just as Maggie took a tray out of the oven. He pressed his cold lips to the back of her neck, making her squeal and squirm. In jeans, a red sweater, and a silly Santa hat, she still managed to look sexy as hell. Maggie's comforting vanilla scent and chocolate chip cookies were intoxicating. So was the ass pressed up against him.

"Merry Christmas, baby," Angel whispered as his arms wrapped around her waist. "Yum, cookies." He reached around her and snatched a warm one off the tray.

Her face lit up at the sound of a car in the driveway. "It's Phillip!"

She fixed her hat and checked her mouth for cookie crumbs. She was excited about Phillip's visit, and actually Angel was too. He'd spoken with him privately earlier this week and felt pretty confident things would be good between them now.

Angel moved toward the door. "I'll go help him with his suitcase."

"Maybe I should greet him first." Maggie's brow furrowed as she chewed her bottom lip.

"I know you're nervous, but I want to talk to him and formally ask him for your hand in marriage."

Maggie wrinkled her nose and frowned. "He's not my father, and I'm not sure this is such a good idea. Why don't we let him get in the house first? I'll ply him with home-baked goodies, and maybe the sugar rush will help…"

Angel laughed. "Maggie Robertson! You're a cookie dealer. No. You're the one who said we marry into families, not just the person. I want to reassure him that I'm going to love and care for you for the rest of your life." He paused and pretended to ponder. "Should I leave out the part where I plan to make you scream my name every night when I fuck you?"

Her eyes widened, and her mouth dropped.

Angel laughed and pinched her nose. "You're such an easy mark."

She let out an unladylike snort. "Definitely leave that part out, and I still hate the F word."

"Okay. Love you, baby."

"Love you, too."

"Marry me?" He flashed a hopeful grin.

"Maybe."

She blew him a kiss, and Angel chuckled on his way out the door. He was still amazed she hadn't figured out his elaborate plan. How he'd managed to pull it off without the nosy gossips in Pine Bluff snitchin' on him was a miracle.

Angel met Phillip at the car with a grin on his face, glad his back was to the window. Phillip looked somber as they shook hands. "Wow. I just drove down Main Street. Does Mom have a clue about what you've done?"

Angel shook his head. "I wanted to be sure to remind you not to say anything. There are so many people involved, it's been difficult keeping my lies straight. I nearly lost my shit when she said she ran out of fuckin' vanilla and wanted to go to the store. I convinced her I needed a stupid washer for a nonexistent leaky faucet and went for her." Angel took the suitcase and slammed the trunk closed.

Phillip nodded. "Hopefully she'll stay put now that it's Christmas Eve. You know she's watching us, right?"

"Yep. Walk with me to the lake? I don't want to go too far so I can keep an eye on the house and make sure she doesn't sneak out to run some dumb errand. We can leave the suitcase on the back porch."

Phillip gave a resigned sigh. "Sure. Look, you really don't need to ask my permission to marry my mom. She's a grown woman, and she pretty much made it plain last time I visited—it's her life to do with as she pleases. This isn't my first rodeo. Been there, done that, got the T-shirt when Dad remarried. I was just shocked at Thanksgiving. I mean, she's always just been my mom. She's happy though, so that's all that matters." He gave Angel a stern look. "And you're going to make my mother an honest woman, right? She's kinda old fashioned..."

Angel had a different opinion but left it alone. "Yes, definitely. I think I've proven that, don't you? I'm the one wanting to get married. Your mom's the one stalling."

"Point well made."

They walked toward the back of the house. The door opened, and Maggie hesitated for a moment on the back porch, a huge smile on her face. Before Phillip could react, she ran down the steps and threw her arms around his neck.

"Merry Christmas! I'm so happy you're here. My baby's home." She gave him a kiss on the cheek. Phillip rolled his eyes, but grinned and hugged her.

"Stop, I'm not a baby." He gave his mother an awkward pat on the back.

Maggie laughed as she stepped back. "You'll always be my baby. I can't help it. I have my both my guys here for Christmas. It's going to be perfect." Her smile was wide and easy, but a lingering look of doubt remained around her eyes.

"I'll be inside in a minute, Mom." Phillip nodded toward Angel. "This one wants to plead his case."

The look on his face was resigned, but he winked when she wasn't looking. Angel bit back his smile.

"Okay. I want to talk to you, too. Um, maybe I should talk to you first?" Maggie looked between them, shifting back and forth on her feet.

"I think I kind of know your feelings." Phillip let out a huge, dramatic sigh.

Maggie blinked back unshed tears. Angel damn near called a halt to the plan to keep her guessing, but Phillip stepped up to the plate.

"I'll listen to what he has to say. I've had a little time to think about this since Thanksgiving. Just give us a half hour, okay?"

Maggie nodded, and the plan was in motion.

She shooed them away, declining their offer to take Phillip's suitcase in the house. "I'm not helpless."

Casting one last hopeful glance at them, she picked up the bag and went inside, closing the door.

"You know she's still watchin' us," Angel said as they ambled toward the lake.

"Get used to it." Phillip buttoned his coat and shoved his hands in his pockets. "Mom's really different now, but she's still nosy as hell."

"Yep. Different how?" Angel glanced back at the house and waved. The curtains snapped shut, and he snickered.

The leaves crunched under their shoes, and their breath misted in the cold air. They walked to the edge of the lake and stood looking at the still water.

"She looks younger, more relaxed. Happy." Phillip picked up a stone and skimmed it across the water. "She and my Dad were never happy. I didn't realize just how miserable we all were until it was over. It was just a way of life." He sighed. "Not that either of them was a bad parent; they just…" He shrugged.

"I know." Angel gazed out over the lake, thinking about his parents. "Unfortunately, they don't give out parenting manuals at the hospital. I guess everyone just fucks around and does the best they know how." He gave Phillip a wry look. "Mine included. They weren't exactly parents of the year. It must be one helluva tough job. You're Maggie's pride and joy, though. You do know that, right?"

"Yeah." Phillip looked away and appeared uncomfortable. "Tiffany's pregnant."

Angel looked at him, surprised. "Well, congrats, I guess."

Phillip snorted. "I guess. Truthfully? I think Tiff did it on purpose to get her hooks into Dad better. But he says he's happy. He wants a girl. What about you? Do you want kids? Mom's kind of old." He looked away red-faced.

"Hell, I haven't even convinced her to marry me yet." Angel stuffed his hands in his hoodie and took a moment to think.

"I love your mother. I know me being here came as a shock for you at Thanksgiving, and I'm sorry for that. In hindsight, I wish we could've explained our relationship better, made it easier for you.

But at the time, we weren't even sure ourselves. And yes, I definitely want to marry your mom and take care of her for the rest of our lives." He paused as he stared out at the lake, infusing the serenity into his very being.

He glanced over at Phillip who stared at him, waiting.

"As her son, you're her number-one priority, and I want you to know I realize that. I'm asking you for your blessing on our marriage. But if you say no…" Angel swallowed and looked down at the ground, his boot rubbing a stone over and over as he voiced his greatest fear. He took a deep, bolstering breath before continuing. "If you say no, I'll leave. I won't make Maggie choose between us. I won't put that burden on her."

"You'll leave if I say no? I mean, after our talk on the phone I thought this was a done deal." Phillip's voice registered his disbelief.

"Yes." Angel met Phillip's questioning look. "I love her more than anything in this entire damn world. Her happiness means more to me than my own. Again, I won't make her choose between us. But if you're okay with the idea of her and me together, I hope we can be friends."

Phillip stared out at the lake. "I can live with that. Just know if you hurt her, I'll kick your ass." He held out his hand, and Angel shook it. "And I refuse to call you Dad," he added with a smirk.

Angel laughed. "Good. And as for your question about children—I'll be honest; I haven't even asked Maggie, so I don't know, but I don't think so. She has you, and my gene pool isn't exactly conducive to a good outcome. I've never seen myself as a father."

Phillip shifted on his feet and nodded, looking a little squeamish. "Forget I brought it up."

Angel grinned at the totally different ways they looked at Maggie. To him, she was sexy as hell, vibrant, and full of life. But he did feel much like Phillip looked right now when he thought about his own mother and her affair. He guessed parents always seemed asexual to their kids.

"Can we just leave it at I love your mom?"

"Yeah. I'm sorry about the way I reacted last month. I mean, she's my mom…" He wrinkled his nose and shuddered.

"I get it."

They shook again.

"I think we've made her sweat it out long enough." Angel looked back toward the house.

Phillip nodded, then looked at the ground. "I, uh, met a girl a few weeks ago when I was skiing, and I can see how love kind of changes things. Not that we're to that point in our relationship or anything, but damn, she's all I can think about. I think I'll go see her tomorrow, if Mom doesn't go apeshit on me for leaving early. Natalie lives a couple of hours from Atlanta. I can stay with Dad…"

"You're preaching to the choir about how love changes shit. Tell me about this girl. Do we need to have a talk about safe sex and commitment?" Angel laughed when Phillip punched him in the arm.

Maggie peered out the window at Angel and Phillip. Her heart was so full of love for these very different men in her life. The conversation looked intense. She bit her lip and gripped the counter, forcing herself to stay put. If only she had super powers to hear their exchange.

She couldn't imagine her life without either one of them. For nearly twenty years her son had been her world, and she was optimistic that they were on the way toward a closer relationship now that she was in a better place. The last few conversations on the phone with him had been good and given her hope. But, the nagging fear remained. Would her love for Angel drive a wedge between them? If Phillip didn't come around, what would she do?

When the two shook hands, her hope soared. It had to be a good sign. Two minutes later, her happiness plummeted when Phillip scowled at something Angel said and took a swing at him.

She tore out of the house and down the steps, but it was over before she reached them. Coming to an abrupt halt, she stood in front of them. Her heart stuttered as she looked from one to the other. Neither said a word, dammit. Angel rubbed his arm, and Phillip kept his head low.

"Well?" She crossed her arms in front of her chest and waited.

"Well what?" they answered simultaneously. They smirked, apparently unable to conceal their amusement at her expense.

She glared daggers. "Fine. I guess neither one of you wants to eat today. Pity, I guess I'll just have to take the bread and pumpkin pie to the homeless shelter." She turned and gave a pretend huff. It turned to a squeal of surprise when Angel grabbed her, throwing her over his shoulder with her butt in the air.

"Don't watch this, Phillip, 'cause I'm gonna beat your mama's ass for threatening to give my pie away."

"I'm not seeing a thing. Give her a swat for the bread, too," Phillip encouraged with a laugh.

She gasped when Angel spanked her butt twice as he carried her into the kitchen. He made up for it with a searing kiss when he lowered her back to the floor, much to Phillip's disgust.

"Knock it off, you two. Kid in the house!"

"Then don't look," Angel growled. He gave her another kiss before letting her go with a laugh.

Maggie took Phillip by his arm and walked with him upstairs to his room. "Thank you."

Phillip looked down at her and shrugged. "You're happy. That's what matters, and I'm sorry about Thanksgiving. Dad told me not to be such an ass."

"He did?"

"Yeah. He basically told me to grow up, that everyone deserves happiness. He's um, changed, too. I, uh…" He frowned and jingled the change in his pocket. "Tiff's pregnant," he blurted. "I didn't want you to hear it from anyone else, but I hate ruining your Christmas by telling you."

Stunned, Maggie paused for a moment before answering. "It doesn't ruin my Christmas. I wish your dad and Tiffany well." She surprised herself, realizing she meant it. Resentment toward her ex and his new wife now seemed trivial in the grand scheme of things. Angel had taught her how to live in the moment.

"Hey, Mom?" Phillip blushed, and he began to jingle the change in his pocket again.

"Yes?"

"I've met a girl…"

Chapter
Twenty-Three

The next day Maggie waved good-bye to Phillip as he drove away after lunch, headed off to see his newfound love interest. They'd spent an enjoyable Christmas Eve and Christmas morning together, and she was sad to see him go. Fingering the #1 Mom necklace he'd given her this morning, she used her other hand to dash away a tear.

"Aw, baby. Don't cry. He said he'd be back on spring break." Angel pulled her close, and she snuggled in to his new red-plaid flannel shirt, feeling safe and loved. He smelled of syrup and bacon, having served breakfast at the homeless shelter, allowing her time alone with Phillip.

Sniffling, she replied, "I know. I'm sad to see him go, but these are also tears of happiness. My life is perfect right now."

"I'm glad your life is perfect." He sighed.

He seemed a little on edge as he slung an arm around her shoulders. They headed back into the house to the warmth of the fire. The lights on the Christmas tree made the room extra cozy, and the lingering smell of Christmas lunch permeated the air. Angel sat on the couch, and Maggie curled up next to him, her head on his shoulder, hand over his heart as they gazed at the fire.

"I love the picture you sketched of the bed and breakfast. It's perfect over the fireplace. And the cookie cutters Santa brought me were lovely."

He shrugged. "It wasn't much, but I'm glad you liked them."

"I know this Christmas must be hard on you," she murmured, kissing his jaw.

He didn't say anything, staring at the fire.

"Angel?"

"Yeah?" He gazed down at her, and his lips curved into a sexy smile.

"Are you okay? Was going to the homeless shelter hard? Are you getting sick?"

"Sick? No, why? And no, it wasn't hard at all. I'm going to volunteer more, as a matter of fact."

"I'm glad. But, well, you slept in a T-shirt and pajama pants last night…"

"I thought I was pushing it that I was in your room with your kid here. We're not married."

She scoffed. "It's the twenty-first century. I'm sure my son knows we're having sex."

He chuckled but appeared lost in thought.

"Did you like your gifts? You sure you're okay?"

"I'm fine. Just thinking about how different this Christmas is from the last few. And yes, I hit the jackpot. Shirts, a phone, sketchpads, *and* markers?"

"To use in the sketchbook."

He laughed at her stern look. "Yes, ma'am." The black Labrador by the fireplace stirred in his sleep. "And Graffiti is by far my favorite present."

Emma and Kenzie had delivered the dog last night. She'd gone to the shelter on the outskirts of town to get him the day before Phillip arrived, and the Pattersons had been nice enough to keep him hidden until it was time for Angel's surprise gift.

"I still think that's a silly name for a dog."

Although he'd answered her questions, she could tell his mind was a million miles away. Nervous energy surrounded him. Something was wrong. Was it holiday blues? Missing his mother? Something Phillip had said? Or she had done?

His new phone rang out "Demons" by Tech N9ne, and Maggie shook her head. If anyone was not into rap, it was Damien. He'd set her ringtone as Rod Stewart's "Maggie May."

Angel answered the phone and walked out of the room. Maggie's eyes filled with tears. Maybe she was feeling normal holiday letdown, or perhaps it was Phillip's hasty departure. No, in her gut she knew Angel was keeping something from her, and it poked at all her old fears.

Maggie sighed and flicked an imaginary piece of lint off her pants, reining in her unease.

Angel walked back in, still looking anxious.

"Everything okay?"

"Yeah, Damien and Dad said to tell you Merry Christmas."

She didn't hide her surprise. "You spoke to your father?"

Angel pursed his lips and exhaled. "Not by choice. Dad grabbed the phone from Damien. He sounded okay, but Damien said he's missing Mom. Apparently, he won't talk about it and has buried himself in work. Damien said he's cut back on the drinking, though, which is good. Typical Dad, he's never been one to verbalize his feelings. They're having a quiet Christmas, nothing big."

Maggie walked to him and stood on her tiptoes, kissing his cheek. "Maybe someday you and your Dad can sit down and talk. You need your family."

"You're my family. Marry me?"

She grinned. This was more like it. "Maybe. Someday."

"What will it take to convince you to marry me?"

"No secrets," she retorted and slapped a hand over her mouth, wishing she could take it back.

"Okay, then. Come with me." Angel stood and marched her toward the back door. Grabbing his beanie and coat, he helped her into hers.

"Where are we going?"

He tugged her toward the door. "No more fucking secrets. I know you know I've been keeping something from you."

"It's Christmas afternoon," she protested as he opened the passenger door to the truck for her. Graffiti followed and hopped in first, taking up most of the room in the cab. "And I don't think it's right to use the F word and Christmas in the same sentence."

He slammed the door shut, walked around to the driver's side, and got in without a word. Puzzled, Maggie kept quiet. Graffiti licked her face and barked, ready for an adventure.

"We're going in to town? Nothing's open…"

"I know." He bit his lip and tapped the steering wheel with both thumbs.

The dog yelped and wagged his tail. Petting him, she stared out the window. Her mouth fell open as the truck slowed when they came to the city limits.

"Oh. My. God." Her eyes widened as they passed building after building with the words, "Marry Me, Maggie" scrawled on the windows. Every single business on Main Street had been tagged, bombed, or wildstyled by Angel.

He parked the truck and turned toward her, taking her hand in his. His clear blue eyes danced with amusement. A lazy, seductive smile formed on his lips. "Merry Christmas, baby. Marry me?"

"Angel, you're going to go to jail! You promised no illegal activity…" Maggie gasped, turning to look out the window again.

"Nah, I did it legit this time. It's just soap. Every business in Pine Bluff gave their permission and will have clean windows tomorrow."

Before she realized it, Angel had hopped out of the truck and opened her door.

She stepped out, with Graffiti on her heels. Angel knelt before her on one knee, looking up at her with a face full of love and promise.

"Marry me, Maggie?" Pulling a box from his pocket, he flipped it open to reveal an antique, princess-cut emerald with a diamond on each side. He slipped it on her finger and held her hand.

"Oh my God, this ring…when? How?"

He laughed. "It was my mom's and always my favorite. Dad and Damien agreed I could give it to you. Do you know how many people have been in on this? It's been insane! The mayor, all the business owners, Phillip — even Emma. She met Damien halfway to Atlanta to pick it up for me. The emerald reminded me of your eyes."

"It's the most beautiful ring I've ever seen."

"So? Will you marry me?"

Unable to speak for a moment, she stared at the man kneeling before her. With her free hand, she stroked his cheek.

"Maybe," she whispered.

His face fell, but his eyes locked with hers. "Just maybe?"

"Maybe next year." She bit her lip, waiting for his reaction.

"Next year?" He shouted, rising to his feet and facing her. He swept the beanie off his head, threw it to the ground, and stomped on it. "Fuck!"

She giggled. He turned around, looking hurt.

"Think about it, Angel."

Realization dawned. "Next year is next week, right?"

Maggie nodded and threw herself into his arms, kissing his cheeks, his forehead, and his lips.

"Yes, it is. And yes, I'll marry you!"

"Fuck, Maggie," he groaned. He kissed her deeply.

"That, too," she replied with a saucy grin. "But not next year. Now. Let's go home."

"Yes, ma'am."

The End

The series will continue with Damien Sinclair's story in
The Redirection of Damien Sinclair

Author's Note

Addiction is a complex brain disease that is manifested by compulsive substance use despite harmful consequence. People with addiction (severe substance use disorder) have such an intense focus on using a certain substance(s), such as alcohol or drugs, to the point that it takes over and controls their life. They keep using the substance even when they know it will cause problems. But there is hope. There are a number of effective treatments are available, and people can recover from addiction and lead normal, productive lives.

The first step on the road to recovery is recognition of the problem. If you, or someone you love has a substance abuse problem, you can call SAMHSA's National Helpline: 1-800-662-HELP (4357) It's a confidential, free, 24-hour-a-day, 365-day-a-year, information service, in English and Spanish, for individuals and family members facing mental and/or substance use disorders. This service provides referrals to local treatment facilities, support groups, and community-based organizations.

Acknowledgments

Jessica Royer Ocken: Some think I'm crazy because I always say editing is my favorite part of the process, but it's because I work with you. You make it fun, you make me work, and you make it coherent. Someday, I might learn where to properly put a comma, but I doubt it. Thank you!

Coreen Montagna: You catch the mistakes that slip through the cracks and format the inside to make it beautiful. I know I drive you crazy, but you put up with my hysterics. Thank you!

Shannon Lumetta: Your crazy graphic skills always amaze me. I think you're a mind reader because you always seem to know what I want when I can't visualize it myself or have unreal expectations. The cover is perfect.

Gel Ytaz: Your teasers are always spot on, I'm so happy I found Tempting Illustrations. We make a good team.

To Katie, Vickie, Jill, Carrie, my beta readers who encouraged me and yet kept things real.

To the Cain Raisers, especially Michele, Eunice, Jo, and Susie, for always spreading the word about my stories.

My SLOBS, you know who you are. You answer my questions, let me vent and pick me up when I'm down. We laugh and cry together and someday I hope to hug each of your necks and buy you a drink.

Stephanie Phillips and SBR Media: Your encouragement keeps me going. Thank you for believing in me!

About the Author

During the day, Nancee works as a counselor/nurse in the field of addiction to support her coffee and reading habit. Nights are spent writing paranormal and contemporary romances with a serrated edge. Authors are her rock stars, and she's been known to stalk a few for an autograph, but not in a scary, Stephen King way. Her husband swears her To-Be-Read list on her e-reader qualifies her as a certifiable book hoarder. Always looking to try something new, she dreams of being an extra in a Bollywood film, or a tattoo artist. (Her lack of rhythm and artistic ability may put a damper on both of these dreams.)

Website: nanceecain.com
Blog: nanceecain.com/blog
Goodreads: goodreads.com/Nancee_Cain
Facebook: facebook.com/NanceeCainAuthor
Reader's Group (Cain Raisers): facebook.com/groups/Cain.Raisers
Twitter: twitter.com/Nancee_Cain
Pinterest: pinterest.com/nanceecain
Instagram: instagram.com/nanceecain
BookBub: bookbub.com/authors/nancee-cain
Newsletter: eepurl.com/bhFMtX
YouTube Channel: bit.ly/2xsU6Ad
Spotify Playlists: open.spotify.com/user/12184539074

Books by Nancee Cain:

Paranormal Romance (Angels)
Saving Evangeline
Tempting Jo
Loving Lili (novella)

Contemporary Romance (Pine Bluff Novels)
The Resurrection of Dylan McAthie
The Redemption of Emma Devine
The Rehabilitation of Angel Sinclair
The Redirection of Damien Sinclair
The Reinvention of Jinx Howell
The Reintroduction of Sammie Morgan
The Realization of Grayson Deschanelle

Contemporary Romances

pine bluff

Although each of the titles in this series can be read as standalone stories, this is the preferred reading order:

The Resurrection of Dylan McAthie

The Redemption of Emma Devine

The Rehabilitation of Angel Sinclair

The Redirection of Damien Sinclair

The Reinvention of Jinx Howell

The Reintroduction of Sammie Morgan

The Realization of Grayson Deschanelle

The Resurrection of Dylan McAthie
A Pine Bluff Novel

Maybe You Can Go Home Again

Hounded by paparazzi, Dylan McAthie—the former lead guitarist for Crucified, Dead and Buried—craves quiet anonymity to regroup and sort out his life. An accident leaves him dependent on the family he once ran from, with no choice but to return to the small town of Pine Bluff, Alabama.

Hired by Dylan's estranged brother, private-duty nurse Jennifer Adams remembers the charming boy Dylan was before fame and misfortune. And she notices he's developed a knack for blaming everyone else for his problems, rather than bothering with introspection. She's not having it.

Despite their clashes, as her patient heals, the chemistry between them grows undeniable—until scandal finds Dylan again, threatening to destroy the progress he's made and the couple's growing respect and affection. Can Dylan fix what fame has so easily broken? Or will his public resurrection mean the death of any relationship with Jennifer?

The Redemption of Emma Devine
A Pine Bluff Novel

A Little Shake-Up in Life Can Be Devine

Emma Devine is on the run and fighting to survive. Her tortured past makes trust difficult, especially where men are concerned. But she has no choice other than accepting the help of the man who catches her shoplifting on Christmas Eve.

When not stopping shoplifters, David Patterson leads a quiet life in Pine Bluff, Alabama, working as a high school teacher. His random act of Christmas kindness brings unexpected joy to his life, as he finds himself drawn to the mysterious Emma. When she leaves, his world is turned upside down, and his dreams are changed forever.

Four years later, Emma returns in search of long-overdue redemption. But despite an undeniable attraction between the two, trust is an even greater issue now — for both of them. Can they find their way to a place of understanding? Or have yesterday's mistakes destroyed their chance for a future together?

The Rehabilitation of Angel Sinclair
A Pine Bluff Novel

Love — the Hardest Addiction to Kick

Angel Sinclair arrives in Pine Bluff, Alabama, determined to make amends for his past and move on. But that changes after a chance encounter with a beautiful inn owner, and instead he finds himself pursuing two things that haven't been in his life for years: love and trust.

Still reeling from a bitter divorce, Maggie Robertson wants to focus on making her business a success. Getting involved with anyone in this gossipy little town is the farthest thing from her mind...until she finds herself tempted by a younger man.

Neither Angel nor Maggie can ignore the sizzling heat between them. But Angel's secretive nature soon fills Maggie with doubts about the man she's allowed into her heart.

Was she wrong to believe love could conquer all? Is their age difference an obstacle they can't overcome?

The Redirection of Damien Sinclair
A Pine Bluff Novel

Sometimes You Get What You Need

Acclaimed divorce attorney Damien Sinclair has witnessed more than his share of love's ugly aftermath. He keeps things black and white, preventing anyone from getting too close. But his illusion of control fades when an attempt on his life leaves him struggling with PTSD.

Enter Damien's childhood friend, the free-spirited Harley Taylor. Shrugging off the awkwardness of their teenaged fling and her broken heart, she appoints herself his caregiver. The man needs to learn not to take himself so seriously, and she's hellbent on snapping him out of his brooding funk.

After a decade apart, Harley and Damien find their attraction is stronger than ever. Could Harley's sunny disposition be the bright spot Damien needs in his life? Or will their differences overshadow any hopes of a future together?

The Reinvention of Jinx Howell
A Pine Bluff Novel

Can Love Unmask Their True Selves?

Hiding behind her wigs and heavy makeup, Jinx Howell masks her insecurities — which even she doesn't understand — with bravado, slashing through life with reckless abandon. Lonely, but unwilling to get close to anyone, she finds the ideal solution: a hook-up with the campus's most notorious heartbreaker.

In similar fashion, Mark "Two-Time" MacGregor protects his heart and keeps himself unencumbered through a string of one-night stands. A chance meeting with the edgy Jinx in a dark alley seems like destiny. She claims to want sex with no ties, making her perfect. *Like attracts like.* But this girl with a switchblade has more hang-ups than he does, which is a hell of a lot.

When tragedy strikes, Mark's hit-and-run lifestyle takes a backseat to his need to protect the broken girl whose secrets are unraveling. Along the way, both of them will find their truths unmasked. Can they forge a real relationship, or will they give up on their romance as jinxed?

The Reintroduction of Sammie Morgan
A Pine Bluff Novel

Can Life Get Any Crazier?

Still reeling from the tragic deaths of his wife and daughter, Matt Tyler trudges through life, caring for his young son, managing his cantankerous father, and working as much as he can. Despite his best efforts, bills are piling up and his vindictive in-laws seem determined to take Luke away from him.

Things change when he stumbles upon Sammie Morgan — with a car that won't run and her mother's ashes in the backseat. Best friends growing up, Matt and Sammie have spent years apart following very different paths. Now they've both run out of options. Without a dime in her pocket, Sammie has nowhere to go. And Matt lacks the stable home life he needs to fight his former in-laws.

Their hasty solution? A marriage of convenience.

But how convenient will this reintroduction be if it means Matt and Sammie have to relive the most painful parts of their past?

The Realization of Grayson Deschanelle
A Pine Bluff Novel

Sex, No Strings Attached

Despite a high-profile clientele, fashion photographer Grayson Deschanelle prefers being behind the lens, away from public scrutiny. After his movie star girlfriend dumps him, he flees to his stepbrother's remote cabin to hide from the paparazzi.

Caught by surprise, Grayson finds Lissy much different than the girl he's known for years. She's no longer a child — though her teen-aged crush is still very much intact. Snowed in with her, he tries to fight his growing attraction. But being with Lissy brings what his life is lacking into sharp focus.

The ice melts, and they return home. When their families discover their secret, Grayson must decide what kind of life he truly wants — and whether he'll fight to keep Lissy by his side.

Paranormal Angel Romances

Although each of the titles in this series can be read as standalone stories, this is the preferred reading order:

Saving Evangeline

Tempting Jo

Loving Lili (novella)

Saving Evangeline

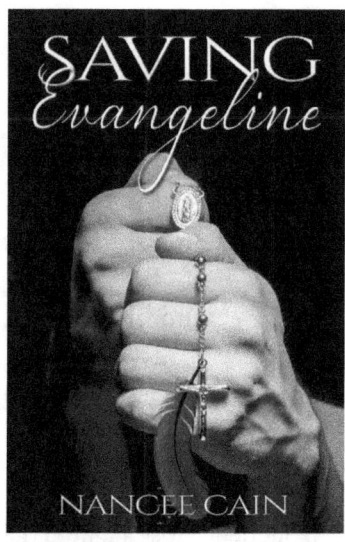

Evangeline is the town pariah. Everyone knows she's crazy and was responsible for the death of her last boyfriend. Even her mother left her and moved cross-country. Lonely and desperate, Evie decides to end her life.

Rogue angel Remiel longs to return to Earth, but there's just one problem. He tends to invite trouble and hasn't been allowed back since Woodstock. The Boss sends him to save Evangeline, but there's a catch: he can't reveal his angelic nature, and he must complete the task as *Father* Remiel Blackson.

Forced together on a cross-country trip, a forbidden romance ignites and love unfolds. A host of heavenly messengers tries to intervene, but Remiel and Evangeline are headed on a collision course to disaster. Will his love save her, or will they both be lost forever?

Forbidden love is hell…

Confident and quirky, Jo Sanford thinks her boss is God's gift to women—and she couldn't be further from the truth. Devilishly handsome, Luc DeVille will stop at nothing to lure his administrative assistant right into his arms—and bed.

Over Rafe Goodman's dead body…

Rafe, Jo's best friend, refuses to sit by and watch as Luc tries to win the heart of the woman he's always protected. After all, Rafe is her guardian angel. Suddenly, Jo's caught in the middle of a battle between good and evil. But the closer she gets to the fire, the hotter it burns. Now, Jo's going to learn that when love battles lust, Heaven and Hell collide.

Loving Lili (novella)

Their lovemaking is hot and dirty. Their break ups are nasty and epic.

Tired of taking the blame for every wicked thing that happens on Earth, fallen angel Luc DeVille decides to write a tell-all-book exposing The Boss.

Sharing a long and passionate history, Luc is shocked when Lili Nix arrives to interview for the job as editor. Immediately the verbal sparring begins, but the sexual chemistry remains combustible. Fascinated by this heavenly creature, Luc changes his game plan. After all, she's the only angel who has ever held his attention and understood his intentions.

Being in this world, but not of this world, is a lonely business. Can two lost angels connect and make it last this time?

www.ingramcontent.com/pod-product-compliance
Lightning Source LLC
Chambersburg PA
CBHW060544260626
47161CB00003B/1041